A Novel

The Gathering

AT THE

Be a Beer-liever!

CHURCH STREET

BREWERY

Christopher K. Horne

The Gathering at the Church Street Brewery

Published by Wisdom House Books, Inc.
Chapel Hill, North Carolina 27516 USA
1.919.883.4669 | www.wisdomhousebooks.com

Wisdom House Books is committed to excellence in the publishing industry.

Book design copyright © 2021 by Wisdom House Books, Inc. All rights reserved.

Cover and Interior Design by Ted Ruybal

Published in the United States of America

Paperback ISBN: 978-0-578-67539-8
LCCN: 2020923296

1. FIC029000 | FICTION / Short Stories (single author)
2. FIC074000 | FICTION / Southern
3. FIC026000 | FICTION / Religious

First Edition

25 24 23 22 21 20 / 10 9 8 7 6 5 4 3 2 1

TABLE OF CONTENTS

DEDICATION

The author is thankful to Will for his bold and insightful comments.

There are no words adequate enough to thank my wife, the near-perfect example of a selfless human being. By your personal sacrifice, and through heavenly teachings, you taught me the true meaning of love.

To my son, Ben, in the words of Jimmy Valvano, "Don't ever give up, don't ever give up."

ACKNOWLEDGMENTS

Thanks to my students who inspired the book.

FOREWORD

Because it is a novel, the reader is alerted that the dialogues are approximations, as are most other elements "quoted" in the book, and the actions and rationales of the characters are as interpreted/created by the novelist, rather than being so closely rooted in reality as to be a testimony. And yet, this comes so very close to realism.

We hope the readers of The Gathering at the Church Street Brewery will be both entertained and edified. It has been my pleasure to work again with Dr. Chris Horne.

Douglas Winslow Cooper, Ph.D.
Walden, NY
Spring 2020

PREFACE

Fiction is often closer to the truth than nonfiction. So, often, others have said, or written, what we wish we had the skill to state. Still, we must have the courage to try, and this is what I have done. In this novel, life experiences reveal characters special to me. Commit your time and patience, and I will tell you a story. Thank you for reading it.

Christopher K. Horne, Ph.D.
High Point, NC
ChrisHorne111@gmail.com
www.christopherhorne.com
Spring 2020

Chapter 1

CARLTON

Carlton awakens, alone, for the first time in forty-one years. His tears, quietly rolling down his cheek, are reflected in the framed glass protecting his bedside picture of Dot and their two grown children.

What am I living for, now? Carlton asks himself. *But if I go to the gravesite and place some flowers, it will make me feel better. I know she hears me when I talk. And I know I need to go see her, but I don't know if I can get out of bed.*

His house is quiet now. No more pots and pans rattling prior to her breakfast call. No more sipping coffee together and chatting on the back porch.

When the kids left for college, we thought we were in heaven, having so much time for each other.

Carlton hears silence as he walks slipper-less to the kitchen. He opens the refrigerator which is nearly empty. Missing are the eggs, bacon, and bread for toast that Dot would prepare every day—she was the cook; she was the one who kept the refrigerator full, who made weekly trips to the grocery store.

Damn it: I just don't feel like going to the store.

With his window down, he smells the flowers along the gravel driveway that circles the cemetery just a few blocks from his home. He parks his car and walks up the hill—sweat beading on his forehead from anticipation as much as the beaming sun. A monument to Jesus overlooks the ten acres of grass and headstones. Its Jesus statue is a towering figure among cemetery-goers like Carlton. His outstretched arms and figure, with white face, are now discolored due to the fifty-plus years of weathering.

God, I miss her. God, why do the good die young?

"Dorothy, are you there?" Carl whispers. She can hear him, he knows.

He sits down on the hard-concrete bench within a few feet of her grave.

Sobbing, he pulls out a letter she wrote to him a few weeks before she died, while in hospice care. Again, he reads it:

> Dear Carl,
>
> I have been trying to write this for a while, but the morphine and pain have drained my energy and interfered with whatever writing ability remains. I have been married to the most extraordinary man for forty-one years. I was planning for us to have at least another twenty together. However, we do not get to choose. From the day we wed, to the amazing birth of our two children, and our walks along the New River, just months ago, I have never loved another

> man. We shared so much happiness. I truly believe
> that God, our grand architect, put us together. I want
> more time with you, Carl, but it seems that's not
> going to happen. When I'm gone, please don't weep
> for me; instead, cherish the memories and pray that
> God will give you peace.

Carl, struggling, tries to read more, but he fails and retreats back to his car.

He used to drive an old pickup truck to the furniture factory he worked at for thirty-something years until NAFTA brought cheaper labor from Mexico. His layoff notice, a few years ago, was welcomed; retiring with Dot made him happy. Now, the once handcrafted chairs are shipped from Mexico to North Carolina showrooms. In his days at the factory, men and women worked hard to feed their families—many were Vietnam vets or single mothers.

Now, Carlton drives a new F-150 pickup truck around town. He parks it in his garage, and, like his careful craftsmanship of fine furniture, his garage is clean and his tools organized. Each drawer of the tool chest holds wrenches cleaned after each previous use, and there's not one oil spot on the garage floor.

Dot's car still sits next to his shiny white truck. The couple used to cruise Main Street in her car, holding hands as they walked, visiting an ice cream parlor every Friday night before going to see a movie.

Finally arising from bed, Carl looks at Dot's portrait in the kitchen, then steps into the garage, eyes her car, and slowly takes a seat in his truck.

He's not sure how he's gotten to this place of utter loneliness. How has his life unraveled, leaving him sitting in a pile of used tissues, unfulfilled wishes, and hopeless dreams?

His plans had been her plans. They were big. All hope and dreams came crashing down after Dot lost her battle to breast cancer. This was not the life he envisioned. That was for sure.

"Surviving the Death of Your Spouse" is an insulting read, suggesting I cannot grow as a person without forming new relationships, Carlton throws the book in the kitchen trashcan. He walks around the house mumbling to himself. The phone rings. His daughter, Emily, calls and tries to counsel him on grief, as if it would help.

"As numerous research studies have demonstrated, bereavement by a spouse is a major source of life stress that can leave people vulnerable to later problems including depression, chronic stress, and reduced life expectancy," Emily explains to her dad, trying to help, but sounding too teacher-ish.

"I don't need this right now," Carlton says.

Emily pleads with him: "Daddy, I know you are lonely. You should visit the church you and Mother attended. There are some really compassionate folks who go there."

As Emily continues to plead, all Carl can think about is his time as a foot soldier, taking gunfire for his platoon and receiving over a dozen shrapnel wounds. He realizes he is literally fighting a different kind of battle—loneliness and despair are his enemies now.

Like many Vietnam vets, Carlton's stubbornness and grieving would forsake the care offered from his immediate family—daughter, Emily, and son, Eddie. He needed healing of his soul, but the wound was deep, maybe too deep. Emily and Eddie both live several states away and have their own families to care for and manage.

Carlton has still been lonely for friendship. Many of his colleagues from the factory are deceased or suffer from PTSD or illnesses they blame on Agent Orange.

Carlton hangs the phone up, his hand still holding the receiver, pondering what Emily said about church.

Friday arrives, and before Carlton visits Dot's gravesite, he stops off at Johnson Brothers' BBQ. Johnson Brothers' makes more food than just BBQ; they also serve breakfast and dinner. The marque sign outside their storefront reads: "Fight Truth Decay, Study the Bible Daily."

However, Bible verses are of little comfort to a man grieving his lifelong friend, partner, and soulmate. Carl finds some solace in the place—the waitresses feel sorry for him.

The forty-something waitress, Donna, says, "What ya having today, Carl?" Most of the time, Donna has a stern look on her face; she's a single mother of three who quotes Bible verses and pours coffee.

Carlton sits down at his usual table—the one nearest the cash register. Everyone has to pass by him, even the men from the church, who gather every Friday morning for Bible Study.

"I don't know what I want today," Carl responds to Donna with a soft voice and a depressed look.

"Where's your better half?" Donna asks. Carl doesn't respond, but his eyes start to water.

He looks across the room, seeing the men's group. He knew of the Men's Bible Study, having attended church with them before Dot died. The preacher walks into the restaurant after Carl sits down.

"Hi. Carl, good to see you," the preacher calls out on his way to the corner booth. Carl sits quietly—no newspaper or Bible, no smartphone or other reading material, just thoughts of Dot. With his head down, he responds to the preacher: "I'm making it," he lies.

Donna brings Carl his order of eggs, grits, and toast, with black coffee. The coffee is so hot the steam rises up and clouds his glasses. The room, too, is already hot on this summer morning.

Carlton finishes his breakfast and pays the cashier. On his way out, the preacher sees Carl with his head down, glasses fogged up, making his way across the parking lot to his truck.

Driving to the cemetery, Carl passes The Church Street Brewery, a gathering spot on Main Street.

The Church Street Brewery started as a food truck parked in an abandoned parking lot just three years ago. The bar, also called "the watering hole," by the local crowd, has curb appeal: outdoor seating, a big firepit, and live music. The Brewery, as it's also called, is the newest addition to uptown retail drinking establishments since the closing of many clothing and furniture stores in the heart of the city. Breweries have been popping up all over town, complementing restaurants.

At The Brewery, food trucks show up to offer tastes of the next big thing, long before it is the next big thing. Whatever you eat will taste a whole lot better with a side of future bragging rights. Carlton drives around town thinking about Dot and the next big thing. On most nights, a crowd of two or three dozen assembles outside. The inside bar is the taproom, where the ambiance is cozy and the different beers are plentiful.

Maybe this evening, I can stop by The Brewery and meet someone, Carlton muses.

"Do you need any life insurance?" the radio announcer says.

Carlton thinks, *the life I had was with Dot—I need a life, not life insurance! Dot was not a beer drinker. Maybe I should not stop by Church Street tonight.*

The Brewery used to be an old 5,000-square-foot furniture manufacturing store with old wooden floors and a sinking roof, but now it's a beer haven with LED lighting and modern plumbing. The firepit heats customers outside in the fall, while, inside, conversationalists try to warm the hearts of each other, drinking their favorite wine or beer or cocktail.

For every ten men that show up at Church Street, on their busiest night, Friday, there might be three women. Some older women come from the rich neighborhood two streets over, and some younger girls from the nearby university. Carlton didn't go to college. He attended "the school of hard knocks"—the Vietnam War. He didn't get a Vietnam University varsity sweater, but he came home alive.

Finally, Carlton arrives at the grave of his dear Dorothy. He reaches for his back pocket and pulls out a picture of her. He carries it around with him everywhere he goes. "You are beautiful. I don't mind looking at you all the time," Carlton says. "I miss you so much. And Emily says she misses you, too."

The next day, Carlton sobs, as the hot North Carolina summer sun beats down on his back, perspiring, due to the walk from his truck to the gravesite bench. Carl had always been a God-fearing man, raised by farmers who practiced the Ten Commandments. He played football in high school as an offensive lineman. He utilized his physical strength to build camps, tents, and huts for his comrades in the jungles of Vietnam. It was during the war that he grew to hate the Vietcong, but, there, he fell in love with a seventeen-year-old girl named Trinh. When Carlton was told he would leave Vietnam in 1969, he asked Trinh if she wanted to go to the U.S. with him, but she refused. She did not want to leave her family. Trinh was not meant to be, and true love came with Dot.

Carl wanted to die with Dot. This lonesome feeling is like being in a desert with nowhere to go. He decides to visit The Brewery not to make memories but to find a friend to listen to his pain and heartache.

Outside, the sun is setting behind the nearby two-story apartments, and The Brewery's firepit is aglow. The firepit is recessed into the concrete wall. Sandstone cobbles edge the five-foot diameter lava-rock-topped pit that blazes with gas-fed flames. The fire warms Carl's skin and lights up the small world around him, as he slides a wooden chair up near the circular knee-high wall surrounding the pit.

Chapter 2

DAVID

For a man of fifty-three who's been divorced three times, the professor has, in his mind, solved the problem of lust quite well. On this Wednesday afternoon, he leaves campus around 1:00 p.m. and drives to Fayetteville. Precisely at 3:00 p.m., he pulls into a well-manicured condominium community.

He calls the agency to let them know, "I have arrived to see Ms. Sonya."

The agent responds, "Press the buzzer at the front entrance."

Waiting for the professor at Door 415, she is dressed in a red satin ruched party dress. She opens the door: "Hi."

David says nothing but makes a low-frequency grunt. He walks straight to her dimly lit bedroom. Her oak furniture sends a strong signal of stamina and endurance with its color, much like her skin: warm, golden, a buttery brown caramel.

She stands in the doorway between the fireplace den and her much-larger king-sized bed. Her right hand immediately reaches for her belt.

Even at fifty-three, the professor dresses like a teenager—jeans and short-sleeved golf shirt. His wavy dark hair needs a wash, but he smells okay.

He undresses and places his jeans and shirt on the love seat, then turns around to see Sonya disrobing. He admires her harmonious back from across the room as sunlight washes down her thighs. He pulls the covers over him, lies back, and watches her. She slides into bed beside him.

"Have you missed me?" Sonya asks.

"I miss you daily," David replies. He strokes her lovely body, as she fully stretches out.

Sonya is Hispanic. Her looks alone led her from Tijuana to Dallas. Then, she followed an 82nd Airborne soldier to Fayetteville. She discovered that her looks and sexuality could pay off more than being a Walmart employee under the control of her US Army Ranger ex-husband.

David is old enough to be her father, though, technically, one can be a father at around thirteen. David has been in her little red book for over two years. He sees her to fill his obsessive need for pleasure. Wednesday has become an oasis for lust and desire.

Done, and preoccupied with his body, the professor slips his pants back on and moves to the love seat, leaving a sprawling young lady tucked under the sheets. At fifty-three, slightly overweight, losing hair, he has the "dun-lap" disease: his stomach "done lap" over his belt—gravity taking its toll.

Despite her occupation, Sonya is modest and rather docile and quiet in bed. In fact, after making love, she tends to ask moralistic questions.

"What do you teach, professor?" Sonya asks. He looks at her with approval. Then, she rolls closer to him. Propping her head with her elbow, her soft, athletic, five-foot three-inch body stares at him. He is mesmerized.

"Religion," David replies.

"Do you think God approves of my services?"

"God is most likely worried about other things than your services," David says.

"You seem to believe that God exists. You should be able to show me God."

"Sorry, but I do not possess God, as if He were an object I could show you," David says.

"Do you know what God is?"

"God is the Master Clockmaker," David says. "He made the clock, wound it, and then left it alone."

"So, is He or She not watching me sell my body to strangers?"

"My faith, Deism, believes that a personal god does not exist, even though this god created the world. However, the god of Deism left the world to be governed by natural law," David replies.

"Natural law?" Sonja responds. "I am breaking the law by engaging in these favors."

"Yes, by human law, this is illegal, but you ain't telling, are you?"

"No, I care too much about my job," Sonya replies.

"But have you suffered any punishment from God for this?"

"Not that I know of," Sonya replies, and then she sits up, grabbing for her pink nightgown.

"I assume you get checked out medically?" David asks.

She hesitates for a few seconds, staring at herself in the large dresser mirror at the end of the queen-sized bed: "I do get regular checkups with my doctor."

David thinks, I've never seen her shower before our meeting. That reminds me, I need to get my prostate checked. The last time I had my physical, the doctor said his "finger test" did not "feel right."

Sonya continues to question David about morality and sexuality.

"Do you think these are big enough?" Sonya asks, pointing to her youthful breasts.

"Yes, but I am not a 'breast-man'," David replies. "I like a firm, slim body."

"Are you offended when a woman wears skimpy, seductive clothing in public—say, at the grocery store?"

"No. She has the right to wear what she desires," David says. "I find all sorts of women attractive."

"I never wear seductive clothing in public," Sonya replies. "Sluttiness is distasteful."

"Very well," David adds. I like the sluttiness. I am happiest when I'm with Sonya.

Because he takes pleasure in Sonya, and because that pleasure is never-ending, he has an affection for her that has given him wings. She makes him fly. He thinks this affection is reciprocal. But, down deep, he knows that this lust and fondness is not true love.

He is lucky to have found her. And to some extent, she is lucky to have found him.

For the one-hour session, he pays her $450—money he could save for retirement or even a new car or to give to charity. But half of the $450 goes to Discreet Companions, LLC. Sonya is not too bad off, however, since the company owns and supplies her apartment—No. 415 Fairness Ave.

Although their relationship is not love, he wants to see her in her own time. Maybe he will invite her to the University's Christmas party. He might even think about taking her to one of his religion seminars, where he leads discussions on God, morality, and the origins of life.

He envisions an all-nighter with her, but he worries she will see him for who he really is—impatient, rude, and calculating, especially the morning after his dirty deed.

Professor David's temperament is abrupt, gruff, and stubborn. He has tenure, and he is still cerebral but complacent. But he is an expert in religion.

His problem is nine inches long. Not his penis size, but the distance from his head to his heart. He has a heart problem for people, especially for his students at the University, where empathy is almost nonexistent.

David has a piss-poor attitude. Everyone at the University, including the Chair and the Dean, knows it. He gets by, though, because he has tenure.

He suffers some sort of multiple-personality disorder and is a calculating flirt with female students by coming across as being interested in their coursework. Then, sometimes, in the classroom, he has panic attacks and goes off on a student for using a cell phone.

By his international academic peers, he is considered a scholar. He lives within his income and is fairly comfortable being alone. Although, as a Deist, he believes in God the Creator, he has yet to accept the notion of heaven.

Back to his life solution—he has, in his mind, solved the problem of lust. His sexual temperament, though intense, is not passionate but rather mechanical. Were he to choose an animal to represent his passion, it would be a snake. His intercourse with Sonya is wet, lengthy, intertwined, but simultaneously abstract and noncommitting. The two trust each other, within limits, more than they would a casual acquaintance or a one-night stand. During their sessions, she speaks to him as though she knows his life story cover to cover. She has heard his stories of his three ex-wives and of his three daughters— one from each spouse.

He spent most of his childhood and married life around women. As his wives fell away, and his daughters moved away, they were replaced by mistresses. The company of women has cultivated his new makeup—one of being a lover of women and, to an extent, a womanizer.

Sonya knows he drinks alone, mostly beer. But about his professorship job and religion research, he says little, not wanting to bore her.

He earns his living at a university in High Point.

With his height, decent looks, prestige, tannish skin, and flowing hair, he has always attracted some women. If he stares at a certain woman, she is likely to be attracted to him. This is how he had been operating for years.

But now, with graying and thinning hair, and gravity working on his body, passionate returned glances can only be garnered with hard emotional work. At fifty, his sex-magnet powers began failing him. Thereafter, if he wanted a woman, he would have to learn who she was, as well as investigate her interests and how to pursue her. Sometimes, to pursue her meant to buy her.

At the University, he secretly had affairs with the wives of older professors who had married younger women. He met them at bars or at university social functions. He would work the scene by talking about his research and some of the books he wrote, mostly novels about spiritual matters and self-improvement, or New Age self-help books. The women enjoyed the novels.

He found Sonya from an online ad from Discreet Companions. She was described as the "Brazilian Babe, exotic and lovely." Her photograph shows her with a long, sleek red dress, a deep V-neck top, and a rose lining her long dark hair. Her ad promised, "Afternoon Delight."

David has a discerning idea of how prostitutes converse with each other about the men they see. Escorts try to tell stories to old men; they laugh and tremble at the same time. Like a young girl on an elevator with several old men, she shudders at their winks and passes.

After over a year of visits to see Sonya, as he is leaving her apartment, she announces something he has resisted thinking about.

"My mother is sick with cancer, and I need to go and care for her. I will need to take a break from our meetings. I won't be here next week."

"How about the week after that?" he asks.

"I'm not sure; Mom's condition is not good," she replies. "You better phone before you come."

"Can I have your number?"

"Phone the agency; they will let you know my status," Sonya replies.

A week passes, and David calls Discreet Companions.

"Can I speak to Sonya?" he asks.

"Sonya has left the agency," a woman says. "Would you like an introduction to one of the other hostesses?"

"Sure," David says.

He spends the evening with Emily in a hotel room off Interstate 95. This girl is skinny and tall, Caucasian, no more than twenty-one years old. She is inexperienced and has difficulty in following his lead.

"What do you do?" the girl asks, as she slips off her tight jeans and purple polyester blouse. The hotel room was dark, and sirens could be heard nearby.

"I do e-commerce," David says.

He does his deed to her. No passion. No smiles. Just an exchange of $300. The girl pockets $150, which is $75 less than Sonya.

There is a new staff assistant in the Psychology Department, which is in the same building as Religious Studies. Her name is Claudia, and he pursues her over the course of a few weeks, until she agrees to lunch with him at the nearby Indian restaurant. She is originally from Finland and is employed to assist research on human personality disorders.

She does a lot of paperwork filing grants for psychology professors to submit to the National Institutes of Health and the American Psychology Association. Over Indian food, Claudia complains about how Americans are so terse and rigid, and about the neighborhood she lives in.

"There is too much crime in America," she says. For the past six months, she and her husband and son have been waiting for their immigration status to change.

"In Finland, we have serious immigration laws. But, here, I can never figure out what paperwork is correct and what the procedures are."

"Really?" David says, smiling at her. And while she moves her head down to take a bite, he is enchanted with her figure.

"The older generation in America does not understand," she says.

The next week, they go out again, a Wednesday. He drives her fifteen miles to Greensboro so he won't run into any colleagues. They have sushi for lunch, and she complains again. He is mostly silent. On the way back to the University, he thinks about Sonya. Then, he is reminded of the Discreet Companions ad Afternoon Delight.

She is surprised by his stopover at his home.

"I need to pick up some materials for my research," David says. "Please come in."

She makes her way to his den and sits on the couch. His walls are full of family photos, including all three ex-wives.

"I thought you were married," she says.

He yells from his study, "I am not," and he continues: "I had three wonderful marriages that ended in divorce."

The woman is both confused by and fascinated with the professor.

A casual conversation over marriage and research turns into sex on the couch. It was a catastrophe.

Kicking and scraping, she works herself into a froth of excitement that in the end only deters him. He thinks of Sonya, while he has sex with this new staff member. He brings her a towel for her and for the couch and drives her back to the University. They talk no more between his car and the building. He avoids her the next day . . . and the next week.

He ponders while reading A History of God: I should stop this nonsense. I could get a castration. I could stay home and drink beer and watch HBO. There is phone sex and video sex. All I need is a camera. I hate the aging process. I miss Sonya. I need to transfer this sexual energy to something productive. But I have tenure and security. I want to be free. Castration? Animals get it. I can ask my doc about it when I go for the prostate exam. Since I'm not married, there are no aesthetic concerns. I should close the chapter with Sonya, too.

The next day, he phones Robert, a former cop turned professor, who he met at a University social.

"Hello, Robert," David says. "We met at the President's BBQ last month.

"David, from the religion department?"

"Yes, I was wondering where I could purchase one of those GPS trackers."

"Why do you need one of those?" Robert says. "North Carolina's cyberstalking law prohibits a person from installing a tracking device without the person's consent."

David lies and says, "I am concerned my wife is cheating on me."

"I'd hire an attorney before planting a GPS tracker on her car." Robert says.

"Thanks for the advice and best of luck in the new academic year." David says and hangs up the phone.

He hires a cheap private investigator to plant a GPS device under Sonya's car. Within a few days, he knows she is traveling from her mother's house in Raleigh to her home in Fayetteville. Her home is near Fort Bragg, and she is married to an Army Commander. The PI also provides David with her home phone number.

He phones her at noon on a Wednesday, thinking her family would not be at home.

"Sonya, this is David," he says. "How are you doing? I miss you."

The phone silent. A vacuum.

"I don't know a David. And there's no Sonya here," she says. "Whoever you are, please do not call here again," she yells.

David pushes the red "end" button on his cell phone. He wonders about her husband: Do they make love like we did?

After class on Wednesday, he decides to get a little exercise by walking past the student center toward the baseball field. The Greenway is a modern escape to a dense campus in High Point.

Along the Greenway, between the baseball stadium and student center, he notices one of his students ahead of him. He recalls her name is Lily from his Religious Studies course. She is a decent student, a B student who sometimes misses classes.

He notices her walk is slow and methodic. Most students have their heads in their cell phones, but she does not. She looks around as if the trees and scenery are attractive. Could it be she is sending out signals?

His womanizing nature kicks in. He catches up with her.

"Hello," the professor says politely.

She smiles back at him. Her eyes are fixated toward his chest. She is much shorter than him and also thinner. Her black hair is long, surrounding a wide face, like a Scandinavian. She is wearing a miniskirt and a greenish halter top, with black tights and a silver belt buckle that matches her earrings.

Does she realize he is a womanizer, a fifty-three-year-old sex-crazed man? Some would say he is a pervert. Like all women, she is sensitive to his persistent attention and the gaze from his brown eyes.

"The weather is nice right now, isn't it?" David says.

"This is my favorite season," she says. "I like to walk the Greenway in the early fall after classes."

"Do you live nearby?" the professor asks. "I'm sorry; I mean are you from around here?"

Again, she smiles at him.

"Yes, down the Greenway and over Centennial Street is my apartment."

"Can I invite you for a drink?"

Silence descends as the two resume walking. Her pace is slightly faster now. But she turns to look at him, and their faces meet in a natural rhythm with their footsteps.

"Okay," she responds.

"Well, turn this way," he says at a Greenway intersection with a city street.

One of his steps lands in a puddle, and she turns and laughs at him.

They walk a few hundred more feet until the Greenway ends on a nice residential street and a gated community where the professor has lived for more than thirty years.

He unlocks the security gate, and they walk side by side to his front door.

"Can I take your bag, Lily?" David asks

"Sure, but I have to be back by 6:00 p.m. for theatre practice," she says softly.

He turns on the lights inside his condo.

He gestures for her to sit on his plush couch. He can see perspiration on her forehead from the sun beating down on the Greenway. She is both excited to be in the home of a tenured professor but cautious, knowing he seems to be a little too friendly.

He is motionless after she sits down. He stares at her. She then lowers her head, being evasive in a foreign place.

Every smart woman knows the world is just overflowing with players, Lily thinks. Is he a smooth talker or a sincere man?

Her beauty makes him swallow. He takes a deep breath and walks to the kitchen.

He opens up a bottle of wine and turns on some soft jazz music. This is what I do to get them to like me now that I am old, he thinks.

But this girl is thirty years my junior, and I have just brought her into my home, where only I live. This is my palace.

"Are you enjoying the course?" the professor asks.

"I liked the study of Jesus."

"Jesus was an amazing figure in the history of religion," the professor responds.

"He was empathic toward all peoples," Lily says. "I admire his humility."

"The religious perspectives on Jesus vary among world religions," the professor adds.

"The Survey of World Religions course you teach is very interesting," Lily says.

"I am most interested in pantheism and Islam, more than in Christianity," the professor adds. "Jesus was good to women."

Lily ponders: Jesus was good to women. The professor seems nice with women, too. Is he a smooth talker? He has charm and a strong, sexy demeanor. Is he a typical ladies' man? He doesn't treat women with quite the respect they deserve.

"What are your career plans?" the professor asks.

"I want to be an actor in theatre," Lily responds. "I'm getting my Bachelor of Fine Arts here."

"Why are you taking a course in world religions?"

She becomes silent. Her long eyelashes move in time with the beat of her finger on the couch. "My father died a few years ago, and I always wondered about God as portrayed in the Bible."

"You mean like Moses and David and all the Old Testament characters?"

"Something like that," she responds. "I want to know who my spiritual father is now."

David leaves the den for a moment and grabs some dishes from the refrigerator, then pieces together a meal—spaghetti, salad, bread, and some wine.

"Do you always cook for yourself?" Lily asks.

"I live alone and always cook by myself."

"But what about all these photos of women?" Lily responds.

"I had three wonderful marriages, and each produced a daughter. But each one ended in divorce."

Lily feels warned. Divorce is not a good thing, and three times makes him . . . she ponders. But he is so nice to me.

"If you like this kind of food, you should marry a man who cooks," he says.

She smiles and answers, "I don't like to cook, so maybe that is a good idea."

They sit together on the couch. She has eaten very little, and he has all but cleaned his plate. His wine glass is empty, and hers is half-empty. He goes to get a second bottle of Chardonnay. It's 5:00 p.m.

For a moment, she contemplates life as a young married woman to a tenured professor. She finishes most of her spaghetti and all of the salad. She sits back to finish off the remaining wine in her glass. His perspiration has gone. She folds her legs, leaving her miniskirt high on her thighs for a moment.

"I see you enjoyed it," he says. "I don't have dessert, sorry."

"That's okay" she says, nodding.

He reaches for the fruit bowl on the kitchen bar: "Unless you want an apple or a banana," he says. "I didn't know you would join me today."

He smiles at her. She is quiet, thinking he can tell that she's nervous. She looks for her bag and leans forward, as though she wants to leave.

"Don't go yet," the professor says. "It's only 5:00 p.m."

"Let me show you more of my home." He grabs her hand and leads her up to see the rest of his home. He escorts her to his living room, where the floors are hardwood. "Do you like to dance?" he asks.

He inserts one of his video cassettes into his machine. The song is called "Come Home" by One Republic. It's a love song with piano and violin accompaniment and male vocals. Standing side by side, they watch the dancers and listen to the song. When the song is over, she walks into the hallway and finds his piano.

"Will you play something for me?" she asks.

"Rock or classical?"

"Jazz, please," she responds. "Something like I first heard in the den."

Looking a bit like Billy Joel with longer dark flowing hair, he plays, and she is mesmerized. She walks around the home, finds his study, and sees the other family photos.

Lily asks the professor, "Do you get lonely?"

"Yes, sometimes," he responds. "Now, I make do with whores."

She chuckles, thinking he is joking, not knowing he has visited Sonya for several years every Wednesday.

"Can I offer you a gin and tonic?"

I never took a drink from a practical stranger, but he's a professor, she thinks. "Can I have whiskey and coffee, instead?"

"Sure," he says. His kitchen cabinets are lined with liquor. Afraid she might be nervous, he mixes the drink quickly and returns to her. Then, he touches her left shoulder, fully bare, in the halter top she is still wearing. "Stay the night with me," he whispers.

Holding the Irish coffee, her lips touch the rim of the cup. She now holds him in high esteem but says, "Why?"

"Because you are with the professor," he responds.

"You're three times my age."

"A woman's beauty is meant to be shared," the professor says. His hand is still on her shoulder, but he moves it down to her back. Perspiration returns to her back, and he can sense her heart starting to beat fast.

"What if I already share my beauty?" she teases. She holds the drink in one hand, her other hand placed on her miniskirt, which rides below her hip. She alternates licking the rim of the cup and asking, "Why . . . why should I stay?"

"You should share your beauty more often," he says.

His words slide from his smooth-talking mouth as smoothly as the creek stones that line his condo and as strong as his iron-door entrance. Under his sudden spell, she feels completely protected and cherished by this man's words.

He then quotes Shakespeare: "She's beautiful, and therefore to be wooed; she is woman, and therefore to be won."

But like a chameleon that changes colors instantly, her mood suddenly shifts from adventurous passion to being a moral young lady who is a student. His smooth words were not a good move on his part. Too much romance and too quick. Typical of an older man trying to capture a young, sexy college student.

Her smile now loses its playfulness. She puts down her cup across the hall on the kitchen counter. She will not join him in bed.

"Changed your mind so fast, young lady?" David says.

"I better get back to studying," she says.

He walks her outside back to the Greenway. The sun is about to set in High Point.

"What a lovely evening," the professor says. "Shall I walk you home?"

"No," she says. "I will be fine."

Like most tenured professors at the University, he is allowed to offer a Special Topics course off-site.

"I have this Q&A World Religions session next Wednesday at The Church Street Brewery," David says. "Would you be interested in attending?"

"I heard about that place from my girlfriends at High Point," Lily says. "That sounds like fun—beer and God."

"Then, good night," David says.

Chapter 3

KATHERINE

"I'm writing a novel," Charles explains. "No one will believe my story, and writing has opened up so many thoughts."

Abigail doubts Charles after he told her about his encounter with a single lady at The Church Street Brewery. That evening, she and Charles decide to attend a Chamber of Commerce social in celebration of Charles's new business opening. They visit The Brewery not for beer; Abigail abhors it. She had an alcoholic grandfather.

Charles calls Abigail on the phone and invites her to the Commerce Social. Abby is a dental hygienist who likes a "clean mouth in more ways than one." She and Charles live private lives, with little social interaction with the business community.

Attending after-hours socials that include alcoholic drinks is not an activity Abigail looks forward to. She prefers sit-down dinners with family—part of the family values she had learned from her own family of seven in the 1970s and 80s. Nevertheless, she wants to support her husband in his efforts to promote his new business.

The social would not last long for the pair. Abby, still dressed in elite scrubs, remains outside the main social area at the outdoor firepit. She wears a white sweater; the fall temperatures chill her. While talking to patients all day, she sees the firepit, visible from three cardinal directions in Uptown High Point. The pit is like a multi-sensory stimulator, as Abigail's attention is on it and her husband, in this brief visit to The Brewery.

Charles grabs a gin and tonic and gets Abby a Dr. Pepper. "I'll check on you in a bit," he whispers to Abby.

Abby responds, "I'm going to wait outside by the firepit. There are too many people in here."

The taproom at The Brewery is a long, somewhat intimate, space with clear glazing along its front, giving dramatic and tantalizingly open views into the old town of High Point, where furniture manufacturing was once thriving. It lends itself to a rewarding interaction and successfully affords a discerning beer-lover an environment for full appreciation of the beer that is being sipped.

The Brewery also serves wine, as many of the so-called "Emerywild" crowd prefer grapes over grain.

Charles mingles a bit in the taproom area. Academic and industry figures are present, including professors from the nearby university and High Point civic leaders.

His ego was popping after landing a new contract and a new business. He spreads around a few hellos and then decides to join his wife; he could see, through the thick crowd, Abigail talks to an old grey-haired man. Charles recognizes him as Jim, a community activist and attorney, whose family knew Charles's father back in the days of segregation.

As Charles strolls to the exit door after exchanging business cards with a few community leaders, a short, stocky lady with bright lipstick and straight shoulder-length hair smiles at Charles, as though they knew each other from some previous encounter. In fact, Charles had never met her before.

Charles moves closer to the woman as he travels in the direction of the front windows. The sun's rays reflect off an outdoor metal pole grazing her hair.

"Hello," says the lady, catching Charles off guard, while he gazes through the taproom window over the short lady's head.

Abigail is conversing with Jim.

"How are you?" Charles responds.

"I'm lovely. Actually, I am Katherine," she giggles, while smiling from ear to ear. Her little hands display a pretty pearl ring, while she drinks from a tall glass of red wine.

"I saw you come in with another woman," Katherine says softly. "What brings you here?"

"I started a new business and wanted to meet some new folks," Charles explains. His gin and tonic is all ice by now; he has downed the treat too quickly.

Katherine notices his drink is done. "This place is really nice; it's roomy, and the selection of beverages is the best in town."

"I'm trying to meet new folks. Know anyone who does websites?"

"I'm a graphic designer more than a web site specialist, but I may be able to help you," Katherine says. By now, her tall wine glass was half full.

"Here is my business card. She is waiting for me."

"She?"

Charles points toward a pair who are conversing at the firepit.

"That is Jim," Katherine whispers. "I have seen him around town, always mingling and flirting with women."

"I normally don't give out business cards to men, but I am giving you mine."

"Nice talking to you," Charles smiles as he departs, and then he turns back to see whether she is still watching him.

With one hand holding the wine glass, Katherine uses the other one to insert his crisp new business card into her small purse. Katherine muses, *I really, really like a guy who is taken.* She exits, turning left after seeing Charles and Abigail joining Jim at the firepit.

Abigail heads for home in her SUV, and Charles sets out for their house in his truck. Abigail happily anticipates the spaghetti dinner she and Charles would soon be eating at home. To her surprise, Charles arrives thirty minutes too late.

On the way home, mildly intoxicated, Charles thinks of Katherine's smile and provocative attire, and then calls her, leaving a voice mail message: "Uh . . . I'd like to set up a meeting with you to discuss a marketing plan."

Two years later, Abigail and Charles sit at the kitchen table, while their meal bakes in the oven and soft music plays in the background. The kids are not home, so the house remains quiet. Charles focuses on pieces of paper, with a pen in hand.

"Are you writing another novel?" Abigail says.

They look at each other, but his words come out of his mouth like thick engine oil—slow, heavy, and bland.

Is it because I am tired that I don't say much to her? Charles ponders. *With Katherine, words would pour out like sweet mountain cider.*

"Can I see the draft?" Abigail says, resting her hands on her iPad.

Charles's editor reviewed the first three chapters and said, "You have some good material here."

Taking the pages of the draft, Abigail walks briskly to the den and reads the Table of Contents.

Meanwhile, music by Journey plays on the TV.

"Cut that off please—it brings back memories," Charles mutters.

The Table of Contents includes: "Carlton, the Widower"; "Jim, the Attorney"; "Katherine, the Single Professional . . ."

"Are you going to write about her again?" Abigail asks.

"Who?" Says Charles.

"Kath . . ." Abigail stops from saying her whole name. The scars from the deep wounds remain with Abigail, despite her steadfast love for her husband and children.

"Do you still think about her?"

"Who?" Charles denies he has any feelings for Katherine. He did think about her often, but he convinces himself that Abigail is the woman he loves.

THE COUCH

That Brewery conversation with Katherine turns out to be a stepping-stone in their attraction for each other: beer and conversation leads them from The Brewery to her house and into her bed, eventually.

All those interesting conversations Katherine and I had about art, writing, and Washington, DC, he thought to himself. Dang, that was so stupid, but I was infatuated with her!

Charles recalls asking Katherine, "Do you want to get married? Do you want to have kids?"

"Charles, dear, my perpetual singledom is not for lack of trying," Katherine replies. "For two decades, I had been on-and-off dating, where I initiated communication with countless men."

Katherine goes on to tell Charles, "My mother married in the 1950s, and my grandmother disliked Mom's working so hard to pay the bills, while my father attended dental school. Gram felt a man was supposed to take care of a woman, not the other way around."

Katherine continues her bachelorette story: "For the next ten years, my mother stayed home and raised three kids, while my father built his dental practice. Then came the young dental assistant and the divorce. My mother walked away broke. My grandparents were deceased by then, but I'm sure my grandmother was looking down, saying, 'I told you so.'"

"My mother's financial struggles terrified me. I promised to never let that happen to me. At age twenty-five, I started investing. I saved, accumulating significant assets over the next ten years. As I aggressively built my net worth, I continued my proactive search for a husband. I wanted to love and be loved.

"But when I was thirty-seven, the doctors told me I had cervical cancer, and they removed my cervix and the upper part of my . . ." Katherine barely makes herself heard as she recounts this to Charles on her couch.

"I'm really sorry," says Charles. "I somewhat understand, though—my mother has cancer."

"Charles, I am sorry to hear that," Katherine responds, from her relaxed position on the couch, as she folds her legs and faces him.

The couch is like a Sigmund Freud scene: a psychoanalytic session, with the patient lying down. Adding to this ambiance is her immaculate den full of books and her jazz music playing softly, as Charles sits on the other end of the plush seat.

"Thanks to my parents, I abhorred the idea of marriage," Katherine intoned.

Charles turns his thoughts from Katherine's couch back to Abigail's concern for him.

"Turn that off, please," Charles shouts to Abigail from the kitchen.

"We have not watched *Our Daily Bread* in several days," Abigail says quietly, implicitly chiding him. "The online version of *Our Daily Bread*, inspires me with the life-changing wisdom of the Bible," said Abigail, "The real-life stories are inspirational."

"I can't hear you, Abigail!" Charles shouts. *Communication is the key to marriage. We have lost our keys.*

Making his way back to the den, Charles admits quietly, "Yes, I still think about her from time to time."

Abigail becomes silent. *I don't think he ever fell in love with me. Love is a sacrifice. A man who truly loves his wife won't cheat on her.*

Charles remains speechless. *I just had a limerence for Katherine. At twenty-one years old, I didn't know what I really wanted. Abigail is a solid person, moral and ethical above all and a God-fearing Christian. The problem was I did not truly know what I wanted.*

"Don't write about her!" Abigail rebukes Charles. "Instead, write about your children."

The two snuggle up and watch *Our Daily Bread* on their iPad. *Our Daily Bread* is a source of emotional and spiritual comfort to the couple after twenty-five years of marriage and one affair.

"Don't forget we need some groceries, Abigail. We normally don't go on Sunday nights."

"I'll get dressed, and we can go after the evening church service," Abigail tells Charles. He grabs his things, and the two head off for church.

Sunday comes, as do church services. Abigail and Charles attend church regularly, serving their congregation and rebuilding their marriage. Their brief visits to the Methodist church proved fruitless; instead, it is the sound doctrine and expository teachings by Baptist preacher, Neal, that "girds their loins" in reconciling their marriage.

This particular Sunday is meaningful, as the couple ride bikes and rake leaves together. "I need to go to the store after church," Abigail yells, as Charles finishes raking.

THE GROCERY STORE ENCOUNTER

Church is over. Abigail and Charles plan to pick up some salmon and vegetables and make a nice dinner. But the time is getting late, and Food Lion is close by. However, Abigail prefers Harris Teeter, especially appreciating the diverse food supplies and the seafood and the dairy sections.

Exiting the sanctuary, they feel a new sense of peace together. "Don't forget we need some groceries," Charles says.

"I'll drive; get in," Charles yells. "Did you get the bags?"

"April will want cereal, as always," Abigail reminds him, as the two round the corner of the produce section.

"I hope I don't run into anyone here," Charles exclaims to Abigail.

"Run into who?" asks Abigail. "Do you want to run into anyone?"

"Like who, Jim or Danny or the 'O.W.'?" Charles responds. The store is busy. Sunday night patrons are getting ready for the start of a new week.

Charles considers what his psychologist, Dr. M., told him about not worrying about other people. "You need to worry about yourself and your family and no one else," the psychologist had chided. Dr. M. would ask Charles the same deep question over and over again: "Why do you want to be married to Abigail?"

Charles answers this question to himself now over and over: *She forgave me for my adultery because of Jesus Christ. That is not what he was asking,* Charles counters to himself. *What do you mean she forgives me because of Jesus? Abigail accepted Jesus Christ as her ultimate authority in her life when she was twelve years old and has never wavered from her faith. She forgave me because of Him.*

Abigail had been thinking to herself since she and Charles reconciled their marriage: *Should I confront my husband's mistress?* Abigail told Charles over and over the past year, "I would never give her the time of day for the pain she caused."

What do the psychologists and marriage counselors think about confronting the spouse's lover? Abigail wondered. *I might have more than a thousand things to say to her and many questions I feel she must answer, like how she was able to capture my husband's heart . . .*

Meanwhile, Charles processes his thoughts: "I'm not wasting my time thinking about who we might run into," Charles murmurs to Abigail.

"The insulated bags, for dairy products—I got them," Abigail says, as though not having heard him.

The Harris Teeter's floor plan is such that the dairy section is in the back corner. The section is cramped, but the aisle is long from the front to the back of the store.

The couple walk together to the seafood section, then turn left past the chicken poultry items. The poultry section proceeds through another turn to where the dairy aisle resides. You can be in a grocery store for an hour and never see any friends because the aisle walls are tall and numerous.

"You go get the milk, and I will look for some chicken," Abigail instructs her husband, who is dressed in a suit because he had just left church. Abigail's dress extends beyond her knees, and her high heels make walking cumbersome. Her plantar fasciitis still bothers her after her frequent long-distance runs.

"Why did you wear high heels, Abigail? Those are going to make your plantar fasciitis worse," says Charles.

Abigail had begun running as a way to cope during the heartache of the affair. *I recently have admired again her newly-found goal of running a marathon; she is devoted to her family, and she told me her legacy was our children,* Charles continued to mull over why he wanted to be married to Abigail.

I like almond milk, but I think she likes some other milk. Why didn't I get clearer instructions from her? Communication is the key to a successful marriage.

For the moment, Charles could distract himself—think about his research, the mountain house, or his family—but then Katherine came to mind: *I'd never run into her here; she shops in Greensboro at The Fresh Market. But I do remember vividly her hair and her figure.* Charles's thoughts are moving toward fantasy, so he stops.

Thoughts, emotions, behavior—Charles knows what to think about, what to act upon, and what not to act upon.

Damn! He thinks. *Is that her?* By the cheese section stood five feet of feminine compactness and style. *I loved sleeping with her because her petite body allowed me to do things that taller women can't.* His thoughts are out of his control.

Don't do it.

But from a scientific perspective, shorter women also have a lower center of gravity, meaning they have an awesome balance, making tricky positions as easy as pie, Charles recalls his analysis of the passion, and the positions, they once shared.

Stop! No more than five seconds passes as he tells himself, *God, I got to get out of here.*

Charles's mentor told him that, if he ran into the O.W. (nickname for Katherine), to walk away since there is nothing to say. "You already wrote her a letter, and that should be enough closure," his mentor had told him.

Charles can see her back as she totes bottles of wine. She reaches for cheese through the glass door at the end of the dairy section. As he squirms toward the front of the store, they pass each other but, this time, only six feet apart.

I really want to talk to her again, the temptation comes for Charles.

Thoughts. Emotions. Behavior.

"Charles," the firm gentle voice—like an elementary school teacher—he remembers so vividly. "Charles, come here!" Katherine calls out. He moves away, slowly, then faster. Her voice gets weaker and weaker as he reaches some fifty feet away toward the front of the store, where the sunlight comes in.

Patrons hear her shout to the man she thought she had a future with. Only a year earlier, Katherine was empathetic and hopeful that their six-month relationship would take on a new meaning. Then, Charles was telling her he was no longer wanted by Abigail.

I will not stop walking. I will turn the corner here and end up in the restroom, where I can wait this out, Charles assures himself.

No, I'd better check on Abigail, and where she is now?

Abigail is a patient shopper. She likes to take her time. Charles makes a long U-turn and comes back behind Abigail, who approaches the dairy section. Then, he sees Katherine literally run into Abigail, as Katherine searches for her old lover.

"Hey, I know you slept with my husband!" Abigail accuses Katherine. "You met at The Church Street Brewery. Do you still go there and pick up married men?"

"I am sorry," Katherine replies. "I am truly sorry."

Standing five-foot-and-eight-inches tall, the lean Abigail towers over the stocky, stylish, five-foot Katherine. Charles had told Katherine, while they were in the affair, that Abigail was the kindest person she would ever meet. But this encounter would create a different impression.

Abigail pushes her grocery cart to the side and faces Katherine. In the corner of her eye, she also notices Ashland, the preacher's wife. Ashland was an outspoken lady, but her "hello" would be squelched for the first time by Katherine.

"Hey, Abigail," Ashland shouts.

Abigail shouts back, "Hey, I'll get back to you."

"Who are you?" asked Katherine. "We are talking now, so excuse me . . ."

Ashland recognizes the two women, who are face to face now, discussing a hot topic. Abigail looks down on Katherine, as a drill sergeant glares at a new Marine recruit.

Ashland is Abigail's prayer partner and was a source of emotional comfort during the affair. Ashland also never shops at Harris Teeter on Sundays due to church responsibilities with her husband, preacher Neal. Katherine doesn't often shop at Harris Teeter, either. The encounter with all three has to be more than a coincidence.

"Listen, the affair is not one to remember, and I want to put this all behind us, but what you did broke the moral code," Abigail admonishes Katherine. "Women do not do this to other women, especially to married women."

Abigail points her finger straight down by her side, a gesture she got from her father when he was feeling "righteous anger."

"When I found out about the affair, I screamed at him for the first time in my life, my voice cracking as I cried day and night."

"I am sorry," Katherine repeats, "but he led me on, thinking your marriage was almost over, and I deeply cared for him."

The red lipstick Katherine wears is now wet with perspiration, as the conversation starts to heat up. The grocery tote Katherine is carrying, which is full of wine and cheese, is weighing her down; her glasses are about to fall off her nose. Sweat starts to accumulate above her lips.

Then, the love of Jesus that Abigail abides in speaks through her to Katherine: "During the marital strife and family crisis, while Charles's heart was with you, I got on my hands and knees and prayed for days and hours for healing." As tears well up in Abigail's eyes, she continues: "Despite being wounded by Charles, I prayed for him daily, hourly, minute by minute at home, and at work. I even prayed for you, Katherine."

Abigail's parents and her devotion to God and family helped shape her response to an unfaithful spouse.

"I am sorry," Katherine replies.

"You don't have to say you're sorry; I already forgave you," Abigail says quietly. "Forgiveness only requires one person, and I forgave you and Charles on my own in private during my prayers to Jesus."

Katherine's eyes tear up. Her right eye has a freckle—something unique about her that was caused by a virus, as she had told Charles on her couch one day.

As Charles hides near the bathroom, he sees Katherine's back from one aisle over, and the conversation appears civil but intense (eyes wide open, Abigail looking down on Katherine). He knew Abigail had saved the day and put full closure to the affair; the encounter at the grocery store was likely a miracle.

Was this encounter with all three women really a miracle? Charles wonders.

Miracles have existed in history, and two-thirds of Americans believe in them, according to a 2016 Barna Group poll. But two-thirds of Americans do not believe in marriage restoration, and breaking the marital moral code is frowned upon by the majority of Americans. Charles and Abigail had proven her work colleagues and society to be wrong.

Essentially, a miracle is an unusual manifestation of God's power designed to accomplish a specific purpose. The consistent Christian recognizes that God's power is constantly displayed in the clockwork operation of the universe, perhaps a continuous miracle.

Most definitions given for the word "miracle" are not complete. The popular Christian author and broadcaster, former atheist, C.S. Lewis, writes this in the introduction to one of his books: "I use the word 'miracle' to mean an interference with Nature by a supernatural Power."

On this day, the encounter at the grocery store was a miracle in Charles's mind, like a rare astronomical conjunction of three independent bodies. Three unlikely women meet face to face.

"I don't know that I can fully understand your Jesus," Katherine tells Abigail, "but you will never hear from me again."

Katherine left for The Brewery to pick up some beer and then headed home . . . this time with no married man, but rather with a secret.

Chapter 4

JIM

New retirees, Deborah and her husband, Johnny, pick up Danny in their CRV around 9:00 a.m. Danny, dressed in a suit, exits his garage workplace and slams the car door. "Did you need a biscuit, hon?" Danny offers Deborah.

"No, I just want to get this thing over."

"Well, why do you think Charles wants this meeting?" asks Johnny. "He already received a partial payout." Johnny drives Deborah and Danny to Jim's office, arriving at the 9:30 meeting.

"When are these estates going to be settled?" Deborah asks Danny. "I want my money now."

Johnny, Deborah, and Danny sit down at the long conference room table. The conference room is where the firm's principal, Jim, a seventy-something poster child copy of his father, meets with clients or community leaders. Today, the attorneys and heirs are meeting to respond to concerns that one beneficiary, Charles, has over the handling of two estates, having multiple issues and complaints.

Meanwhile, Charles has to prepare to meet the siblings who have kept him out of most of his mother's asset distribution. *I wonder what happened to her diamond rings, Charles ponders. They gave me six Bibles from her stash of books, but they did not disclose her jewelry. It is the Bible they may need the most.*

Four years prior to the meeting, Charles had called Jim's law office and spoke to his assistant, Ray, who stated that Jim's colleague, Jack, was handling the estate. Ray went on to confirm, "Charles, your name is all over the will and estate papers; I don't think you have anything to worry about—you are the executor, with power of attorney and health proxy."

Charles was, indeed, executor with power of attorney for Asher Anderson, Charles's stepfather and his mother's (Mary's) third husband. She had died after a long battle with cancer.

After Mary's death, Danny showed up at Asher's home each morning to bring over breakfast and talk secretly with caregiver Patty. "If Asher needs anything, you call me, Patty—not Charles or Abigail," ordered Danny.

Danny was still a single man living at his workplace, and his immediate family was unsure of his relationship with his extended family.

Charles had uncovered Danny's greedy strategy years earlier when discussing their father's rental properties. Charles stopped by Danny's place of business and wanted to receive wisdom from his elder brother, Danny, hoping his words would offer guidance on life and financial investing. Charles walked toward the auto shop, which smelled much like paint, and the cloud of fumes briefly hid the dirty-looking Danny, who walked out the garage door.

"You ain't working today?" Danny chided Charles. Danny was known for smart remarks that hid his insecurities as a short, divorced man.

A few years earlier, while Danny and his wife were divorcing, she asked Danny for half of the value of the home they shared. Danny would not agree to her request. So, the ex-wife took Danny to mediation and threatened to sue him. Danny's ex-wife had to hire an attorney to resolve their asset issues, including Danny's attempt to devalue their first home. Despite Danny's evil tactics, Charles looked up to Danny as a possible surrogate for their dead father.

Charles had offered, "I'm interested in buying one rental property that I worked on as a teenager with Dad. Are you interested in selling one of the many you have, Danny?"

Danny smirked, looked at Charles, and said, "You don't want one of those." Then, he turned away like a coward.

The ancient practice of primogeniture was the first-born male's right as the eldest son to succeed to the estate of his ancestor to the exclusion of all others. Primogeniture, in ancient times, was a system of inheritance in which land passed exclusively to the eldest son, partly to help keep it undivided. Until the Industrial Revolution, this system severely restricted the freedom of younger sons, who were often forced into the military or the clergy to earn a living.

So, Danny—controversial and often despised and feared among his immediate family—was doing "good deeds" for Asher: bringing him breakfast, pushing him around in the wheelchair, and flattering his elderly acquaintances in the cafeteria at River Landing. Danny always came to see Asher when Charles and Abigail were not around, as though he did not want them to catch his act—cowardice.

Danny had rationalized this behavior as doing all these virtuous deeds for his mother, unaware his actions appeared to Abigail and Charles as though he was plotting his revenge and manipulating Asher. For the previous eleven years, Danny despised "the old man," and then later, he wanted to be best buddies with the multimillionaire.

"Mama, I worked so hard on your mountain property. You know Charles doesn't care about the farm," Danny complained to his mother several months before she died of cancer. Danny's complaints to his mother were just façades of manipulation and dishonest business practices, as he did not share the funeral arrangements with Charles or Abigail. Danny was a schemer, and Asher had no choice in elder manipulation.

Charles suspected Deborah's cold shoulder toward him was because she either had negative and irrational emotions toward him or saw the dollar signs with Danny's new-found obsession with Asher. When Charles and Abigail confronted Deborah about Danny's hidden agenda, Deborah resorted to "you have to ask Danny about that," rather than thinking independently about the best alternative or taking a neutral position on the issues.

Four years earlier, Asher had a minor falling accident. In previous wills, Asher always had a co-executor or back-up. But the subsequent will was altered so that Charles was no longer the executor, and there was no back-up. Danny had manipulated Asher—now ninety-eight years old—into changing the will. "Asher, Charles is too busy, and Abigail has her hands full, so you better let me handle your estate," Danny had begged the old man.

Charles wondered why, since he was the executor, Asher's attorney or Asher himself had not informed him of the executor change. Most elderly folks don't change their wills when they are about to die, when they are physically and mentally weak. For Asher's prior will, Mary was the executor, and Charles was the back-up. Then, Asher changed the executor to Charles and wrote his nephew, Chuck, telling him about the alteration.

Asher had been recorded on tape as saying that Charles was to be the executor.

DJ informed Charles of the meeting they had been requesting from the estate lawyer, Jim, for several weeks. DJ had discovered some serious flaws in Danny's probate filing of the will.

Danny's self-image was faulty, his jealousy of Charles raging, and his revenge for the mountain house deed-change was brewing. Thus, Danny attempted to act as an attorney, to control everyone, but he had lacked the formal education or experience to enable him to do so correctly.

His drinking buddy, Jack, the first lawyer to represent their mother's estate, had been careless in managing the estate, and he left off Charles as one of the co-trustees of the large bank account. Charles would later learn Danny did this intentionally.

Charles's attorney, DJ, arrived at the same time as Danny and Deborah. Rather than be on time at 9:30, Jim, the principal, was missing, but his paralegal, Sharon, received Danny, Deborah, Johnny, and DJ into the conference room. Attorney Richard was also present but only for the Mary Anderson estate. The conference room walls lined photos and plaques, with the name "Jim Mashburn" prominent on all walls and desks. Jim wanted everyone to know he was important, and anyone who entered the conference room knew who was boss.

"Good morning, everyone; I am DJ Saintsing, Charles's attorney." DJ was a young stud, not quite cocky or arrogant but confident—now a partner in a reputable law firm in Winston-Salem. Charles had met with him a month earlier, explaining to him how the two estates of Mary and Asher comingling is fishy.

"Here is the big box of accounting records for the estates," Charles said. "I had to go to the courthouse and make copies myself because Jim's firm and Danny rarely informed me of the transactions."

DJ sat at the end of the conference table—a non-verbal strategy, bold—to show authority. Danny was sitting at the other end of the conference room table, rubbing his face and bowing his head—tactics of a telltale sign of dishonesty. Danny didn't speak to DJ, since Danny wanted to exclude Charles from anything of monetary value in their mother's estate. DJ explained that he was representing Charles to review some of the issues with the estate paperwork. A concerned Danny, dressed up in a business suit, put his hand on his forehead and stared at the floor beside him, as to disregard the younger DJ. Meanwhile, Deborah nudged Johnny to her right and whispered, "Where is Charles? When is this estate going to close out? I just want my money."

Charles was on his way to the meeting, driving slowly to arrive after everyone else. The late arrival was not typical of the teacher, who started his lectures at the University on time, every time. But that day, Charles pondered and prayed that a seed of unity could be sowed for the long-lost Spencer family. "God, help me to say the right words, and You be pleased," he appealed. His late arrival, passive avoidance, most likely had hurt the overall desire for family unity in the past four years, contributing to the bickering of the siblings and lack of open communication.

Parking his truck at Jim's office, a suited-up Charles walked by Danny's Ford F-250 carrying the legal file storage box of estate papers he amassed as heir to his mother's estate and co-trustee of the co-mingled Asher estate.

"God, here he is!" Deborah whispered to her husband, Johnny. A nervous Danny says nothing.

Charles walked straight into the law office. "I am here to see Jim Mashburn," he politely told the receptionist.

"I think they are in there . . ." said the receptionist, pointing toward the conference room down the hallway.

Charles thought, *why is there a Jaycee Jollies' photo of my father and Jim's father in "blackface" on the receptionist's desk? That is racist.*

Charles had met Jim once before, face to face, four years earlier in his office, when the estates' issues first commenced. "There sure is a lot of money in this estate," Jim had smirked to Charles. "Your daddy and mine were best buddies."

Charles contemplated this: *The love of money is the root of evil.*

Charles had shown up at the first and only attorney-client meeting, but Danny had not—only Jack came. Jim was waiting around in the reception area, making flattering comments about an old photo of his father and Charles's father. The principal of the firm, Jim, attempted to appeal to Charles's emotions with the photograph of him and his father with Charles's father. Then, Jim remarked about how much money was involved in the Asher estate. It became clear that Jim was in the game only for the money, and not for a win-win outcome.

A few days after that meeting, Charles's first attorney sent a letter to Jim:

Dear Jim,

I wanted to follow up on some of the items that we discussed at your offices the other day. This obviously can get a little sticky when we have two Co-Trustees who do not get along or communicate with each other, and each is separately represented.

In reviewing the Application for Letters Testamentary, I noticed that only Danny was listed as the Trustee of the Revocable Trust, which is the beneficiary of the estate. I've spoken with the Clerk's office, and they have made a notation on the estate file that Danny and Charles Spencer Stanton are the Co-Trustees of the Revocable Trust. This is necessary, as each will have to sign off on the Final Accounting when the probate estate is closed.

Up to the present time, Charles has been pretty much been kept in the dark. He was not listed on the Application for Letters Testamentary as a Co-Trustee, and he believes that this was done intentionally. I have told him that this was merely an oversight in the court paperwork that has now been rectified.

Please be aware that Charles Spencer is a "numbers

guy" and takes his appointment and the fiduciary responsibility that goes with that appointment to heart. He is also aware of his potential personal liability as a Trustee should there be issues with the payment of the possible estate taxes. I know that the two brothers do not get along, but, because of them being Co-Trustees, there must be open communication between the two of them and the three residuary trust beneficiaries.

Please let me know when the information is available to bring me up to date on the trust assets and the communication with the beneficiaries as to a good time to meet as soon as possible.

Regards,
Keith (Attorney representing Charles)

Progress in the estate eventually had gone nowhere, and Charles was rarely informed on legal transactions by the Mashburn firm. Mostly, one or two rudimentary letters, with no phone calls or meetings.

Fast forward four years: entering the conference room with a file box in hand and facing all four persons, Charles noted that Johnny sat on the middle side, Deborah to his right, and Danny on the end. Deborah's smile baffled Charles; this nonverbal cue suggested she was taking anti-depressants again. Charles had learned to wait until some had introduced themselves before flashing his own pearly whites.

Why would my sister, who didn't respond to my letter, and now sides with my brother over Mom's money, be smiling at me? Charles wondered: *She used to look slimmer; has the stress Danny has caused her affected her health?* Charles set down the large box of estate records.

It would've taken two knives to cut the tension in that room. In the partially-dimmed room, DJ stood up to greet Charles, while his siblings and Johnny remained sitting. Only Johnny's expression appeared genuine. Danny's facial expression was changing from grimacing to looking away. Danny was hiding something, as his eyes did not remain fixed during the initial greeting and introduction. This physiological reaction indicated to Charles that Danny felt uncomfortable, fearing to be trapped by questions he didn't want to answer. Charles recalled Danny having said years earlier, "Only the strongest survive in the wilderness." Charles thought, *Danny must fear that he is in a dangerous situation such as facing a human or animal adversary.*

Deborah was also blinking her eyes and smiling more often than normal. "When stressed—for instance, when someone knows she's lying—she may blink five or six times in rapid succession," was a passage Charles recalled from a book on negotiating behavior.

In walked Sharon, announcing that Jim is too busy to meet in the conference room but would have a few moments in his office for Charles's attorney, DJ. Attorney Richard remained passive taking no leadership in the matter. "I think we better meet separately today," DJ said to the siblings and the paralegal.

Charles was standing and facing his siblings and Johnny, and there was no interaction, nor eye contact. DJ attempted small talk with Danny, who said, "I'll go talk to Jim." Charles figured the seeds of unity would again fall on rocky soil.

Prior to that day's meeting, Charles had asked another attorney about

Jim and his behavior, "Can Jim be trusted to explain the mishandling of the estates?"

Charles's theory that Jim was politically motivated was affirmed by the other attorney's comments: "He is really a politician, only caring about his image in the community. You better be careful when money is involved."

Those who happen to live or work with a narcissist know all too well how problematic the forging of solid, honest relationships can be. For a narcissist, almost everything is about him and his hidden agendas. This attorney meeting included a narcissist and a politician: Danny and Jim.

Any area of conduct that is legal, yet potentially unethical, is an attorney's duty to communicate clearly. According to the American Bar Association, a lawyer, as a member of the legal profession, should seek a result advantageous to the client but consistent with requirements of honest dealings with others, and a public citizen having special responsibility for the quality of justice.

DJ accompanied Charles to the smaller room down the hall. "Why can't we all meet together and discuss my concerns?" Charles inquired of DJ.

"Your siblings were bickering over the delay in handling these estate matters," DJ responded.

"Delay? It's been four years waiting on Danny and Jim to communicate the transactions," Charles exclaimed. "As a co-trustee, Danny is supposed to inform me."

Charles had written a letter to Jim several weeks prior: "According to GS 36C-8-802, the trustee shall administer the trust solely in the interests of the beneficiaries. GS36-8-803 goes on to say if the Trust has two or more beneficiaries, the trustee shall act impartially in managing, investing, and distributing the trust property," Charles explained. "Furthermore, as co-trustee, I must agree to any transactions of the Asher Anderson Trust. I have only been contacted once by your office in 2016, where I signed the Fidelity Trustee agreement. Since that time, the Fidelity Trust was debited in full, and your office did not provide me information on this transaction. Moreover, your office did not provide me with details on access to the Trust. Upon visiting the Clerk of Court's office, I found the accounting statement shows multiple transactions from the Trust and that I am unaware of their details. In your Trust Ledger Statement of November 23, 2018, there is a payment to River Landing Retirement Home for $6954.59 and another payment to Mashburn et al. LLP for $226,803.87. Additionally, the statement ends on January 28, 2019. Are there additional transactions your office conducted in the Trust of Asher Anderson without my knowledge? Moreover, I received the Federal Schedule K-1 of interest on inheritance after I filed my income taxes—July 15, 2020 by Accountant Amy. This was unethical and motivated by Danny. I will be glad to sit down with you and discuss my concerns. Until we do so, and the Trust Statement concerns are rectified, I will not be signing any closeout agreements. Please reread GS-36C Article 8, and then contact me at your earliest convenience. I am available by telephone."

DJ left Charles in the small room and went back to the large conference room to meet Jim. But he remembered that Jim will only meet in his office. So, DJ asked the executor, Danny, if he would meet together with Jim. "Why don't we go and discuss these issues with

Jim. I have given both of you the questions prior to this meeting so you will know their contents," DJ exclaimed. So, Danny and DJ made their way to Jim's office, neither saying a word.

"Hey, buddy, you want to grab a drink at The Brewery for lunch?"

Jack excluded Jim. Meanwhile, Sharon was in Jim's office, sitting down at his computer. "Do I need to tally up all these numbers in the estate accounting ledger?" Sharon asked Jim.

"I think the total comes to about nine million, and we need to get about four percent of this money," Jim's deep voice asserts.

"What about Charles—does he have to agree to the four-percent fee?" Sharon asked Jim.

"Don't worry about Charles," Jim responded. "He's the baby boy and is not concerned with our fee; Danny will talk him into it."

For the moment, DJ and Danny stood next to each other outside Jim's office. One wearing a suit, one in jeans. Danny with head down, jaw moved crooked, and eyes moving around. The thin office walls allowed conversations from Sharon, Jim, and Jack.

"That's right, the baby boy with all that education can't keep up with Mama's estate," Danny mumbled to himself while moving his hand to his mouth. When lying, people often cover their mouths because this unconscious body language represents a closing off of communication. Also, when lying, people tend to cover vulnerable body parts, which they feel are exposed and vulnerable.

Facing Danny squarely, DJ said, "Danny, let's get Jim's attention, in order to go over why Charles was left off the estate transactions."

Danny changed his facial expression to a rolled tongue in his mouth but kept his hand on his mouth and repeated himself: "The boy is an old man now and took the mountain house from me and cannot keep up with Mama's estate."

Meanwhile, Charles was waiting in the small conference room by himself with the large legal file storage box, notebook, and tape recorder. *Jerry taught me to use a hidden tape recorder in big meetings with narcissistic old men because they often forget what they said or lie, thought Charles. This Jim really loves himself, with all these plaques photographing his community activities. He's riding his father's coat-tails, just like Danny rode my father's. Jackasses.*

"Sharon, I really appreciate your help with the Anderson ten-million-dollar estate," Jim said as he walked up behind her chair. "Do you want to join me for drinks at The Brewery after work?" Sharon had joined the firm several years before, after her secretarial role at her church went away once membership declined. She was a God-fearing lady, but Jim's flirtatious comments, and her recent separation, had hurt her self-esteem deeply, so she liked the attention Jim gave her. Jim wanted everyone to think he was a father figure to the forty-something Sharon, but in reality, he was merely a flirt.

Jim had stopped wearing his wedding band twenty years ago, when he went through a so-called "mid-life crisis." Jim's wife rarely came to his office. Jim's flirtatious behavior and drinking habit was nothing new; he was known around town as a controversial community activist—one with unethical business practices, drinking, and flirtatious behavior that was noticed by just about everyone and accepted by most.

The lack of attention from Sharon's distant husband made her seek attention elsewhere, so she started wearing revealing attire at work.

Squarely facing Jim's doorway, DJ politely added, "Hello, Jim. Can I discuss the estate issues with you?"

"I suppose I have some time, but I'm going to the new brewery this afternoon," and as Jim sat down and Sharon was leaving, he added, "Danny Boy, come on in, my friend."

DJ took a seat in front of Jim, while Danny was beside Jim in a lower chair, and DJ marveled at the corner office. The corner office is a symbol of success and power. It is the modern-day throne room where Jim would rule the firm and plot his community activism. Jim would beckon people to his presence and cast down rulings, hirings, and firings. However, his castle was everyone else's dungeon.

The eyes are the windows to the soul, and this was especially true with Danny and Jim. Like a bulldog in heat, Jim nor Danny would look at DJ eye to eye. "One of the issues with the Trust, Jim, is that Charles was not notified of most of the transactions in this ten-million-dollar estate," DJ protested. DJ had a habit of staring directly at the other person, eye-to-eye; he had learned in law school that honest negotiation was done face to face. Danny remained silent with his hand covering part of his mouth and looking down.

DJ noticed that Jim's chair behind his large desk was higher than the rest of the chairs—the two he and Danny were occupying. DJ thought to himself that this simple office arrangement creates a subtle psychological dynamic between Jim and the opposing attorney. The opposing attorney is stuck in one place, while the interrogator can freely move around the room. *Similar to a throne, Jim sits higher than me,* DJ thought. With these two pieces of furniture, a message was subconsciously sent: Jim and Danny were in charge, and DJ, representing Charles, was not.

Charles told DJ in their first face-to-face meeting that he wanted a win-win agreement. "What do you want me to do for you, Charles?" DJ exclaimed. "I do see smoke coming from all your mother's accounting records in the legal storage box, but I can't find a gun."

In a quiet tone of voice, Charles replied, "When a person needs to communicate something vitally important to another person, face-to-face conversation is usually the method best suited to produce a win-win scenario or build trust. A phone conversation is less effective than a face-to-face meeting; even the use of a mediator may be necessary."

Charles knew Danny felt that he deserved all of his mother's property, based on his informal suggestion to acquire Charles's interest and ownership in an earlier 2001 face-to-face conversation, with Mary present. The conversation had taken place at the forty-acre mountain house property, informally in the grassy meadow, rather than at a previously scheduled formal meeting at a table, where everyone would know the agenda beforehand. After Danny and Charles worked on the stone wall together, his mother had asked the boys to meet in the meadow. "I want to buy you out, Charles; you don't want this property," Danny had pleaded, trying to manipulate Charles.

Charles had been taken aback and immediately said, "I was with my father when he was dying on this property, and it is too sentimental to let go."

Charles had disagreed with his brother's position that he deserved all of the mountain property based on Danny's claim that he'd kept it up and performed all the work. Charles's philosophy had been based on a common principle of inheritance: the parent chooses how to divide her estate, not the child, not the heirs.

Now, with Jim and Danny in charge, and DJ representing Charles, years later, the baby boy could not reach a win-win. As his eyes were either closed or looking around, the seventy-something Jim stated to DJ, "My father started this law firm in 1948. He helped build this city, and I will be damned if I'll let some young attorney like you try to dictate how I handle these estates." Jim then added, "Where did you go to law school, anyway?"

"Wake Forest—with honors, sir," DJ responded.

"I thought you went to Campbell, like Jack," Danny smirked. "Or was it that negro school in Durham?" DJ became irritated that the two men were basically teaming up against him.

"I'll handle all the closeout stuff," Danny countered.

"Danny, Charles has to sign off on all final paperwork, and he does not agree to the appraisal you had performed," DJ stated. "And speaking to Charles, the reduction in 'fair market value' (FMV) of $265,000 to $125,000 seems incorrect relative to construction costs to gain legal access to the Big Horse Creek Property."

Charles had told DJ that, based on 2019 construction data, the cost to build a bridge and dirt road from any of the three cardinal directions (W, N, E) would not exceed $55,890 to $77,252, depending on the materials utilized. Since the tax value was $265,000 in 2019, the appropriate fair-market value was $265,000 minus ½ ($77,252 + $55,890) = $198,429, worst case.

"I don't agree with the technical method or the business manner in which the appraisal was ordered and performed," DJ objected. "Do you have any idea what it costs to maintain that property?" Danny slammed his hand down on Jim's table and yelled. "I nearly broke my back and still suffer from a torn meniscus keeping that place up."

"Well, if y'all could get your matters in order, I'm going to The Brewery," Jim said.

"Gentlemen, I can see we're not going to come to any agreement today," DJ said. "Let me go talk to my client, and I will get back to you."

DJ headed back to the small conference room with Charles, while Deborah and Johnny waited in the large conference room. "You've already been paid $41,000. Is that really the one-third value of the mountain house?" Johnny asked Deborah. "It's worth much more than that," Deborah said.

"Why could we not all meet together in the large conference room?" Charles pleaded with DJ. DJ confirmed that, before he arrived, Charles's siblings were already bickering about the time delay of settling the estates and that he knew right away they were not going to be team players.

"What kind of vibe did you get from Jim and Danny?" Charles asked.

DJ sat down and confirmed the narcissist behavior of Danny. "Your brother sure does think highly of himself," DJ chuckled. "And Jim is not too far behind."

DJ was unaware that Charles had both audio recordings and copies of old wills, where Asher Anderson had agreed with Charles on his executor role. Danny had secretly manipulated the ninety-eight-year-old multi-millionaire to change the will and trust. A breach of fiduciary duty, based on comingling the estates and embezzlement, was documented by Charles. But at this attorney meeting, DJ was interested in finding a win-win agreement, and Jim was more interested in leaving work for Church Street than honestly discussing some of Charles's concerns.

DEBRA

Debra sits on a white floormat in her bathroom, examining the rows of medications lined up on the shelf of the vanity—neat piles of green and white boxes of blood thinners, a rainbow of pill bottles, and painkillers worth thousands of dollars. She studies the labels: Percocet, Zofran, Maxeran, Dexamethasone.

Debra ponders the directions: *Take daily. Take twice daily. Take with food. Do not crush. Do not chew. Take as needed.*

She wonders if a one-month supply of drugs can save a sick person's life. *It probably will if I consume them as directed. Chew them, crush them, and don't take with food.*

Take handfuls at the same time. But the order matters. I must swallow an anti-nausea pill first so I don't vomit up a $248 cancer pill.

Debra has taken cancer medications for over two years, not wanting to die. The fifty-eight-year-old Debra remembers the day she and her husband, Don, brought the drugs home. On the afternoon of June 10, 2017, she was discharged from The Cancer Center. As she changed from her hospital gown into jeans, she let out a sob: "The cancer has spread down my leg," Debra said. "And I don't know what to do about it."

Don is sixty-three years old and has suffered from high blood pressure for nine years. He was a firefighter for twenty-five years. The firefighter, unlike most athletes, wears thirty to forty pounds of gear, which increases the workload and also insulates the firefighter, impairing all usual means of dissipating heat.

When he was fifty-four years old, his job as a firefighter led to a heart attack. He and Debra liked to call it a "silent attack," but soon the doctors told him the attack was caused by a leaky heart valve.

"Don't worry, honey, we'll get through this together," Don attempts to console Debra. "I'll make some dinner now."

"You shouldn't make high-cholesterol meals, like hamburgers and French fries!" Debra complains.

"We have to enjoy something in life, so why shouldn't that be burgers and fries?"

"Can you bring me my jeans?" Debra yells from her bedroom. "I'm tired of wearing hospital gowns."

The short, bulky Don leaves the den for the bedroom, grabs the Levi's, and takes them to Debra, who's seated in the master bathroom.

"They are a size eight—smaller than usual," Don whispers, as he crouches closer to her.

"Help me get these pants on, please," Debra says.

Her body has grown so thin from the medicine that her jeans keep sliding down, even with her belt cinched as tight as it can go.

Don helps her get to her feet. "Here ya go," he says. "Now, pull them up."

Don is already winded from the short walk and from assisting Debra. His high blood pressure has left him with poor cardiovascular health.

"I'll make some hamburgers," repeats Don.

"Ever since I started taking these meds, my appetite has gone to shit," Debra replies. "Can we just sit and watch a good movie?"

In the two years after her diagnosis, uterine and ovarian cancer have galloped through her body at a ruthless pace, laying claim to her kidneys, her lungs, and her liver. In its wake, blood clots formed, threatening to block her arteries and veins. One clot had already clogged the vessel carrying blood to her liver, causing the organ to swell so large that it extended across her abdomen and hogged any space that rightfully belonged to food. Each day became a balancing act in blood consistency: too thin, her kidney bled profusely; too thick, clots threatened to move into her lungs and kill her.

Don makes the burgers, even though Debra knows Don's diet is supposed to be low in cholesterol.

Don carries a dinner tray with the hamburgers, buns, French fries, and fruit into Debra's bedroom. Debra lies on her bed, her facial expression gloomy. Her cancer diagnosis has created feelings of depression, anxiety, and fear about her future.

"I'll sit up here with you, and we'll eat together," Don leans over and whispers to Debra.

"I don't know if I'm even hungry anymore," Debra responds. Next to her bed, on the nightstand, is a journal she's kept since her cancer diagnosis. She never had much interest in writing, but now, she thinks, *This journal is a valuable asset that my children and grandchildren can read one day, after I am long gone.*

"I'll turn on the TV," Don says. "Do you see the remote?"

"I've kept it in the drawer on your side," Debra responds, "ever since you started sleeping in the other room."

Don fumbles the silverware on the bed, while stretching to open the drawer.

"Do you read this anymore?" Don asks Debra, pointing to the old Bible sitting next to the remote.

"What?"

"Your grandma's *King James Bible,*" he replies.

"From time to time," she says, "I read it, and it gives me solace, like the children do."

Don can't help but notice how weak she really is when he feeds her. Her mouth opens at a slow pace, and her eyes are fixated on the flowers sitting on the dresser.

"Here, let's eat," Don feeds her a small piece of hamburger.

"I know I've gained weight," Debra whispers.

"You're so weak, you need to eat more," Don admonishes her.

Debra considers, *During my year in treatment, I learned that chemo interrupts the brain's ability to metabolize carbohydrates, which results in "chemo brain." Once one is off the chemo, the brain goes back into functioning normally, for the most part.*

"I was able to lose a lot of weight and exercise before I got this cancer," Debra says. "My joints can no longer take the pounding of intense exercise, and I can barely walk, even at a moderate pace."

"Maybe we can ask the oncologist when we can exercise again," Don adds. "Take a sip of this water, honey."

Detecting my sensitivity around this subject, my oncologist trod lightly around the fact that the little pill designed to keep my type of breast cancer from returning was most likely also responsible for my unwanted weight gain, as well as the inability to lose weight at an acceptable pace.

At home that evening, right on schedule at seven o'clock, Debra had taken her cancer medication, and then she vomited it up.

"Don, I need a warm rag for my head."

By morning, she is peeing out blood clots, and she can't eat or drink.

"We better call the oncologist," Debra whispers to Don.

"Okay, my blood pressure readings are high again this morning," says Don, as he goes to the phone.

"Hi, Becky, this is Don Swinger. Debra is having serious reactions to the medicine this morning."

The nurse consults with the oncologist, and he agrees to meet with them at 11:00 a.m. at the hospital Cancer Center. Debra had been home less than twenty-four hours, but she had wanted some time in that familiar environment.

Home again, Don and Debra lie down on their queen-sized bed, on top of a white-and-beige quilt they received as a wedding present thirty-three years ago. On the other side of their open window, a bird taps its beak on a metal air conditioning vent. Debra lies on her left side; her right side aches too much to place pressure on it. Don nuzzles in behind her and puts his nose to her back, where he imagines the diseased kidney to be. The two weep like that together for half an hour, as Don inhales deeply and pretends that he is drawing the cancer out of her body and into his. Moments later, Debra says, "Let's go to the hospital."

The stocky Don dresses in jeans and a plaid, long-sleeve shirt, and he grabs his newspaper and car keys.

"We'll take the truck, dear," Don says.

"Can you take my overnight bag, honey?" asks Debra.

"You won't be staying overnight, will you?" Don replies.

The song *Glory of Love* by Peter Cetera plays on the radio. It's Valentine's Day.

The ride to the hospital becomes another meaningful time of reminiscing.

Don's truck is a 4x4. As he escorts Debra to the truck using one hand, the other one carries her overnight bag.

"I'm too weak to get up into this truck," Debra exclaims. "But I like being 'high up.'"

The sun is shining, and High Point is alive with cars going up and down Main Street. The truck is about to pass a few churches in Uptown.

"I want to stop at the grocery store and pick up some chewing gum," Debra tells Don.

"Okay. Harris Teeter?" Don replies.

"Yes."

"I'm going to wear my bandana." Debra adds. "I don't want anyone to see me like this."

"Can you make it by yourself?" Don asks.

"Yes, I want to do this alone," Debra responds.

As Debra comes down the canned goods aisle, she spots a woman she has not seen in years. The woman comes toward Debra with her cart and asks, "What have you done to your hair?" Debra thinks to herself, *Is she disapproving of my hair partially covered with my bandana? Her face confirms her disdain for my short, curly, post-chemotherapy hair.*

Before Debra can respond and before she realizes her friend's question was both misinformed and hurtful, the woman looks at Debra with a look that seems to say, "Bless your heart," and she remarks, "It used to be so pretty."

Debra squares up her body to the woman and responds quite honestly, "Chemo. These are my chemo curls coming out of my bandana."

The woman completely misses that information and keeps on talking.

"Your appearance has surely changed since I last saw you," the woman rudely tells Debra.

Debra is wearing a coat, so the woman cannot see the weight loss.

"Nice to see you," Debra says as she walks off. *Words have power. So many times, I've wished I could have either taken back something I said or spoken more comfortingly. There have been times in my life when my tongue slipped. As the Bible says, the tongue is a two-edged sword. It also says in Proverbs, "Death and life are in the power of the tongue, and those who love it will eat its fruits." Having gone through the difficulties of hair loss, however, I am more aware of the tremendous power of words. I know that so many well-meaning people struggle with what to say to others, especially during the crisis of a serious illness.*

Debra carries nothing but her purse. She grabs the chewing gum, exhausted from the conversation, and walks slowly to the front checkout counter.

Don is waiting for her just outside the front door. He comes out and assists Debra back into the truck.

"How did it go?" Don asks.

"I ran into Gracie Saintsing," Debra's voice cracks. "She has no idea what I am going through."

"What do you mean?"

"She said, 'you sure have changed a lot,'" Debra exclaims. "Can't she see I've lost most of my hair?"

"I'm sorry. I should have gone inside with you."

"The most comforting words I received were, 'I'm sorry you are going through this,' Debra says. "Nothing more needs to be said."

Don turns his truck back onto Main Street, and the two head south.

Debra is still talking to herself. *Every person dealing with cancer knows that things might not turn out 'okay'. To offer false reassurance is not comforting or encouraging; rather, it diminishes a person's feelings because it discounts the lived experience of an unpredictable illness.*

"That is where we got married years ago, First Baptist Church," Debra tells Don. "Let's turn down Church Street and see it."

"They're doing a lot of construction across the street," Don replies. "We might not be able to get the truck next to the old sanctuary."

"Across the street, the sign says, 'Coming soon—The Church Street Brewery,'" Debra says to Don.

"They are remodeling the old factory," Don replies. "I've put out many small equipment fires in that old factory."

"The factory you said has the chemical storage vault underground?" Debra asks.

"Yes—that is the one. OSHA violations for sure now in 2019," Don says.

Debra asks Don to stop and pull into the parking lot, where she can see the old church. She can't help but see among the backhoes and construction activity the brewery going up.

The Church Street Brewery. I've never been to a brewery, especially one next to where I was married. Maybe after my hospital visits, I'll have enough strength to go, Debra muses.

"You remember we walked out of the church sanctuary to this spot in the parking lot, and I threw the bouquet at least 20 feet?" Debra comments.

Don replies, "You have a strong arm, probably from your days as a softball pitcher."

"We've been through some bumps in our marriage, but you're a good man, Don," Debra whispers to him as she stares through the truck window.

Dust from the construction work on The Brewery is settling on Don's truck.

"We better go, or this sandstorm is going to keep us here for good," Don snickers to Debra.

"Maybe we should just stay here and die," Debra responds. "From what I've read about cancer patients like myself, that might be the best thing to do."

The truck gets silent. Don backs up and pulls away from the construction side of the parking lot to the other end that faces the steeple and the cross.

"Debra, stop!" Don says, then adds, "I'm sorry to raise my voice at you."

"I don't want to die, yet," Debra sobs.

"You have been the love of my life for over thirty years," Don's voice cracks. "You mean more to me than life itself. You're not dying because I'm not going to let that happen—so let's go see the oncologist, and he will get you back on track," Don continues.

Don pulls his truck out of The Brewery and onto Main. The hospital is just two blocks away from the construction site and the new stadium in Uptown High Point.

As Don pulls into the hospital parking lot, Debra reads the hospital building's sign to herself: *"The Cancer Center." My doctor did a biopsy, so he will probably tell me the prognosis today. I've got ovarian and uterine cancer. How will Don handle all these female problems? I know he loves me, but we have not had sex in two years.*

"Here, let me help you walk in," Don maneuvers Debra out of the truck.

"I don't need a wheelchair," Debra responds to the senior citizen volunteer who brings a wheelchair to the truck.

Debra and Don enter the large double-pane glass sliding doors. The ceramic tile walls are full of names of donors to The Cancer Center: Hayworth. Morgan. Millis. Adams . . .

The words on a sign directly in front of Debra say, "You do not know how strong you are until you have to be strong."

"Hello, Debra, come on back," the oncology nurse says, welcoming her and Don. "Dr. Haresh will be in to see you soon."

"Why is it so cold in here?" Debra asks Don, as he slips into the recliner.

"These are nice rooms here," Don says, evading the question.

The nurse overhears Debra's question and responds, "It helps lower the risk of infection."

Debra thinks, *I already have the worst infection one can have—I'd at least like it to be warm like my bed at home.*

Dr. Haresh arrives and says, "Hi, Debra. Good to see you."

"I really didn't want to leave home but throwing up some blood this morning got me worried."

"There are several causes of vomiting blood. And I'm sorry to say that most of them are very serious and require immediate medical attention," the doctor acknowledges.

"Is that all?" Debra responds. "How about my uterus?"

"A cancerous tumor came back on your pathology report; the cancer has spread to your stomach," Dr. Harsh explains.

"But, Doc, that sounds pretty aggressive, and she wasn't like that a month ago," Don says from the recliner.

"I know, but stage two uterine cancers can be aggressive," the oncologist comments.

Debra tells herself, *It is absolutely possible to be a survivor. However, the doc says it's equally possible that it will kill me. The important thing is that I don't let it.*

"We want to keep you overnight, Debra," the doctor explains. "Nurses can take some blood samples, too."

Debra's head falls back onto the cool hospital pillow. *Cancer doesn't care how old you are. It doesn't care if you smoke or drink or if you use artificial sweeteners in your coffee. It doesn't care if you exercise every day and do nothing to harm your body. Cancer does not care if you have been a "good person." None of that matters now. Anyone can be diagnosed at any time with cancer.*

"Doc, what is my long-term prognosis?" Debra asks.

Don interrupts, "Was it all the hot sauce we ate that caused this cancer?"

"When I removed your uterus and cervix, the pathology report indicated that area was full of cancerous cells. And I'm not sure I got all of them. And now, they've spread to your stomach," the doctor explains.

"I remember two years ago, it all started when I began experiencing slight swelling in my tummy," Debra tells the doctor. "After the surgery, I had serious menopausal symptoms—lots of sweating," Debra adds.

"Your CA-125 test suddenly shot up last time, and we did a laparotomy and found more cells," Dr. Haresh explains.

"But what about the blood from my stomach, now?" she asks.

"Because of your age, we may decide to do a peritonectomy, but I want to monitor you for a few weeks, first."

While the doctor keeps talking, Debra tells herself, *I don't want another surgery. I miss seeing my old friends. They have invited me on trips, and I can't go. I've missed opportunities to go and do things with them. I feel limited. I feel stagnant. But this cancer is not my fault. My life isn't over. It's just on hold. The timing got a little messed up, a little slowed down. But things aren't over for us, so don't forget that when times are hardest.*

Debra thinks about the first sign she saw walking into The Cancer Center, which said, in big bold letters, "You do not know how strong you are until you have to be strong."

Don sits dumbfounded in the recliner after hearing the doctor's disappointing news.

Debra notices Don's face turning whiter than usual.

"I'll leave you two alone for a while," the doctor says.

"Don, are you feeling okay?" Debra asks.

"I feel a little lightheaded," he whispers. "Maybe it was the hamburgers—indigestion, maybe."

"I'll ask the nurse to take your blood pressure," Debra says, as the doctor walks out of the room.

The nurse adds, "Let me get my cuff on you—just a minute."

"Thank you," Debra says. The hospital room is now silent, with Debra pondering her diagnosis and Don seemingly worried about his wife and how he feels, physically, with his history of heart disease and high blood pressure.

"Your top blood pressure number is 145, but your bottom number is 108," the nurse explains to Don, "and what concerns me is the bottom number."

"Did you take your medicine today?" Debra asks Don.

"No, I forgot it, with all the stuff we had to do to get you here."

"Well, you need to go home and take your meds and get some good sleep," Debra admonishes him. "I'll be fine until the morning."

"You really need to get some rest and follow your prescriptions," the nurse tells Don, as she smiles. "Don't worry, I'll take good care of her."

"Okay, honey, I'll go home and get some rest." Don adds. "I really don't feel very good."

"And probably go see your cardiologist on Monday," Debra says.

"Yeah, good idea," Don says softly, walking over to Debra's bedside.

"See you soon, my love," Don leans down and kisses Debra on the lips.

"Bye. See you in the morning, Don," Debra whispers. *My lips are so dry, and his face looks like a ghost. I'm worried about him, but he will do the right thing. He is a good man.*

Feeling sluggish, Don drives his truck home, taking the same route he took bringing Debra to the hospital, passing Church Street and the church where the two were married. *She wants to visit the brewery when it opens. With the damn cancer, will she be able to attend?* Don wonders as he turns off Main Street into his neighborhood.

As he drives into his neighborhood, about a third of the way down the hill on Farris Avenue, his head slumps forward, and he grabs his chest with his right hand, leaving the steering wheel briefly uncontrolled. Don's acid reflux has been occurring all day. He is anxious about Debra and the possibility of losing his wife to cancer. He has been disappointed that his fireman career was cut short with his first heart attack nine years earlier. *Am I having another heart attack? The intense pain in my left arm and chest is unusual. The cardiologist told me not to be alone often. He told me that, if my heart stops being able to function adequately because of a heart attack or some other medical or trauma problem, I may become unconscious and will need CPR to have a chance of recovery. Maybe I should have stayed at the hospital with Debra? But she needs rest and the nurses' care, not mine right now.*

The hospital visit is the last time they were together. After Don enters his home, with family photos all around him, lonely for Debra, he grabs his chest and falls to the ground. Only when he doesn't answer the phone calls from Debra does she alert the hospital; they send an ambulance to their home, but it's too late.

Debra is stunned on her hospital bed, stunned not due to her cancer prognosis but because of her husband's sudden death.

Debra ponders her life, and her tears start to fall. *Now, our home is my home. Don left everything to me; he'd no time to be more deliberate in his will. He gave me his beloved firearms and fishing rods, his damn pager that woke us up in the middle of the night, his collection of model trains, and a bathroom full of drugs that were supposed to save his life.*

The pile of medication in our bathroom—my bathroom, now—is a remnant of a life that no longer exists. I don't know whether to dispose of these drugs or keep them, in case I need them to end my own life.

The widowed are two and a half times more likely to die by suicide in the first year of widowhood than the general population. I am more likely to die of many causes: heart attack, car accident, cancer, and many seemingly random afflictions that are not so random, after all.

After Don dies, Debra's daughter, Sandra, takes care of her during chemotherapy.

"Mom, you need to sit down," Sandra says.

"I want to climb these stairs and see the photos of Don," Debra responds quietly.

"I know you want to, but the doctor said to rest from time to time; it helps you gain your strength back," Sandra says.

"Those pictures up at the top of the steps are wedding photos at the church," Debra says. "I want to see those of the church."

"You're gonna pass out if you don't sit here for a minute," Sandra says.

"And can you take me to Church Street?" Debra asks softly.

"Church Street? Where you were married?"

"The Brewery," says Debra.

"The Brewery?" Sandra asks.

"Yes, across the street from where we got married is a beer joint called The Church Street Brewery," Debra explains.

"If you're passed out for more than four minutes, we need to call the ambulance," Sandra says, trying to warn Debra to take it easy.

"I don't need any ambulance today," Debra chides her daughter. "I want to get out and experience life some more before I die."

"Wednesday, I am not working, so I can take you to The Brewery then," Sandra tells her mother.

"Fine, we will have a glass of wine."

"Doctor said not to have alcohol with your cancer," Sandra replies.

"We will sit in The Brewery and look at the church where your daddy and I were married and drink a small glass of wine," Debra tells her daughter with determination.

"I hope they have some nice chairs to sit in," Sandra says.

"Looks like large glass windows facing the church and high-back chairs," Debra explains.

"Sounds good, Mom," Sandra says. "I'll pick you up around 5:00, and we'll hit The Church Street Brewery."

Chapter 6

YUAN

Yuan is born, in 1998, in the Chinese province of Guangdong, Guangzhou, formerly known as Canton, the capital of Guangdong province—and the home of Cantonese. Spoken by seventy-three million people across the world, Cantonese has a great global influence because most of the early Chinese immigrants came from southern China. When they moved, they took their culture and language with them.

Yuan also speaks Mandarin, as well as Cantonese, and she is enrolled at North Carolina A&T State University to study engineering.

Now twenty-one years old, as a baby girl in 1998, was left by her parents on a bridge in a rural area outside of the growing city of Guangzhou. Her heavily pregnant mother hides herself, along with her first child, on a houseboat on a secluded canal in Shenzhen and waits. The mother has a choice, but she doesn't believe in abortion, even though she is in danger from the authorities and living in severe poverty.

Three weeks later, Yuan's mother gives birth on the boat to a child who should have been aborted under China's Nazi-like one-child policy, introduced in 1979 by the Communist government to reduce poverty.

Yuan's father cuts the umbilical cord with a pair of scissors he has sterilizes from a nearby firepit and all seems to be going well until the placenta stays within the womb. The delivery is a dangerous and tricky situation, but hospital care was nowhere to be found. Fortunately for the couple, there is a small clinic nearby and a doctor who agrees to help without alerting the authorities.

Four days later, Yuan's mother rises at dawn and takes her to a covered food market in Shenzhen. There, the mother leaves a note written in ink brush: "Our daughter, Yuan, was born at 9:00 a.m. on the seventh day of the seventh month of the lunar calendar, 1998. Our poverty has forced us to abandon her. Mercy be to the hearts of fathers and mothers! Thank you for saving our little daughter and taking her into your care. If there is a heaven, may we meet again one day."

Considering that these poor peasants are raised under a vaguely religious pantheism, her plea for heavenly help shows their desperate need for an intimate higher power rather than from nature.

Since 1991, American families have adopted more than 60,000 Chinese babies, almost all of them girls. Adoptive parents often face the grim realities of the child's Chinese birthplace—and cope with the knowledge that their child's happiness came at the cost of another mother's loss.

Chinese mothers risk their future and their family's future because they know their baby can be taken care of by Americans. Chinese mothers of the second baby have grueling and coercive medical procedures they have to endure. Slogans from the Chinese government are brutal such as "Abort it, induce it, just stop it from being born!"

These slogans have been converted into countless human tragedies.

In the 1990s, perhaps 100 million of China's 800 million peasants moved to cities like Guangzhou to find jobs. The infants were left at railway stations, in parks, and in front of police stations. The police were supposed to look for the parents, but most searches proved futile.

Yuan spends the next few months in a Chinese orphanage in Shenzhen, China, a few miles south of the bridge where she was abandoned.

A street vendor in the market heard the baby whimpering during the night as she slept in her bungalow above the street. Then, infant Yuan is hid behind a garbage bin on the cold floor, trapped between high-rise shanty apartments. The street vendor's room on the second floor, by comparison, is relatively spacious—100 square feet in which to sleep, cook, and live. He sometimes struggles to make his 500-USD-per-month rent, after paying for food and other living costs.

I must contact the orphanage and get this baby to them while not warning the police, the vendor decides.

Newly arrived infants at the orphanage are placed in a separate small room, which holds about a dozen baby girls. Two or three untrained minimally-paid women from nearby villages, struggle to support their own families, care for the infants.

China's current one-child-per-family policy makes domestic adoptions difficult. A couple must be childless between the ages of thirty-five and fifty years old before regulations permit them to adopt. Typically, fifty to sixty babies are adopted from one orphanage, per year—more than half by foreigners and the rest by Chinese.

Susan, a single Chinese-American woman works for the United

Nations in New York City meets her new daughter, Yuan—then six months old. Yuan resides in the orphanage only a few days after she was born. Susan is told by her gynecologist that she would never be able to have children.

For American mothers like Susan—women who cannot have children—Yuan's birth mother is a hero. As Susan tells the orphanage caretaker, "The birth mother gives an enormous gift to families who can't have a baby. So, birth mothers, instead of aborting the child, bravely have the child and give it up for adoption.

Susan raises Yuan by herself while living in Long Island, until Yuan is five years old, and then she meets Chung, a Chinese-born engineer working at Bell Labs. By the time Yuan enters high school, she becomes curious about her birth mother, but she only shares her story with a few friends. Yuan's closest friend, Zhuoliang, asks her one day, "Do you know why you were adopted?"

Yuan replies, "Because, when I was a baby, my biological mother didn't want to take care of me anymore."

Zhuoliang responds pointedly, "Didn't want to, or couldn't?"

Yuan is taken aback, then says, "Well, I'm not really sure, I guess."

Yuan ponders what Zhuoliang says and how her adoptive parent, Susan, keeps most of the story hidden: *Who cares if she could or couldn't, or simply didn't want to? I am a smart child who makes good grades, especially in mathematics, and I can draw nice pretty lotus flowers. As far as I am concerned, if this mysterious birth mother did not need me, it's her loss.*

Yuan is now a senior in high school, she notices that something is amiss while she is having dinner with her parents. Susan and Chung look worried. "We thought this might happen," Susan says. "But we didn't think it would happen this soon."

Yuan's mind immediately jumps to divorce, since that was the only thing she could imagine necessitating such seriousness. Instead, her parents sit Yuan down and tell her that her brother, who's one year older than her, called and left a message. Yuan's parents mention that he existed, but, for the first time, they explain to Yuan the adoption story in detail and about her brother. "Your brother and you have the same mother," Susan tells Yuan, "and he is interested in meeting you."

Yuan's dad goes on to explain, "Your mother was only eighteen when she left you in a basket at the street market in Shenzhen."

Susan and Chung are concerned that Yuan's birth mother and brother in China might be after money. Yuan decides, *They said the decision to talk to my brother was up to me, and I just don't want to.* Susan and Chung are so relieved.

But deep down, Yuan thinks more about those biological relatives she never knew. Out of the blue, her brother contacts her via Facebook, introducing himself, and Yuan writes back. This exchange led to an offer to meet, but where?

Yuan is now a healthy, intelligent college student, known by her adoptive parents and friends by the nickname "Yu."

One of her favorite classes is World Religions, an elective she took to help her understand her Chinese worldview and her love of nature, especially lotus flowers.

Despite my association with many Asian people in my career, I never took the time to study their worldview, David thinks to himself. David is Yuan's religion professor, and he plans to interview her for a place in his selective class on the study of world religions. David is a deist, meaning that he believes that God created the universe, but then left it alone after its creation. *Although I have been able to secure this tenured position with multiple research papers on religion, I still have doubts about my faith,* David admits to himself, while preparing for his planned class interviews.

"Good morning, Yuan," David says. "Please come in." His office walls are lined with photos of great thinkers like Aristotle, Socrates, and even artwork of the crucifixion of Jesus. A small green bamboo plant sits alone in David's window. After looking around at the walls, Yuan says, "I like your plant," making no mention of the religious figures or plaques.

David conducts a mutually respectful thirty-minute interview with Yuan. The first question he asks is about the origin of life, to which she responds, "Origin of life comes from a higher power. But I cannot verify my view using scientific methods. So, we have a creator. Life creates everything. Life gives everything emotions."

David thinks to himself, *When she said, "Life creates everything," I surmised that her thinking would be pantheistic, with nature as God. As a deist, I believe God created everything.*

David asks Yuan what she means by "Life creates everything," and she responds that there is a higher power that creates everything. David stops here and doesn't pursue the question further.

David wonders, *Should I have mentioned Jesus?* The next question he asks this twenty-one-year-old Chinese engineering student is about the meaning of life, and specifically, what it means to her. Yuan responds, "Life means gratitude and challenge. Life is sacred to me."

David thinks this answer is interesting: *the meaning of life has something to do with being thankful and striving for . . . what?*

David then asks Yuan, "Is a baby in a mother's womb sacred?"

To which she responds pointedly, "Yes, she is sacred."

The next question is about morality. David asks Yuan if she follows a moral code. She responds, "I have a moral code. In China, people use lotus flowers to describe a person having a moral code. The flower lives fully. However, the flower is still clean. So, good people are the same as lotus flowers."

David thinks to himself: *What? Are lotus flowers her moral code?* David then asks her to send a photo of a lotus flower. "Yuan, I am really interested in the lotus flower," he exclaims. "Can you send me a photo?"

David asks her if a lotus flower is a guide or just an image: "Are there different flowers for different moral principles?" Then, David goes deeper: "Is hatred wrong, and is there a flower for hatred?"

Although Yuan is a hard-working, intelligent young lady, she is a reserved person. She is careful about sending images to her professor. She did send David a photo of a lotus flower. She writes, "Different flowers have different meanings. And we can use flowers to present moral principles." She says to David, "Hatred is not wrong. It is a special emotion, but I cannot use a flower to instill hatred."

David's final interview question was about one's eternal destiny, and he asks, "Do you believe in life after death? Is there an eternal destiny?"

To which Yuan answers, "I do believe in a life after death." She pauses, then exclaims, "And I trust eternal destiny." Her head bowing slightly, she remains curious about David's questions.

David then asks her about where one goes after death: "If there is life after death, where does our soul go? What is the 'essence' of life after death?"

Yuan says, "We may have a soul, and we can become everything." Her face lights up, and she exclaims, "We can become sunshine to warm the earth, grow into a bird to fly, and also become a book to pass on knowledge."

"So, what are your plans now, Yuan?"

"After death is a new start for me. Right now, I want to study, then I can find a good job." Yuan politely adds, "After these things, I will have a happy life, and before my death, I want to achieve my dream—after death, then I can have a new start."

As Yuan rises and makes her way out the door, a sign on the front of David's office door caught her eye: "World Religions Discussion at The Church Street Brewery." Yuan remembers Professor David mentioned that, after exams, he would be offering an informal session in the conference room of The Church Street Brewery.

"Is this not a bar where most folks drink beer?" Yuan muses. However, her interview with the professor got her thinking about life, God, and nature. She decided that she might just stop by.

Chapter 1

GREG

"I think he's a ten-point buck," Greg whispers to his friend, Neal. The two had not spent this much time together in fifteen years.

"There is something about the solace of nature and watching deer that just makes the hair on the back of my neck stand up," Neal explains.

"Four years ago, I fell from a tree stand I'd built myself," Greg replies. "I was climbing up it one evening, about five feet off the ground, when one of the steps broke loose from the tree. The nails had rusted through. I ended up breaking my arm, and it took ten weeks to heal. I also missed the entire hunting season. I missed several prostate surgeries I was supposed to perform. That's the last time I ever used a homemade tree stand."

"Building your own tree stand from wood is a bad idea," says Neal. "It's kind of like using plastic instead of metal to do surgeries."

"That got me thinking that maybe I don't need to bring a gun and hunt; I'll just sit in my truck and watch the deer," Neal exclaims.

The two continue to sit in the tree stand. Greg is sipping on spiked cider, and Neal a Diet Pepsi. The preacher, Neal, does not partake in alcoholic beverages, but he does love the outdoors and nature.

"Do you ever drink beer or wine anymore, Neal?" asks Greg.

"No, not anymore. When the Lord saved me in 1989, I never craved alcohol again," Neal explains.

"Well, it helps me relax after weeks of surgeries, fixing men's bladders and prostates—the taste does something for me."

It's a cool fall morning in Halifax County, North Carolina, and a herd of whitetail crosses the field in front of them.

"Be real quiet; there they are," Neal says. "You aim at the ten-pointer."

"My tree stand is twenty-feet high, and I have been told to aim low when shooting at a deer," Greg says, "and my colleague says to aim normal—maybe raise the sight an inch higher than the center of the deer."

"Well, you aim high because the drop is less when shooting up or down at an angle. The point of impact will be lower than it would be if shooting at the same horizontal distance with no drop or rise, so you must aim high—this is true regardless of whether shooting uphill or downhill, which is counterintuitive to some perhaps," Neal explains.

"I thought you were a preacher, not an engineer, but thanks; that makes sense to an old cowboy doctor."

"Cowboy doctor? You are making $300,000 each year taking out prostates," Neal laughs quietly.

"Let's stay quiet. I think I can get a shot off here," Greg whispers. "You can tell me later about your first deer."

"My first deer? Whoa! That's going back a way," says Neal.

"Let's stay quiet," Greg says.

"An awesome experience for me as a young hunter right after I accepted Jesus Christ as Lord."

"Was it Jesus or the deer that was awesome?" asks Greg.

"If it was not for Jesus, I would be going to hell," Neal responds. "The Holy Scripture says in Saint John that 'Jesus is the way and the truth and the life. No one comes to the Father except through Jesus,' meaning I cannot enter the presence of God without first believing in Jesus."

"You really believe in hell?" Greg chuckles.

"Jesus was tempted by the Devil, and he spoke about hell," Neal explains. "A place of conscious, eternal torment where people experience God's punishment for their sins. Yes, hell is 'the eternal fire prepared for the Devil and his angels,' according to Jesus in Matthew."

"I just don't see evidence for such a place, and maybe the Bible is a collection of myths passed down through the centuries," Greg contends. "Look, the buck is getting closer."

"Hell will be total separation from God," Neal responds. "I don't want anyone to go there."

The beeper goes off on Greg's pager.

"You still have one of those pagers?" Neal asks. "The rest of the world uses iPhones with the internet at their fingers."

"I don't want an iPhone. It would be a distraction from this getaway hunting trip," Greg responds, "but just in case of an emergency, I keep the pager."

The deer make their way closer and just sit and graze in the meadow of clover field about fifty yards from the two men, now deep into their conversation about hunting, Jesus, and urology.

"What is the most urgent call you have received for work?" Neal asks.

"A man had an ultrasound procedure on his prostate, but he had a misfortune, and it was my fault," Greg replies. "And he ended up suing me, but the case ended in a mistrial, and I kept my license."

Neal responds, "Really, is that all that happened?"

"A sixty-year old man wanted robotic surgery; the technology was in its infancy, and the FDA had just approved the procedure; I was thirty-two years old, then, and wet behind the ears," Greg explains. "I nicked his penis during the setup, and it couldn't be repaired without major cosmetic surgery."

"The prostate is a gland that can raise its ugly head unexpectedly," Greg continues. "Patients are usually concerned about longer-term quality-of-life issues such as urinary control and changes in sexual performance."

Neal whispers, "That buck is a perfect ten-pointer, don't you think?"

Both men sit quietly. Words are about done. Greg sees fifty patients a week and longs for silence, solitude, and simplicity. Neal gets his inner strength from times alone in the woods, watching deer, and praying to God.

"Greg, I'm not shooting deer anymore; you take this one."

Greg hears footsteps while he is watching the feeder and surrounding clover fields. He realizes that a large buck is making the noise; his adrenaline level jumps. His large hands—used for a cystoscope, catheter, or needle guide—rest on the trigger of a Ruger M77, its magazine full of 100-grain Federal Power-Shock factory loads.

He looks through the tree stand window to get his crosshairs behind the shoulder of the buck, where the heart is.

The deer ended up being much closer to Greg than he and Neal previously thought. They figured on the buck being about fifty yards out, which, because they were sitting twenty feet up in a stand, would have given Greg a near-perfect shot. Instead, during the deep conversation with Neal, the buck had gotten to about only ten yards away, nearly under the men.

"I can't get a good shot because the height of the shooting window creates a bad angle," Greg whispers to Neal.

"You have waited too long, my friend," Neal whispers back.

Their conversation scares the deer. Neal panics. "Damn it, the buck was standing so close, I could have killed him with a pistol, and I just couldn't get the angle to shoot him with the long gun."

Neal stands up, very slowly and quietly. The buck appears to hear the men talking and turns toward them. Neal freezes, very close to being ready for a shot. He looks away to get the extra two inches he needs. With his head turned, he sticks the barrel out and flips off the safety. The deer runs, fast.

The men see the buck stop about 100 yards away, but by this time, there isn't a clear shot.

"That makes me mad as hell," Greg chides himself.

"Remember, hell is a place you don't want to go," Neal chuckles.

Greg responds, "Because I had just missed what may have been my only opportunity to kill a buck today."

The two men step down out of the tree stand in the pine forest next to the field and start walking back to their trucks.

Greg slams the door. "We better get back to High Point. I have a full list of patients," Greg says.

"One of my congregation members is having a procedure done on his prostrate next week," Neal adds.

"Really? HIPAA will not allow me to name any names."

"I understand confidentiality," Neal responds. "Take care, my friend; we will try again another time."

Arriving the next day at his office, Dr. Greg Hill has a list of patients that includes an eighty-five-year-old woman with incontinence and a fifty-year-old man, Charles, there for a prostate exam. Greg and his staff of nurses see hundreds of prostate and bladder patients each year.

Charles was healthy, a teacher who was thriving in life. His general physician (GP) had warned him that the digital rectal exam (DRE) "did not feel right." GPs use the DRE as a relatively simple test to check the prostate. Because the prostate is an internal organ, the doctor cannot look at it directly.

"Who's on the list today for exams?" Dr. Hill asks Sonya.

"The same ol' crowd—mostly the older crowd, Ms. Ellie, too, and some young fella," Sonya shouts from the nurses' station down the hall where the tall, stocky Dr. Hill is wearing his cowboy boots.

"How young? I'm fifty-nine," says the doctor.

"Did you get one of those deer?" Sonya asks. "Why you want to kill them, anyway?"

"What did you say?" asks Dr. Hill, as he fumbles through the paperwork from patients, his jeans tucked up beneath his white coat with his grey beard down to his chest.

Sonya is an African American urology nurse. She was born and raised in low-income housing near the office. Her mother raised her and her four brothers and sisters on a waitress' salary and hospital cleaning contracts.

"Charles Spencer is the first patient. His GP states in the records that the DRE shows some abnormality," Sonya yells to Dr. Hill, who is now sipping on coffee.

"What's Spencer's PSA?" he shouts.

"4.9," Sonya says. "By the way, last time Ms. Ellie was in here for her annual checkup, she complained about your coffee breath."

"That was the day I rode my Harley to work and during lunch stopped at The Church Street Brewery for chili peppers and forgot to brush my teeth," Dr. Hill responds. "And what does bad breath have to do with bladder control?"

Charles feels out of place. The doctor's office patients are quiet, mostly old, grey-haired men and some women—their facial expressions mostly straight and concerned.

"Good morning, Mr. Spencer. I'm Sonya—Dr. Hill's nurse."

Charles guesses the stocky black lady to be in her forties.

"Call me 'Charles,' thanks," he responds politely.

"I hear you need an exam?"

"Yes, my family doctor, Dr. Garrison, says the DRE did not feel right, and I want to rule out an abnormal prostate."

"He will check you out; slip your clothes off and put these scrubs on."

Dr. Hill's entering the room takes up most of the doorway, and then he slides his chair across the room in front of a sitting Charles. "I'm Dr. Hill," he says, stretching out his bear paw of a hand. "I'd like to do an ultrasound on you to see the shape and size of your prostate."

"You mean an instrument up my ass?" Charles says.

"Sort of. We will insert a probe and needle guide through your backside," Dr. Hill adds. "And I know that sounds painful, but Sonya will make sure you are not in too much discomfort."

The needle guide will sound like a pop gun because it is taking samples of your prostate tissue—twelve samples," Dr. Hill explains.

"Why twelve needles?" Charles asks.

"Not twelve needles. Twelve specimens of your prostate will allow enough samples. Prostate biopsies incur the risk of being false-negative. We don't want that. We don't want to miss something important."

Dr. Hill rises from his seat, cleans his hands, and then states, "When I insert the thin, hollow needle into the prostate, you will hear a sound like a gunshot but not as loud; those are the needles taking and retrieving the core samples."

Meanwhile, Charles texts Abigail to let her know about the ultrasound procedure: "The doctor will do an ultrasound on your prostate. And we'll let you know the results this afternoon."

Sonya escorts Charles to the imaging room: "The biopsy itself takes about ten minutes. I'll give you some antibiotics to take now, and also for a day or two after, to reduce the risk of infection."

Charles could see the ultrasound monitor on the wall. The sterile, shiny instruments were larger than he expected. "Turn toward the wall so he will have good exposure to your backside," Sonya instructs him politely.

"Can I take a photo of the image? I want to show it to my wife," Charles requests.

Dr. Hill enters the room and slips on his surgical gloves. One hand uses the needle guide, while he and Sonya study the ultrasound image.

"Ouch, that does hurt a bit," Charles complains, as the "gun" keeps going off.

The room got quiet as Sonya and Dr. Hill studied the ultrasound image.

"Damn! I apologize. Your prostate is the size of an orange!" Dr. Hill adds. "You are too young for such a large prostate."

Sonya's face turns numb. Charles is quiet. *Great, another hurdle in my life to overcome—an enlarged prostate.*

"It appears to be an extreme case of Benign Prostatic Hyperplasia

(BPH)," Dr. Hill explains. "We will send the samples off for cancer screening and should have the results by the end of the week."

Returning home, Charles feels bloated. He had not eaten or drank much, and he could not urinate. After two hours of abdominal pain, he decided to call Dr. Hill's office.

"I can't breathe well, and the abdominal pain is excruciating," he explains to Sonya on the phone.

"If you don't get up here to the office before we close in fifteen minutes, you'll be in the emergency room tonight," Sonya explains.

He limps to his car.

I can barely walk. How will I drive? I'll run this red light. The office closes in ten minutes, Charles thought. Lord, help me get to that office and not pee all over the place.

"Come on back, Charles," Sonya urges with a slight smile.

"Spencer, I knew you would be back in here," Dr. Hill chuckles.

I can't believe he just said that. Why did he not fix me before I left?

Sonya pulls out a large catheter and says, "If you had not come so quickly, you would have backed up and been in the ambulance to the emergency room."

"Lay back; I'm going to put a catheter in to relieve all the backed-up pressure."

"The catheter will feel like a bee sting or two, but it will release the entire bladder," Sonya explains.

"A bee sting hurts!" Charles murmurs. "God that hurts."

"After three pints coming out, you will feel much better," she adds. "The inflammation from the ultrasound procedure blocked your pee."

A week passes, and Charles returns to see Dr. Hill.

Dr. Hill explains, "The cancer screening results are back, and there is one sample that is abnormal. I recommend you start taking finasteride immediately, and we need to schedule an MRI."

Charles is surprised. *An "abnormal" sample could be cancer. Well, I am a praying man. God created man in His own image. God may or may not answer my prayer now, but I will be thankful for the life He gave me.*

"But, Doc, I don't want to take those pills; they may cause me to have sexual performance issues!"

"Charles, as I would tell my own brother: if you don't take those pills, you will have prostate cells taking over your whole body! Sit down, Charles; this is serious," Dr. Hill says. "I need to remove part of your prostate; any small amount of cancer not removed may spread throughout your body. You are too young to risk this happening to you."

"Dr. Hill, life brings us unexpected situations. I don't know why I have this incredibly large prostate, do you?"

Dr. Hill looks into Charles's eyes and has little to say beyond the medical diagnosis. "When I need some relief, I go deer hunting or to The Church Street Brewery a few blocks from here."

"I don't know why. I almost lost my family just two years ago," Charles mutters, while Dr. Hill looks at Charles, confused by the statement.

"What do you mean?" Dr. Hill says.

"It's a long story, but I'll just have to accept this enlarged prostate and hope for the best," Charles says.

"The enlarged prostate is probably genetic," the doctor says, without empathy.

"I'll see you back in three weeks for the TURP," Dr. Hill states. "It will be done at the hospital surgical facilities."

Trans-Urethral Resection of the Prostate is called "TURP" among those in the field. Dr. Hill will need to put Charles to sleep with general anesthesia.

Three weeks have passed.

After the surgery was done, Dr. Hill speaks to Charles's wife: "He did well in the TURP surgery," he tells Abigail. "I did have one problem, though. I discovered a bladder stone and had to remove part of it before the TURP. The prostate was so large, and part of the bladder stone is still inside Charles; he may suffer some additional pain for several weeks."

The hospital staff were always surprised Dr. Hill wore Harley-Davidson T-shirts under his scrubs. "Did you drive your Harley to the hospital?" Charles asks Dr. Hill, as the MD walks into the room where Abigail is sitting. "I've been riding my Harley all over High Point—it's a replacement for a mid-life crisis," Dr. Hill says.

"I bet you cruise Main Street," Charles says.

"I'll see you in three weeks for a follow-up; in the meantime, I'm going on a week's vacation, but Dr. Ward will be on call."

"Thanks, Dr. Hill. Enjoy your vacation," says Charles, as he chuckles. "Watch out for Harleys and The Church Street Brewery crowd."

"The Church Street Brewery! I probably need to go to a church, not the brewery."

Chapter 8

NADIA

"**G**et in the car!" Nadia's father shouts from the taxi. "You're not dressing like that!"

"But, Father, I have just started shopping," Nadia pleads. Her freedom from home chores is interrupted. Her father, a forty-something taxi driver, makes thirty dollars a day to support his wife and four children.

The streets of Muscat, Oman are vibrant with street vendors selling potatoes, greens, and fruit. Trash lies along the side of the road. Men and women dress in traditional Islamic clothing. Muslim men often wear traditional clothing that fulfills the requirements of modesty in Islamic dress.

The thobe is a long robe worn by Muslim men. The top is usually tailored like a shirt, but it is ankle-length and loose, and it's usually white. Nadia's father, who goes by Ravi, wore such a robe while transporting his customers through the country of Oman, even to the border of the United Arab Emirates and Saudi Arabia and, to a lesser extent, Yemen.

Women have significance within the family unit and make strong contributions toward family decisions regarding various rites of passage. Outside the family, however, women have little authority or privilege. This rule applies to Nadia's family structure.

There are many different types of clothing that are worn by Muslim women. Sharia (Islamic law) does not require women to wear a burqa, but her father demands it.

Nadia was taught from an early age that she is to wear the burqa, the most concealing of all Islamic veils. It's a one-piece veil that covers the face and body, often leaving just a mesh screen to see through.

Nadia liked to "dress down" when she left her father's home for the nearby street market to buy food. She liked to wear a headscarf the Arabs refer to as a *shayla*. The *shayla* is a long, rectangular scarf popular in the Gulf region. It's wrapped around the head and tucked in place at the shoulders.

In pre-Islamic times, the Arabs used to be disheartened and annoyed with the birth of girls. When Nadia's father learned his wife had given birth to a girl, he said, "By Allah, a son is more blissful; a daughter's defense is crying, and her care is but stealing!"

A city of traditional architecture and friendly people, Muscat, Oman, the capital of the Sultanate of Oman, is an eclectic mix of modern and old-world charms. It is also a place with strict religious practices.

His taxi is dirty, as prior riders leave their extra trash in the already sandy back seat. "Why do I have to sit in this mess," Nadia cries. "I said my prayers today, Father."

"You are not to walk around here without your burqa," her father admonishes her. "I am to pick up an American from the airport and take him to the border and into Buremei," he says.

Nadia craved freedom. Life for her, as a fifteen-year-old, was impoverished and boring except for her love of school. She did chores around the house and watched farmers ride into town on horse-drawn carriages. The wheels of the carriages reminded her of the circle and trigonometry.

She dreamed of attending university in the United States, where she could study mathematics and physics. From an early age, Nadia's mother watched her count the fruits and vegetables in the nearby stores. She would take them home, adding them together and making shapes with beans. On the dirt floor in their small house, she drew shapes and made arithmetic and algebraic calculations.

Her father was jealous of her intelligence. He built their home out of mud and hay, using fabric, wood, and metal scraps for the roof. The timber supply was limited. Nadia was eight years old when the three-room house was built, but she vividly remembers the boards and angles and squares—shapes she loved.

"Mom, this is a triangle, and this is a hexagon," Nadia shouts. "How do I make an 'infinity-gon?'" Nadia asks.

"What is an infinity-gon, Nadia?" her mom, perplexed, asks her young daughter.

"Mom, you know what a square is, and you know what a circle is, right?" Nadia says quietly, as she draws on the floor. Her mom is making dinner in the other room, when her father arrives, after driving his taxi all day.

"How about if we make a circle from a square?" Nadia exclaims.

"Nonsense!" her father cries out.

"Squaring the circle is a problem proposed by ancient mathematicians. It's making a square with the same area as a given circle by using only a fixed number of steps with a compass and a straightedge."

"I told you not to be going into my toolbox and taking my construction instruments!"

"You should study the Qu'ran, not mathematics!" Nadia's father admonishes her. He believes the Qu'ran affirms everything that was revealed to all the previous messengers in the past including Prophets Abraham, Ishmael, Isaac, Jacob, Moses, and Jesus.

Meanwhile, through their single window, covered with drapery, the call to prayer and sermons can be heard via loudspeakers from mosques located throughout the city.

"I must leave now. The American businessman needs a taxi from the airport to Buremei, and the border guards will be there. I'm also concerned for him being so close to Yemen," her father explains.

"Can I go with you, Father?"

"Your mom is not feeling well, so I suppose you can, but you must wear your burqa and obey all the rules of Islam. Bring the Qu'ran, and you will study Allah's teaching." Her father packs his bags for the two-day trip.

He does not offer the wife nice words or even a kiss on the cheek. The wife wonders why her husband does not show her any deep affection. *When I asked the sheikh about this, he said it was because men weren't reading the Qu'ran properly.*

"Reportedly, the American is in Oman to work on the government radio station," the father adds.

"Goodbye, wife."

The American would be needed to correct a problem with Saudi Arabia's government antenna system situated in the southern desert on the border of Oman—four hours from the nearest major city, and bordering Yemen. The Saudi Arabian government's AM station broadcast information to its citizens, who relied heavily on AM radio to obtain the news and weather.

The problem was that Iran was broadcasting on the same channel, the same frequency as Saudi Arabia. The Iranian broadcast was full of propaganda that the Saudi Arabian government did not want their people to hear. Why was Saudi Arabia on the same frequency? Because of Iran's political power, Saudi Arabia would not want to threaten them. Thus, the government relied on the American expert to fix the technical problem.

The Americans' European look and demeanor got the attention of Nadia's father as he pulled up to the airport. The drive to the radio station would be four hours, and Nadia was curious about where they would eat and what her father and the American would talk about. Nadia wondered if the American had children and was strict like her father. Did he read the Qu'ran or the Bible?

"Before the American enters this car, I remind you not to talk to him," Nadia's father exclaims.

"Look, Father, at all the shapes of those airplanes," Nadia shouts as she ponders mathematics and squaring the circle.

"You should study the Qu'ran; mathematics won't get you into heaven!" Nadia's father admonishes her. *But I don't see Father studying the Qu'ran,* she thought.

"Nadia, wait in the car, while I take my welcome sign to the arrivals gate," the father said pointedly.

I've never seen so many people waiting at an airport. Look at all these cars and airplanes. I wonder what shape the tall, glass-covered tower at the end of the runway is, Nadia ponders.

I don't see the American. He is supposed to be here. Security is strict for foreigners, her father observes. Everyone at Arrivals was dressed in mostly Islamic clothing, so the American would stand out if he had made it through security.

Nadia's father hears his phone ring, and he picks it up. "There has been a problem with the American at Security inside the airport, and the police have confiscated his bags," the caller says. The caller is the father's client, the one who hired him to pick up the American and take him to Saudi Arabia. The client was a member of the Saudi Arabian government. *I will have to negotiate with the police since the American does not speak our language.*

"Omani Security will allow you to represent the man, and you must report inside the Emirates Airline terminal," the client instructs, then adds, "They have taken his equipment, which he needs for the work."

The father makes his way through the dense crowd of all men wearing thobes. He then finds the American being interrogated by police dressed in all black inside the airport law enforcement agency.

"*Salaam Alaikum,*" which means "hello" in English, the father says to the police officer.

"*Alaikum Salaam!*" the officer responds sharply. The police officers are dressed in black uniforms, carrying rifles; their attire replaces the old khakis of years past.

Charles sees the father coming and rises out of his chair. "Sit down, sir," the officer shouts to Charles.

The father enters the police interrogation room.

"Hello. I am Charles, and you must be . . . ?"

"I'm Ravi, and you got yourself into a mess here."

The police officer and Nadia's father, Ravi, exchange words for several minutes, while Charles fills out several pages of forms. The forms have police insignia, rather than the typical customs declarations.

"Your bags say 'radio frequency transmitter,' which they believe is a unique weapon," Ravi explains to Charles. "They will hold the equipment for a few hours before we can leave here."

"This is my daughter, Nadia," Ravi explains to Charles. "As you know, I have been instructed to transport you to the town of Al Kharkhir just across the Yemen border. I am told the Saudi Arabian Government is expecting you there at 0100 hours."

Nadia, dressed in Islamic garb, including the burqa, sits on the front seat with her father. She has her small notebook with torn edges and a lead pencil. The notebook is mostly full of math equations and the geometrical figures she loves to draw.

"Hello, Nadia," Charles politely responds. Dressed in long pants, a long shirt, and a broad-brim hat, Charles looks like a desert reporter. The arid temperatures stay around seventy degrees all day.

"I want you to know that the war between Saudi Arabia and Yemen may be over, but there still exist rebels in the area, so please let me do the talking at the border," Ravi tells Charles.

"But how about my test equipment?" Charles says. "We'll pick it up after I show you around Muscat," Ravi says. "The Grand Mosque is open for non-Muslims between 8:00 and 11:00."

Nadia continues to doodle in her notebook, solving a quadratic equation. *If I get a minus one inside the square root radical, what number is that?* She is puzzled by this weird solution called a "complex number."

"You must cover up," Ravi tells Nadia, as the three walk through the entrance into the Sultan Qaboos Grand Mosque in Oman. Nadia's wrists and ankles are slightly uncovered, although she'd made every effort to wear suitable clothing.

"Father, look at the low rows of tiles on the floor and the symmetrical layout," Nadia says.

"Why is the men's prayer hall so much bigger than the women's?" Charles says to Ravi. Ravi does not respond.

After two hours of touring the Grand Mosque, Ravi gets a call that Charles's test equipment has passed security inspection at the airport and can be picked up.

The six-hour drive in a Jeep 4x4 from Oman Airport to the Yemeni border includes steep mountains, blue water, and a crashed Russian helicopter on an isolated Arabian Sea beach.

Charles, an adventurous traveler, finds the border concern exciting and nonthreatening. He carries his own journal and considers the ride an opportunity with much "pen time" ahead of him.

The road to Yemen seems to be more of a natural journey than the three-day flight from North Carolina. The highway to Yemen runs along Oman's southern coast, and while the dry season is devoid of grass, camels make their way everywhere along Highway 47.

"We will make three stops before the border," Ravi explains. "First to stretch our legs near the coast, second to have lunch, and third to meet the Saudi official near the border, who will give us our entry briefing. We will travel the Furious Road; remember, please, to let me do the talking if anyone stops us."

The Furious Road rises half a mile sharply over the course of three miles. A spectacular and terrifying marvel of engineering, the road is steep curve after steep curve through some of the highest mountains on the Southern Omani coast.

"We'll stop here for a snack," Ravi explains. When Charles asks where he should put his lunch trash, he is told to just throw it in the road.

As the taxi draws closer to the Yemeni border, the sky seems replaced with a darker one. Ravi decides to stop again to pray. "I must take time for Allah now before we enter the Yemen security point," Ravi says quietly. "Nadia will join me."

"Wow, Father! The lookout tower is a cylinder," Nadia exclaims. "I wonder what equation can calculate it's volume."

"Nadia, it's time for Almighty God, not mathematics," he scolds her.

The lookout point is nearby, at a viewing point with a wall, where travelers can stare down into Yemen from Oman—quite a beautiful scene.

Charles wants to stretch his legs and take a few photographs. Reaching for his camera, Charles is warned by Ravi, "Don't use that! Cameras near the border are strictly forbidden."

Then, Ravi pulls out a handkerchief and falls on his face.

Why do Muslims kiss the ground when they pray? Charles ponders. And why do they bow on the ground? Can't you simply pray while your head is held up in dignity? What is so sacred or holy about the ground that it should be kissed?

Charles respects the Muslim prayer tradition, having observed the ritual in America. "Thank you for driving," Charles tells Ravi, as they get back into the car.

"Muslims do not kiss the ground; they place their foreheads on it in prayer. A Muslim's dignity is found in submission to God, their creator. In prostration, they believe they are nearest to God."

But why did he need to pray for so long near the border? Charles asks himself.

"Everything we do is with the help of God, whether we admit it or not. For this, we should be grateful. We should humble ourselves in our prayer. Therefore, we bow and say, 'All praise is for God the Greatest'— in reverence. Then, we must show humility by touching the ground with our foreheads, saying, 'All praise is for Allah,'" Ravi explains to them both, as he turns his head toward the back of the SUV.

Meanwhile, Nadia doodles in her notebook, drawing squares, right triangles, and cylinders like the lookout tower.

"Father, how do I compute the volume of the tower, when it is not a perfect shape?" Nadia asks.

"Only Allah is perfect, Nadia," her father says, praising God with his hands.

Charles admires Nadia's interest in math. "Have you studied 'SOH-CAH-TOA' yet?" Charles says. "Father, what is So-ka . . . ?" Nadia asks. The taxi starts to slow down, and Charles can see Ravi eyeballing him through Ravi's rearview mirror.

"Nadia, it's time for mathematics," Ravi admonishes her again.

The three passengers of the SUV, each with different motives on this journey, are only one-quarter of a mile from the Yemeni border guard station on a sandy desert road, trapped between a tall mountain and the coast.

TROUBLE AT THE YEMEN BORDER

Charles does not expect to see a convergence of people crossing the border or military blockades, and his first view of Yemen is surprisingly tranquil, except for one dark storm cloud.

After the lookout point, Ravi drives almost all the way up to the border. Travelers are not allowed to take pictures, but there's a machine gun nest where the road ends. This is a serious place—not a place to cross, a place to keep Omanis and Americans out.

Charles sees guards with rifles and dogs. Ravi's SUV slowly pulls up to the guard post. With so much sand in the air, it's hard to see the armed men.

"*Salaam Alaikum,*" Ravi says to the guard. Two other guards exit the stationhouse and surround the Jeep with dogs. Their uniforms resemble pirate garb, lacking the formality of a regular soldier.

"*Alaikum Salaam,*" the lead guard responds. Ravi hands over his passport. One guard sees Nadia and asks her to roll down her window. With his right hand, her father grabs her burqa and tugs her closer to him, making her elbow bump the gear shift.

"Ouch, that hurt!" says Nadia loudly. The guard takes the passport inside the station.

"Hush, do not say anything, Nadia," the father says quietly. The other guard taps on her window. A dust storm starts, and a dark cloud descends on the group, while the sun and the Yemeni countryside are obscured.

Charles looks around; perplexed with the weather and uneasy, the threesome seems to be all alone in a foreign secluded place. No cell phone reception. No cameras allowed. No weapons. This is Yemen, which, three months before, was fighting a guerrilla-style war against Saudi Arabia for border control.

Charles senses a confrontation coming as Ravi is asked to exit the SUV. "*Aayn hi al'awraq alkhasat bk?* (Where is all your paperwork?)," the Yemeni guard challenges Ravi.

Why did Ravi not ask for my passport or Nadia's paperwork? Charles thinks. His camera sits next to him on the seat. His radio transmitting equipment remains in the back of the Jeep, out of sight. The third guard's dog sniffs the back of the SUV.

Charles can see a fourth guard inside the station, appearing to be commanding another person in a chair.

The conversation turns heated as the man pushes Ravi inside the station with his rifle: "Where are the birth certificates for all passengers?" the Yemeni guard yells at Ravi. Another man is being whipped by another guard. *Praise be to Allah,* Ravi thinks to himself. *Please protect me, almighty God.*

"Where are the birth certificates for all the passengers?" the Yemeni guard yells again at Ravi.

"I don't have these. They are not required by Oman-Yemen agreement—only passports," Ravi pleads.

The guard yells to his comrade to bring the American inside: "The American did not show a birth certificate, either—bring him here!" The third guard has Nadia's window down, rubbing his hand along her burqa.

"Stop!" she shouts. "Father, Father!" Ravi and Charles are being accosted and ridiculed for missing paperwork. *This can't be right. Why are they doing this?* Charles tries to understand.

Charles and Ravi are strapped into wooden chairs on a concrete floor. "We don't like Americans," the lead guard says. "More than 10,000 people in Yemen have been killed, and three million forced to flee their homes as a result of almost four years of fighting and no help from America," the guard continues, as his rifle's bayonet edges Charles's neck.

"We will detain you until the Saudi Government hands over our comrades," the guard demands. "The girl will be locked up downstairs."

Ravi pleads with the guard, "We'll turn around and go back to Oman. Please!"

"There must be some misunderstanding . . ." Charles murmurs, as the bayonet scratches his ear.

The third guard has Nadia on his shoulder. Crying, she pleads to her father, "Don't let them take me!"

The third guard yells, "I was young when the war started, and ambitious. I could never have imagined how bad the war would trash my dreams—I hate Saudis, Americans, and Omanis."

Nadia is fifteen. The guard is forty. She is beautiful, clean-cut, and intelligent. He is unshaven, with dirty fingernails and dark teeth.

Nadia is forced into the basement of the guard station. It's cold. Damp. Dark. A small crack in the ceiling between floors allows some light to enter. An old wooden chair sits in the corner. A floor drain reeks of urine. Reddish stains appear on the chair, next to dirty towels on the damp, sandy floor.

"Give me your burqa and put these on!" the guard yells, as he throws her a gown from the upper ground floor. "Put these on so you can look like an American model," the guard chuckles.

Upstairs, the rhetoric increases from the first guard to Charles. "I know what your President Trump said, 'Islam hates us.' I don't like Trump, and I don't like Americans."

Charles recalls what his boss told him before Charles left for the

Middle East: "Islamic terrorists don't just hate America or the West; they hate the modern world, and they particularly hate Muslims who are trying to live in the modern world."

The guard continues: "The Houthis forced our US- and Western-backed leader to resign last year. Now, we hate the Americans."

Ravi is crying and praying to God for his daughter, who he can hear screaming from below. The second and third guard make their way down the steps and shut the door behind them.

Charles cannot believe what is happening. *Will they rape her? Will I live to see my wife and kids again?*

Nadia is held at gunpoint by two Yemeni guards. Then, three of them rush Nadia, push her to the ground, and all three of the men rape her.

The Saudi army arrives two days later, looking for Charles. After a brief shoot-out between the Saudis and the Yemeni guards, the Yemenis surrender.

The Saudi soldiers enter the guard station to find Charles and Ravi tied up in chairs. Ravi is shouting, "Where is my daughter?"

A Saudi soldier comes into the back room and finds a crying, half-naked fifteen-year-old girl.

The Saudi government officials meets the Omani army and takes all three back to Muscat, Oman.

Nadia recounts her story to her mother: "I couldn't talk. Said nothing. The Saudi soldier took off his jacket and put it on me because I was naked. He said, 'I'm going to get you out of here.'

"It was so hard for me to trust the Saudi soldier! There were no other choices. I had nothing else. Everything inside me was gone. So, whatever comes next, it's fine. They're going to cut me; they're going to kill me? Fine. It's better than this. He opened the door and told me to stay behind him, and we started walking upstairs. He opened the door where Father was. He and Charles had been beaten, too. But I was raped."

"They took me to the back of the guard station, where there was this little room," Nadia tearfully explains to her mother. "They told me I could have some snacks."

"That went on for days, nights. And all I got to eat was a glass of milk with an egg in it, raw, mixed in. They said it will give me energy. But when I got energy, they hurt me again," Nadia explains.

"For four days, I was locked in that room," Nadia recounts. "They took off my clothes; they beat me and raped me!"

Two years passed, and Nadia continued to study mathematics in Muscat, while her severe emotional scars were so evident that she didn't like men anymore. She even distanced herself from her father.

She found solace in studying and preparing the F1 Student VISA application to enter the United States, to study at a university.

"Mother, the US President's immigration policy is stricter now," Nadia explains.

In the other room, her father yells, "It's not safe for you to travel overseas; you should study in Saudi Arabia!"

"What happens when your visa runs out?" her mother asks.

"Maybe I will be a mathematician in the US," Nadia responds.

Nadia doodles in her notebook, now solving differential equations and finding the area and volume using Calculus. She is now a senior in high school. She understands how to square the circle and the meaning of the Fibonacci series. She graduates at the top of her class. She is two months away from attending university in the United States.

Wearing her burqa, she takes an airplane flight from Muscat to Dubai and then to New York City, eventually making her way to High Point, North Carolina.

She has enrolled in the School of Mathematics and Science at a university and could not be happier to be pursuing her dream. She takes math and English courses, as well as Religious Studies.

THE INTERVIEW

Nadia is now a college student of mathematics, known by her friends as "Pi" because of her attention to the detail in challenging mathematical proofs, especially "squaring the circle."

Nadia likes to study in the graduate lounge, where professors often hang out, as do other undergraduates sometimes. "Being an irrational number, pi cannot be expressed as a common fraction," Nadia would tell her classmates.

Despite her love for mathematics, one of her favorite classes is World Religions, an elective class she took to help her understand her Islamic worldview and her devotion to the sanctity of marriage.

My time in the Middle East taught me that Arab-born folks are rigid when it comes to their religious beliefs, David thinks to himself. David is Nadia's religion professor, and he's interviewing her in his discerning class on the study of world religions. David is a deist. Like Yuan's interview, this is going to be interesting to be so close to a Muslim student who spent most of her life in Oman.

I have never published on Islamic beliefs, and I just can't understand their idea of virgins in heaven. I still have doubts about my own faith, David admits to himself while preparing for his planned class interviews.

"Good morning, Nadia," David says. "Please come into my office and have a seat." David is a slender, attractive man, now in his fifties, with graying hair and blue eyes, wearing a tie and a button-down shirt.

David's office has a picture of his family: his attractive wife—about twenty years younger than he—and their two small children. Nadia stares at the family photo as she sits down with a notebook in hand. A pendulum moves in one corner of the office, and Nadia's head glances at the motion that reminds her of the horse-drawn carriage back in her hometown in Oman.

"Thank you for accepting this class assignment to be interviewed," David says, while Nadia's face remains unexpressive. Her dark hair is long and flows off her back. She no longer wears the traditional Islamic dress, and David is curious about her attire.

Prior to the interview, David spotted the Arab-born young lady near the front of his Religious Studies class: *I observed her in the classroom as being studious and respectful, often more so than her American-born classmates. Americans make erroneous assumptions about Muslim religious practices, as I learned on my travels to the Middle East.*

"Nadia, I want to understand your Islamic worldview. I have four questions for you, and they are about 'origin', 'meaning', 'morality', and 'destiny,'" the professor intriguingly states, in order to keep her interested.

I was surprised Nadia's worldview is similar to the Christian worldview, except for the critical piece—the Gospel, David thinks to himself.

Her eyes look straight at the professor—her legs crossed, body erect.

"Do you believe in a 'moral code?'" David asks.

"I highly value family and my Muslim traditions, so sex before marriage and sex outside of marriage are strictly forbidden," Nadia states with confidence.

"This view is refreshing, given the often-casual view some Christians and Catholics have regarding the consequences of immoral sexual behavior," David responds. Then, he ponders, *We have only been in the interview two minutes, and the issue of sex has already been brought up.*

"Tell me about your clothing and dress: Do you still wear the traditional Islamic dress? Obviously, you are not wearing it today . . ."

"I stopped wearing a hijab because of some prejudice I felt from some Americans," Nadia says, and goes on to elaborate. Her eyes start to water.

"I especially felt uncomfortable here in the US after Donald Trump took office in 2017," she murmurs.

"I've never felt this type of prejudice." Nadia's eyes continue to water as she speaks up.

David thinks, *I can appreciate her dedication to the Muslim faith and her ideals about work ethic, family, and charity during her fasting period. Her worldview is rooted in tradition and the Prophet Mohammed's teachings.*

Then, Nadia's eyes move toward his family photo, and she says to the professor, "In my home country, I could do nothing to defend myself from my father's abuse. Only by Allah was I able to escape and come to study in the US. My father allowed me to be abused by Yemeni rebels, and I will never forgive him for that."

"Forgiveness . . ." David starts to discuss it and then stops.

"Origin? Where do you come from?" David asks.

Nadia's eyes move from the photo back to the professor: "Although Islam views Jesus as one of the five great prophets in history, I don't believe Jesus is the only begotten son of God."

"You believe in Abraham, as do the Christians, but not the divinity of Jesus?" asks David. "Yes, I cannot believe in Jesus as the Messiah," Nadia responds.

"Meaning? What is your purpose on this earth?" David inquires of Nadia.

"My purpose is to do good works and make Allah happy," she says, as Nadia smiles.

According to the Qur'an, God predestines the moment Muslims will die before they are conceived in the wombs of their mothers. No one can delay his or her own death if it is against the will of God, regardless of the cause of death.

"Where will you go when you die?" David asks.

"I do believe in heaven."

"Do you believe in the virgins as a reward in heaven," David asks. Nadia's face turns red, and she looks down. Quiet fills the room.

"I believe that only God knows where a person will end up in the afterlife, since only God knows a person's works and deeds. God will judge human beings according to His complete justice on the day of judgment." Nadia's breathing subsides after making this assertion.

I may be a deist now, but there is significant evidence for the death and resurrection of Jesus by Christian and non-Christian scholars, David contemplates.

David leans over to collect his papers and says to Nadia, who is about to exit his doorway, "Thank you for the interview and don't forget about the Q&A session after exams. It will be at The Church Street Brewery in uptown High Point."

"Is this not a hangout for the rich crowd?" Nadia asks perplexedly. "Islam forbids me from places like that, but I'll give it some thought."

David smiles as the American-looking, Arab-born college student leaves his office: "Bye, Nadia."

Chapter 9

RAE

"Get your ass back in the house, Rae!" yells Mama.

"But, Mama, Petey and me going to go to the store and get some Now & Laters," Rae yells back.

"I told you to keep quiet," older brother Petey says. "We can sneak under the porch, then when she falls asleep, run off to the store."

"I'll whoop y'all's ass if you leave me!" Mama yells at the two boys from her couch inside the 800-square-foot frame house. "Bring me the mail and watch out for them drug dealers."

High Point, North Carolina is experiencing mild temperatures this Friday evening, which means Section-8 residents spend more time out and about. Driving along Hoskins Street, one knows the front porches of small government-subsidized housing are there for a reason.

The front porch on Hoskins Street is where it all started, especially for thirteen-year-old Rae and his eleven brothers and sisters. The front porch might not seem like an interesting place for the rest of the town, but it was a gallery seat for black families in a poor section of town.

The only mail Mama would get would be a government disability check for $500 per month, plus child support for her eleven kids— ages two to eighteen.

Millions of fathers in the United States do not live with their children. A vast majority of these fathers do not pay formal child support. On the other hand, a significant percentage of these absentee fathers are poor themselves. But even the well-off non-resident fathers may be just as guilty. Mama's child support comes and goes.

The two boys tiptoe across battleship-gray tongue-and-groove flooring and make their way under the front porch to hide. The old porch needs repair—something the government required the landlord to do.

"Them floors got holes all in them," says Rae. "Watch out for the sharp nails."

"Why Mama push that McDonald's trash under the porch?" asks Petey.

"I ain't hiding under there with those dogs and rats!" Rae exclaims.

"Shut up and sit still," Petey whispers to Rae. "The shit smell from dogs under the porch is nasty."

"Old man is sitting over there, and he will see us and tell Mama," says Rae.

"It's about dark, so we can run up to Washington Street grocery store and get some Now & Laters," Petey says. "I've got two dollars."

"Where you get two dollars, Petey?"

"Old white man that comes around here in that white pick-up truck,"

Petey responds as he checks his old jean pockets. "He gave me a dollar bill last week."

"I thought that man was a pimp."

"No, his name is Mr. Walker—some rich man from downtown," Petey responds. "Mama say he likes to make bridges."

"Make bridges?" Rae says. "What do you mean?"

"Bridge the gap between white and black folk," Petey says. "To help us black folk."

"One day, Mama say Mr. Walker just pulled up in front of the front porch and handed out groceries," Petey says. "And he didn't ask for no money in return."

Peeking out the underside of the front porch, the two boys see their getaway, since the neighbors have left their porches, as darkness settles in, and Mama has fallen asleep.

The boys walk side by side up Hoskins Street and turn behind the corner fish market toward Washington Drive. Washington Drive in High Point was once a bustling, vibrant community for African American business owners and educators during segregation.

Dating back as early as 1893, Washington Drive was a hub for black life with the creation of a school for black students. The school was later renamed William Penn High School, where scholars like Booker T. Washington and poets like Langston Hughes came to speak.

The street was home to black doctors, dentists, and High Point's first black-owned hotel, opened by Willis Hinton—a freed slave. Even Martin Luther King, Jr. spoke at First Baptist Church on Washington Drive.

But the boys are not thinking about history in the 2000s, as an older black man wearing a dark overcoat starts to cross the street carrying a brown bag.

"You want a dime bag?" the man yelled. "Ten dollars."

The two boys stood motionless. As the man's coat was opened slightly, they could see something metal tucked behind his belt. The streetlight, which just came on, reflects the metal in his mouth as he yells.

"No, sir," Petey says, and the boys step back away from the street.

"I'm broke as a bitch," the man replies. "Give me your damn money."

About that time, the boys could hear the rumbling sound of an automobile turning the corner onto Hoskins Street.

"Leave them boys alone," Mr. Walker shouts through his truck window, moving his vehicle to shield the boys from the man.

"Mr. Walker, thanks for saving us from that," Petey tells him.

"Y'all need a ride home?"

Rae answers, "No, we'll be fine going to the store up yonder, then right back home."

"Okay, boys, I'll be making my way down your street if you need me," Mr. Walker says and smiles as the two boys walk off.

"Mama's at home, Mr. Walker!" Petey yells back.

Mr. Walker turns his truck into the corner fish market parking lot and gets out. *This area of town is ugly, the ugliness of poverty—dilapidated and boarded-up homes tagged with gang symbols, empty lots littered with liquor bottles and fast-food wrappers, and sterile low-income proj-ects like Hoskins Street,* Mr. Walker ponders all this as he opens the glass door protected by iron bars.

Mr. Walker could see men clustered on the far corner of the parking lot selling drugs, but no one messed with Mr. Walker. He was known around town as a Good Samaritan. As he looked around, he saw few working factories, only empty ones being torn down for scrap, and he felt sorry for the poor black folks like Rae's family.

"Mr. Walker, good to see you," the store clerk says. "What ya having today, catfish?"

"No, I want to buy a loaf of bread and milk," Mr. Walker responds.

"You sure you don't want any fresh whiting?" the clerk asks.

"No, I was wondering about all the houses around here abandoned and boarded up. The one next door is half burned down; the others sit empty, although a few people squat in them," Mr. Walker comments.

"Everyone always saying we don't have jobs around here because of things we lack, but it ain't what we lack; it's what we have: black skin," the clerk responds.

Meanwhile, the man who tried to sell crack to the teenagers continues his slow walk down Hoskins Street in a trench coat on a summer day.

Mr. Walker glances back through the front door, while paying the store clerk for the food.

"Well, let me see if I can help some of those folks." Mr. Walker adds. "I'll be on my way."

"Thank you, Mr. Walker, and come back."

Meanwhile, Rae and Petey have picked up Now & Laters and milk for Mama at the grocery store down Washington Drive. They start making their way back to Hoskins Street.

"We better get back before Mama wakes," Petey says. Walking past one of the half-burned-down houses along Hoskins Street, Rae hears a faint low-pitched sound. The boys remember such a sound from their bedroom, where their two-year-old sister sleeps and cries. But this sound was from the front porch of a dilapidated frame house.

The cry is unrelenting, rhythmic, and comes in short bursts.

"What's that noise?" Rae asks. "I see a cardboard box on the porch."

The cry becomes high-pitched as the boys creep up the wooden steps to see what's inside the box. The old house would meet a new life.

Opening the box, they see a small baby dressed in white clothing, sucking on its fingers. The cry becomes "eehh, eehh" followed by quick, successive cough-like sounds.

Petey says, "That is a baby. We gotta get out of here!"

"No, we ain't leaving this baby!" Rae whispers, as the dark front porch carries the cries, and the boys don't know what to do with the crying baby.

Meanwhile, Mr. Walker stops his truck in front of Mama's house. She's sitting on the front porch.

Mama is a large lady, and she sits on the front porch for work and rest, the same front porch where she snaps beans in the morning and greets passersby in the afternoon—her time to hear things and to talk.

For Mama's menfolk, the porch is a space of socializing and relaxation after a day of working. For young people, the porch is a place to be alone, yet not unchaperoned, when courting.

"Hello, Mama." Mr. Walker leans out of his window and shouts, "I saw ya boys up on the corner."

"I told them not to go—there's drug dealers along that street," Mama responds, while holding a tin bucket between her legs.

Her upper body is large, and her legs extend out in front of the old rocking chair toward the old porch railing made of pine 2x4s. Her left hand reaches for green beans, and her right throws the beans into the bucket. The early evening air makes for cool nights and warm conversations.

She is quite fond of Mr. Walker, as he has been a kind man, giving her food and money the past year. Mr. Walker is a God-fearing man in his fifties, formally educated; after years working in construction, he took over the family furniture manufacturing business.

"Please come up on the porch and sit awhile," Mama shouts to Mr. Walker.

Mr. Walker is dressed in his dark suit after a long day as owner and manager of a furniture factory near downtown High Point. He has a mustache and smokes a pipe.

Meanwhile, the two boys who just discovered the crying baby on a porch just two blocks away gather their thoughts.

"Mama is going to kick our ass if we tell her we gotsa baby," Petey moans.

"We better tell Mama about this," Rae says, as he pulls on Petey with the other hand, while carrying a plastic bag of Now & Laters and a quart of milk.

Mr. Walker sits down in an old rocking chair—paint peeling off and its armrest unsteady. He is eager to hear how Mama is doing.

Mama moves carefully in the rocking chair with her long cotton gown. The grain of the wood is showing after the gray color has faded. The rocking chair creaks and groans as grain scratches the dirty porch floor.

The rocker is important to her. She takes particular comfort from rocking in it. She sings old Gospel hymns when she is worried about her children, and then the rocking comes fast and rhythmic. When she tries to relax and remember the good ole days, she rocks slowly.

"I used to sing those hymns up the street at Church Street," says Mama.

Then Mama's rock slows, and she says to Mr. Walker, "When I was a child, after church, the preacher would come by and sit with my mother on our porch. She would serve cake and coffee; the porch is our outdoor living room."

Mr. Walker just sits and listens and whispers, "Yes, Mama, but are you worried about these drug dealers and drive-bys?"

"The Lord is going to protect me and my children, Mr. Walker," she explains, continuing to rock, but now finished with snapping her green beans.

Mr. Walker pulls out his pipe. Mama likes to see him light his pipe.

"I bet that gives you almost complete happiness—you always smiling when you smoke, Mr. Walker," she says this as she grins, then she adds, "You always smelled like pipe tobacco, too."

Mama is everybody's mama on Hoskins Street in High Point.

Mama and Mr. Walker hear someone yelling up the street.

"Mama, Mama, we found a baby; we found a baby," Rae yells from the side of the street toward his rundown house, where Mr. Walker's white truck sits in front of the porch.

Mama jumps out of her rocking chair and yells, "Rae, get up here!" The front porch flooring can be heard moving.

Mr. Walker rocks slowly and says nothing. He is still wearing his fedora hat and smoking his pipe—a scene not common in this part of town. He stands up, peering down on Mama now walking slowly toward the street. Mama and Mr. Walker believe the boys may have found a stray kitten but not a baby.

"We were on our way back from the Washington Drive grocery store when we came to Downing Street, and we heard the baby crying," Rae says.

"What color is the baby?" Mama asks.

"It's a white baby, Mama, and very little," Rae explains. "And we should go back there and get it before someone else does."

Mama looks at Mr. Walker and asks, "Can you go up there and see about that baby?"

Mr. Walker extinguishes his pipe and tells the boys to come with him: "Get in the truck, Rae, and you, too, Petey; let's go see about this baby."

"Turn on Washington Drive and right before Downing, over there," Petey explains, as he points out the truck window toward the direction of the old house and crying infant.

The boys had heard cries, but Mr. Walker had believed that a raccoon or baby deer was the source, but their investigation had clearly proven otherwise.

Mr. Walker could not believe his own eyes. "It's a little baby wrapped up in a plastic bag," he says to Rae.

As he walks toward the abandoned house, half gone due to fire, he thinks to himself, *Who in God's name would leave a baby on the front porch? Is someone still living in this burned-out house?*

Smelling of old charcoal and burned timbers, a cardboard box sitting two feet tall against the hardboard siding, with the tops closed, holding a precious life, awaits the man.

"Rae, help me lift the box, and we'll take her to Mama first and see if she recognizes the child."

"She is probably hungry," Petey says.

"I bought some milk from the store," Rae tells Mr. Walker.

"That is very kind of you, Rae, but new babies this little should not drink that kind of milk," Mr. Walker explains. "But we need to get her some food soon."

Mr. Walker, Rae, Petey, and the newborn baby take a ride back to see Mama on Hoskins Street.

Arriving back at Mama's house, they see she is rocking fast on the front porch, and then she stands as she sees Mr. Walker pull up.

"Careful with her," Mr. Walker tells Rae.

"I am. Mama, look, here is the baby!" Rae yells.

"Not so loud, Rae!" Mama says. "This ain't our baby, and the police will be coming for her."

The baby is now whimpering and trying to open her eyes, still coated with afterbirth. Her umbilical cord has been clamped with the kind of plastic twist-tie used to secure a garbage bag.

"It's real young," Petey says to Mama. "Not old at all."

"We better call the police right now," Mr. Walker tells Mama.

"We don't get to keep it?" Rae responds.

"Rae, that is a tiny white baby and ain't no way we gonna keep it," Mama responds. "Now, you and Petey get back in the house."

"Mama, please," Rae contends.

"Alright. Wrap her up in something first," Mama tells Rae. "She has gotta be a little cold."

You could see the joy on Rae's face as he holds the newborn, wrapped in swaddling clothes.

Mama is always trying to keep me from learning. I want to see how that baby breathes and if she moves her arms, and who is going to take care of her cuz I could do that. Who would leave their baby all alone? Rae thinks to himself.

"911. What is your emergency?" the operator says to Mr. Walker.

"I have found a newborn baby in a cardboard box on Washington Drive," Mr. Walker tells the operator.

"What is your address now?"

"I am at 206 Hoskins Street, with a white pick-up parked out front."

"We will send an officer to you right away."

"The law in the State of North Carolina is that a mother has thirty days to relinquish her infant. She does not have to give her information at all. She can go to any fire station, police station, or hospital," the police officer explains to Mr. Walker.

Ever since my youngest daughter died of a brain hemorrhage, I've longed for another girl. My wife cannot have children anymore, Mr. Walker muses.

"Good evening, ma'am; I'm Officer Jones. What can I do for you?"

"My boys heard a crying baby up on Downing . . . Here she is," Mama says.

"I'll have to take her to the hospital and have her checked out. She will stay there for thirty days unless the biological mother comes forward," the police officer explains to Mama and Rae.

"Abandoned babies are unfortunately not at all unusual," the officer comments. "Too often, babies are abandoned in terrible conditions like this. We've had babies left in bathrooms and other horrible places."

The police launch an investigation and learn from bystanders that a pregnant woman had been seen near the area where the baby was found.

The woman was apparently homeless all her life and was abused by drug dealers in the area, including being raped under the bridge that crosses over Washington Drive.

A day passes, and Mr. Walker drives by to check on Mama. He finds Rae on the front porch.

"Mr. Walker, what happened to the baby?" asks Rae.

"Well, it's a girl, and she is in an intensive care unit."

"Can I go see her?"

"I can take you to the hospital, but you can only look at her from behind the glass window of the ICU," Mr. Walker explains.

"Okay," says Rae. "I would love to go see her."

"You best get your homework done, Rae, if you want any chance of a life outside of these projects," says Mama.

I want to go to college and be an engineer, not like the ones driving the trains next to Washington Drive, but the ones that make cell phones, Rae tells himself.

Mr. Walker and Rae visit the baby every day in the hospital, and they learn the biological mother has not come forward.

Mr. Walker decides to go through with adopting the baby girl, who is now only four weeks old.

"She's gaining weight and smiling a lot. She's an easy baby who loves to be held and sung to, and, overall, she's thriving now," the hospital nurse tells Mr. Walker.

"Rae, what do you want to call her?" Mr. Walker asks.

"How about Robin?" Rae adds. "That is Mama's real name."

"We will call the baby girl Robin," Mr. Walker says, adding, "And I'll let you come see her whenever you want, Rae."

"Thank you, but, for now, I better get back home and help Mama and do my schoolwork."

"You are special, Rae; don't forget it."

Mr. Walker drives Rae back home to the worn-out Section-8 house on Hoskins Street. Rae's dream is only partially broken.

Rae slips up the front porch, now holey and squeaking.

"Get your ass back in the house, Rae, and do your homework!" says Mama.

Mama's husband died when Rae, who's her second child, was just seven years old. Life became dramatically different for Mama and the boys.

I really miss my daddy. Mr. Walker was like a daddy to me. Now that he has the baby girl, I may never see him again, Rae dwells on his loss.

Tears start to well up in Rae's eyes, *Daddy always helped me with the heavy boxes or carrying groceries inside. He kept close watch over me and Petey and everybody else. He told me to be careful because danger lurks in the streets.*

It's in this part of town, littered by check-cashing storefronts, liquor stores, and carry-outs, where mothers like Mama struggle to make ends meet and keep their children safe. And it's in this part of town where too many black young men like Rae have to navigate life alone.

Not long after his father's death, Rae and his siblings started skipping school and missing curfew. Typical teenager behavior turned into serious crime. More than once, one of the boys ended up being led away in handcuffs by police. Their mother, for her part, sought help—from the school system, the courts, the government. Only Section-8 housing money came in, and her efforts fell short.

Two of the boys have been in the criminal justice system, and the youngest has had several stints in drug rehab. Only Rae has not been arrested by the police and remains out of juvenile detention.

So, what happened?

Would their lives have been different if their father had lived? What did these young men need in their lives that their mother could not provide?

For some reason, Rae has so much courage and kindness in his heart to help people like the abandoned baby in a cardboard box. But life would be different as soon as he graduates from high school and seeks acceptance at a nearby university.

A year passes, and Rae enters college in High Point, North Carolina. Originally, he wanted to be an engineer, but having experienced poverty and finding the abandoned baby, he now wants to major in psychology or social work.

Raymond is now a healthy, hard-working college student, known by his friends by his nickname, "Rae."

But deep down, Rae could never forget Mr. Walker, the abandoned baby, and how hard Mama was on him to do his schoolwork. Her well-meant verbal abuse and the loss of his father took a toll on his emotional stability.

Most people look at black boys like Rae and say that they're bad. But counselors who understand black teens say that they're hurting. Their behaviors are acting out the pain. They're just trying to meet their needs—the need to be included, to be loved, to be welcomed, respected, and wanted.

One of Rae's favorite classes is World Religions, an elective he took. He wants to know more about God, Christianity, Islam, and Hinduism. Rae thinks, *Hey, we all worship the same god.*

What does it mean to be a Christian? Mama used to take us to the white church on Church Street. She was trying to fit in with the white people, but it didn't work out so well. Only Mr. Walker stayed friends with us, Rae recalls. *After Daddy died, I just wanted a place and a space to be respected. I prayed for my daddy to come back to me, but that was like praying to a brick wall. I've heard of Moses and Jesus, but they lived thousands of years ago. What does it mean to be a modern Christian?*

"Welcome to World Religions," Professor David states to his class.

"How's it going?" Rae says. The rest of the class turn to see who spoke up.

David muses at the outspoken young man. David is Rae's religion professor, and he has interviewed him on the study of world religions.

Like Nadia's interview, this is going to be interesting: to hear from an African American student who spent most of his life growing up in an impoverished inner-city with racism and little time spent at church or reading religious books.

I have never published on African American beliefs, and I look forward to hearing Rae's perspective. Some of the most spiritual people in America are black people.

Rae knocks on Professor David's door.

"Hey, professor, is this an okay time?" Rae's voice stays smooth and calm.

"Absolutely, Rae; I was looking forward to you coming in today," the professor nods. "Rae, I want to understand your worldview. I have four questions for you, and they are about 'morality', 'origin', 'meaning', and 'destiny,'" the professor adds.

Rae sits slightly hunched over with torn jeans and his cell phone still in his hand.

"If you don't mind putting that phone away, we can have a better interaction," David notes politely.

"Oh, okay, but you know I like to take notes on my phone," Rae says.

"Do you believe in a 'moral code?'" David asks.

"You mean like morals, like the Ten Commandments, Moses, and all that stuff?"

"Yes, is there a set of rules that guide your life?" David responds quietly.

"Mama always told me to treat others like I wanted to be treated," Rae explains. "I once found a baby in a cardboard box and took it to the police . . . Is that following a moral code?"

"That's very interesting. So, you found a baby and returned it to the local authorities?" David asks. "Have you ever stolen anything?"

What kind of question is that? Because I'm black, he thinks I'm going to steal some homework or something like that?

"Well, doing the right thing is treating a black man the same way as a white man," Rae states. "This university is mostly a white institution, and I have no interest in Jesus. I wasn't raised a Christian, and I haven't had much experience with church, except for a white church in downtown High Point. Campus ministries here are all white Christian organizations."

"Thanks, but can we slow down a bit?" David asks. "So, do you or do you not believe in Jesus?"

"I'm not sure; all I know is that, when a number of racial incidents happened on campus, I was offended," Rae explains. "But then I met a group of black Christians who looked like me, who were out there praying and protesting."

"Protesting?" David asks.

"Yes, when those white neo-Nazis killed people up in Charlottesville, Virginia, the black students held signs in opposition," Rae states. "They were being the people God created them to be; they were unapologetic about being black, and they seemed to love God. There was something fascinating about that, something that I didn't feel when I wandered into predominantly white organizations on campus."

"That's interesting, Rae. I'm glad to see you've found people you can relate to," David says.

"I really want to learn from everyone," Rae says.

"Let's move on to the next question: What is the origin of life?" David asks.

"You mean like where do we all come from?"

Professor David nods his head, his white face straight, and his arms relaxed on his table, making notes.

"Mama had eleven children. She never got an abortion, and I found a three-day-old baby one time in a cardboard box. I would never throw that away. Each of us are unique, and Mr. Walker said I was special, so I think something special must have created us," Rae states firmly to Professor David.

"Do you believe in the Big Bang, or has God created us all?" David asks

"I haven't read the Bible, yet. Mr. Walker told me to start with *Genesis,* where it says, 'In the beginning, God created the heavens and the earth,'" Rae explains.

"The beginning is the question," the professor smiles, responding to Rae.

"We don't know when the beginning was. Were the first humans born 6,000 years ago or 100,000 years ago?" Rae asks.

David sits back slightly and studies his notes, while Rae glances down at his iPhone, but the young man is seemingly satisfied with the discussion.

"I liked what we talked about," Rae says politely.

"Thank you for the interview, and don't forget about the Q&A session after exams. I'll add three points to your final exam score if you show up. The Q&A will be at The Church Street Brewery in uptown High Point."

"Is that where the First Baptist Church is?" Rae asks perplexedly. "Mama used to take us there when we were little, but there was some racism, so we never went back."

"Well, let's hope there is no racism here," the professor adds.

"Maybe it was not racism, but some of them made Mama feel real uncomfortable in the church service, and that's not very Christian-like!" Rae explains. "But I might see you at the Q&A. Do I need to pull up my average?"

"If you want to pass this class, you need a C, which is a numerical average of 73," David says.

"I understand," Rae says.

"Goodbye, Rae," says David

"Later," says Rae.

Chapter 10

CHRISTINE

D r. Queenan phones his daughter: "Christine, sweetie, something has come up at the University," he says. "I won't be able to make it to your dance recital."

"But you promised me, Dad."

"Your brother is having some difficulty adjusting to college. He's pledging Delta Upsilon Chi."

"Pledging DUC is crazy, Dad. Do you realize how much alcohol and drugs are done at that house?"

"I don't allow drugs and alcohol at this university," her father replies. "We have very tight security here."

Through her window, she can see a hazy morning view through their academic aerie. The University seems to have doubled in size since she became a freshman just seven months ago. But like a gangly eighteen-year-old, many of the thoughtlessly erected buildings— barely ten years old—were being torn down to make way for shinier dorms, new academic labs, and a brand-new student center.

"Mike told me that, at DUC, they grind up pills into powder and snort it," Christine says. "He's going to kill me if he finds out I told you."

"I'll protect you from anything, sweetie."

"Mike said they haze new kids coming in and make them do all sorts of crazy things."

"Does Mike do the hazing?" asks her father.

"According to Marshall, Mike is the ringleader."

Her father thinks, *If there is a problem with Michael, I will deal with it. He's a good boy. He was at the top of his class in high school, and all the kids on campus like him. He's got a sales and marketing sense about him, just like me. A businessman to be, and maybe a motivational speaker.*

"I'll ask Jeff what he knows about the fraternity," her father says.

"Who's Jeff?" asks Christine.

"He's Head of Security at the University."

"You mean the bald guy that drives the golf cart around?" says Christine.

"He used to drive the new students from my office to Starbucks. Now, he has his own office and manages a team of security and transportation officers."

Christine says ruefully, "I remember when he picked me up on the front lawn last year."

"We won't talk about that, okay?"

"Why, Dad?" says Christine with mock innocence. "Was there a problem or something?"

"I said there would be no alcohol at any sorority or fraternity. You were found drunk and belligerent in the front yard of Theta Phi Upsilon."

"Pugnacious?" Christine says.

"Be-lig-er-ant, which means you were hostile with the police who were dispatched to check on a report of excessive noise," says her father.

"I don't have a drinking problem, Dad."

"Really, Christine?"

"Really, Dad, this is part of being a freshman."

"This was your third offense on campus," her father says. "You've had repeated meetings with the RA, and it doesn't seem to help."

"I'll be fine. Did Mom get my dance clothes cleaned?"

"Well, the police wanted to take you in for disorderly conduct. But Jeff talked the police out of taking you to jail."

"Yelling out loud toward the police is considered disorderly conduct?" Christine is not convinced.

"Yes, the city has a noise ordinance that restricts loud music and loud voices, and the University is not exempt."

"I think it's fine if me and my sisters have a little fun," Christine says. "We have to study to pass our classes, and we need a break now and then."

"You need to do more than just pass your classes. You are making As and Bs, aren't you?"

Christine makes a face. "Can you talk to my religion professor?"

"What do you mean 'talk to your religion professor?'"

"Dad, you are the president of this university," Christine says. "You can talk to him—he'll listen to you."

"I am the President, and we hire only the best educators to teach here. Furthermore, the Department of Religion includes four PhDs and an internationally respected professor, Dr. David Kirkman."

"Well, Professor David Kirkman gave me an F for my midterm grade, and he even gave me an F on my essay."

"An F!" shouts the father. "No one in the Queenan family makes Fs!"

"Dad, you are the President. Can you talk to him?"

"Yes, I will talk to him, but he is a tenured professor now."

"Tenured?" says Christine. "What's that? So what?"

"It just means I can't fire him unless he does something morally wrong at the University."

"What would that be? Not showing up for class?"

"No, things like unprofessional behavior, like sexual misconduct."

"He's not bad-looking for a professor," Christine says with a smirk. "Call him, now, Dad!"

"I have several meetings today, but I'll call him after. You can be too demanding, Christine."

"I'm busy, too. Today, I have the country club get-together with Mom, then I am going to get my nails done and a spa treatment."

"You did that last week," Dr. Queenan says.

"I get them done every week, Dad," Christine says. "Mom gives me a hundred-dollar bill each week. A girl has got to look good."

"Well, then, what do you do with the hundred-dollar bill *I* give you each week?"

"I need that for the sorority parties and my meals."

"Your meals!" her father yells, as he jumps out of his chair, standing between his executive oak desk and the other window, which faces the grand entrance to the University. "Your meals are already paid for in the forty-thousand-dollar tuition."

Dr. Queenan leans back in his wingback chair and peers out the large third-floor window overlooking the campus. From his vantage point, he can see the new baseball field, the new student center, and several new modern dorms. The campus is growing. His political influence extends beyond the campus, into the city administration and police department.

Dr. Queenan's busy schedule leading the fast-growing university has left little time for his daughter, Christine, and his son, Michael. Although he knows exactly what to say to other rich parents sending their kid to his private school, his permissive parenting has not taught him about limits and self-control.

"Where are you now?"

"I'm at home playing with Banker," Christine says.

"At home! You are supposed to be in class today."

"The professor told us attendance was not part of the grade so . . . I'm going to the country club after I finish in the hot tub."

"How about the job interview I got for you. Did you follow up?"

"Not yet, Dad, but I will."

"Bye! I need to go, now." He hangs up the phone just as his secretary knocks on his door.

"Anything I can do for you today?" The secretary inquires.

"Please set up a meeting with Dr. David Kirkman."

"The professor in the religious studies department?"

Despite his hair loss, Dr. Q. manages to slick it back with gel, covering most of the grey and provide a relatively youthful look for a sixty-something executive, a father of four making a million-dollar salary at a private-club-like institution for higher learning.

"Yes, thanks—that's him," Dr. Queenan says, as he fixes his purple tie and dark suit jacket, then organizes his papers and contractual agreements on his desk.

Dr. Queenan ponders, *I don't know what I am going to do with Christine. Her drinking needs to stop. I know it's normal for young kids to try alcohol, but I am hearing more reports from Jeff that drinking has become a bigger problem on Greek Row. Christine is such a loving young lady. She is a social butterfly, good looking. Looks can take you a long way. I don't want her to flunk out of here. I'll talk to her religion professor soon.*

Meanwhile, Christine finishes up her hot tub time at home. It's 11:00 a.m.

Most people driving past the well-manicured green hedges and clean fenced-in tennis court would think of a public pool for their family. However, Emerywild Country Club is the most exclusive private club in High Point.

After its construction in 1923, Emerywild soon became the central gathering place for High Point's civic and business leaders and a popular recreational and social destination.

Every Sunday, Christine's family comes together for lunch at the club—her home is just a block away. Rather than walking, or driving their car, Dr. Queenan hires a chauffeur service to take the family to the club. They arrive in style.

The chauffeur service includes a long black limousine that seats six comfortably. David "Petey" Logans unlocks the door to his polished black Lincoln Town Car, a stately vehicle that stands out among dusty economy cars. The new-car smell fills the limo, with its leather seats and complimentary beverages. The short Petey, an African American dressed in a formal black suit, climbs into the driver's seat and closes the door, disappearing, along with the secrets of his clientele, behind dark tinted windows.

Petey has been escorting the Queenan family for several years, since police were called to their residence for a reported hate crime. Dr. Queenan likes the privacy of the service. Christine likes the service, too.

The limousine arrives at 11:30 a.m. on Sunday, pulling up to the front gate of their brick mansion on Rotary Drive.

"Doc, I'm here," Petey says, after pushing the security control keypad on one side of the concrete driveway, while roses bloom on the other side.

"Petey, it's Mrs. Queenan," the wife says. "Pull on up. We're still waiting for Christine."

Petey pulls the elegant black Town Car into the grand portico on the front entrance. He jumps out of the limo and opens both rear doors.

"Hello, Petey—thanks for picking us up," Dr. Queenan says, as his back holds open the front oak door. The front door of the mansion is so wide that two people can exit without touching each other.

"Hello, Petey," Dr. Queenan's wife says, through the front door. She's wearing a white satin dress. Dr. Queenan is wearing his usual dark suit and purple tie.

"We're waiting for you, Christine!" Mr. Queenan yells back, through the house.

"I'm finishing my hair! Just a minute!"

Dr. and Mrs. Queenan both enter the limo. "She's been so into herself ever since she started at the University," Mrs. Queenan whispers to her husband.

Christine looks like a Barbie doll: curvy, blonde, fit, and trim. She wears a skater dress—a tad less casual than a cocktail dress, but fancy. Her mom bought it for her at Saks Fifth Avenue on their Christmas trip to Manhattan. The black dress is an elegant fabric and covered with jewels. Her purse carries her brand-new iPhone and her cigarettes.

"Let me in!" Christine yells. "Shut the door behind you, Michael."

Mrs. Queenan chides, "Christine, that's rude. Mr. Petey can hear you."

The limousine has a no-smoking policy, but Christine decides to light up anyway.

"You're not supposed to smoke in here," Dr. Queenan says, as the family of four settles into the limo for a one-block drive to Emery-wild Country Club.

"Darling, you think we could see the construction progress at the University before we go eat?" Mrs. Queenan asks.

"I'd be delighted to show you. Petey, drive me to my office."

"Yes, sir, Doc," Petey replies.

"Put the cigarette out, sweetie," Christine's father says. "I don't know how you smoke those things."

"I credit a girl in my middle school English class with getting me interested. We would sneak out behind the back door of Westminster Day School and smoke cigarettes."

"And no teachers saw you?" Mrs. Queenan asks.

"Yes, Ms. Pumple confronted us, but when I told her who my father was . . ."

"That's no excuse!" Dr. Queenan complains. "Now, your lungs are taking a beating from the smoke . . . and so are we!"

Changing the subject, he adds, "At the University, we have seen tremendous growth in the last five years, and we're not done growing."

All four peer out the tinted windows of the limousine. They see red brick buildings designed with Georgian architecture influences. There are wide paths and plazas made of clay pavers in colors and textures that complement the buildings.

"Wow, look at those gardens," Mrs. Queenan comments.

"The campus is home to 2,000 different kinds of plants and 200 separate kinds of trees," Dr. Queenan says.

"The baseball stadium is incredible," Michael says.

"Who's that gentlemen by the new construction?" Christine asks.

"That's Will," Dr. Queenan responds. "He runs a large construction business in High Point and is doing a lot of work in Uptown, as well."

"Donors give thousands . . . no, millions of dollars, so my father has a grand salary," Christine purrs.

"I've managed to raise millions, and now we have a new library, construction of a new academic facility, construction of a new admissions center, and even a Division I ice hockey team. All in a day's work."

"I'm so proud of you, Darling," Mrs. Queenan says.

"Petey, you can take us to the club now," Dr. Queenan directs the driver.

The limousine drives slowly through the campus, exiting onto Martin Luther King Drive. It turns back west toward Emerywild, but before it does, it immediately passes Washington Drive.

The limousine passes an old abandoned playground and basketball court. A weathered old sign says "Washington Drive Park."

"Washington Drive Park—all the black kids live over here," Michael says. "I never saw them at Westminster."

Christine adds, "They attend Central and then A&T; I doubt they can get in here."

"Jazz great, John Coltrane, learned to play the saxophone at William Penn High School on Washington Drive," Dr. Queenan says.

The University is comprised mostly of rich white men, and they have yet to get actively involved in redeveloping Washington Drive or building up the community that is only two blocks from campus. The complacency of the leaders is part of the painful history of intolerance and bigotry in High Point.

Washington Drive in High Point is now mostly quiet, with one grocery store. Poor black artists attempt to revitalize the essence of the street by painting rundown buildings.

Washington Drive is not far from where Petey grew up. He can hear the rich white family in the back of his limousine as he drives them from the University to the country club.

Petey thinks to himself, *Damned rich white folk talking about my roots. I grew up in the projects across the street. I went to public school, like all kids should. Christine is just a privileged white girl. Yeah, I am nice to them cuz I want to get paid, but I don't like them . . . well, at least how they think they are better than us. God says we are all created in His image, so we must be of equal value. My hard hours and unsteady pay . . . They have no idea what it's like. I try to do my job well, with dignity, even though sometimes I don't get a break. Doc tells when and where to go. He ought to be thankful I ain't told about some of the crazy kids I've seen around his campus and off campus. I've even seen Christine hanging out at bars uptown, when she's supposed to be in class. I ain't telling Doc about that.*

The wooded neighborhood of Emerywild is full of stately mansions and manicured lawns, and streets cleaned especially well by the City. Other parts of town don't get this special treatment.

Emerywild is made up of about a hundred homes on lots that average about two acres in size. They have an average market value of $482,500, about $460,000 more than where Petey grew up.

What's unique about the area is that almost all these homes have circular driveways that stand out. The wealthy people can't be bothered to back out of their driveways.

"See those driveways?" Michael says. "The rich only go forward and never backward."

"Are you going forward, Michael?" his mother asks pointedly.

"You bet I am," Michael says. "I'm going to be the CEO of a private university one day, like Dad."

"How're your grades, Son?" Dr. Queenan asks.

"Fine. I've managed a C average and pledged Delta Upsilon Chi."

"I've heard some reports from the security team that DUC can get a little rowdy on Friday nights," Dr. Queenan comments. "Is that true?"

Petey pulls the limousine into the country club. The two-hundred-foot-long driveway to the country club is lined on both sides by rows of six-foot-tall green hedges. The front portico is at least fifteen feet tall and thirty feet wide with painted oak columns and gold-plated handrails.

The family enters the reception area. Emerywild features a ceremony lawn and a large plantation-style clubhouse. The club features a newly renovated boardroom and auditorium. The backside dining area seats a hundred, with beautiful golf course views.

Petey parks the long black Lincoln in front of the eight-foot white double-door entrance. The Queenan family all exit and climb up the steps.

"You'll wait for us until I call you," Dr. Queenan directs.

"Yes, Doc, I'll wait in the parking lot," Petey says. The family enters the lobby and is greeted by the tuxedoed host who escorts them to the back dining room overlooking the eighteenth hole.

Petey prepares to pull the limo out from under the portico to the parking lot next to the pool.

"Wait! I forgot my purse," Christine yells, turning toward the portico outside. "Petey, get it for me!"

Petey thinks, *Damn, that little girl is so demanding.* He gets back out of the driver's seat, opens the rear door, and looks in the back seat.

"I don't see it, Christine."

"It's in there; get it and bring it to me," she replies, standing outside next to the massive oak door and looking down on the limo's sunroof.

"I still don't see your purse. What does it look like?"

He didn't take my purse, did he? I don't trust those blacks, she thinks.

"Alright, I'll come down!" Christine walks meticulously with her high heels, stepping back down to meet Petey at the back of the limo.

"You must have dropped it, but I don't see it under the car," Petey says.

"It must be inside, in the back seat," Christine replies. Then, she pokes her head back in the limo. The darkness of the inside and bright outdoor sun temporarily blinds her, and the aroma of Petey's air freshener has now been eroded by the cigarette smoke she generated on the twenty-minute trip from the University back to the club. Even bystanders and those walking a few feet away under the portico see, hear, and smell the commotion.

Petey is on the other side of the limo looking in—one knee on the leather seat and one hand reaching under the dark rear console. A bottle of champagne has been opened, and he thinks, *Doc does not do that—must be Michael or Christine popping bottles. Someone will have to pay for that—twenty-five dollars a bottle from the Main Street Wine Bar.*

"What's this baggie?" Petey asks. Christine's purse has opened, revealing the dope.

"Don't you tell anyone—give me that!" Christine says, and she grabs the long purse strap next to Petey.

Petey sits down. One hand now holds the bottom of the purse, while he rummages through it with his other hand. Christine pulls on the strap and yanks the purse away from Petey, the baggie flying toward Christine. "That's not yours!" Christie says, and firmly collects the white rocks, while also sweeping some out the limo onto the portico driveway. She bumps her head on the door frame backing out and says, "Shit, leave me alone!"

Like a kid caught with her hand in a candy jar, Christine is caught with crack by Daddy's limo driver. Her perfectly caked-on makeup and low-cut dress mean little now.

Christine thinks, as she clamors to get her purse and dress fixed, *Will he tell my father? If he does, Dad won't tell the police or security at the University. Dad always looks out for me.*

Petey shuts his door and walks around to the other side of the limo, momentarily catching a glimpse of Christine's tanned leg bent at the knee as she tries to put her heel back on. In one of her hands is her purse, partially open and revealing a plastic bag and a pack of Marlboros. In her other hand is her shoe, as she fumbles while shoving it onto her tanned foot.

In that moment, Petey sees that his dignity is more admirable than being a rich eighteen-year-old white girl whose father is a king living in Emerywild, a girl who is a spoiled child who could go to prison for possession of crack. But he says nothing. He waits in the club parking lot, obeying his orders.

Christine makes her way back inside, to the dining room. Her father had just gotten up to find her—frustrated that she was momentarily missing.

"Where have you been?" Dr. Queenan questions her. "We have been waiting for you, and Dr. Brown said he saw some commotion outside with Petey."

"I'm fine. Can't you wait a minute for me? I needed to fix my hair."

Dr. Queenan admonishes her, "Don't you think it is rude to have the waiter stand here, while you fix your hair? Ever since you started at the University, you have had this attitude."

"Honey, it's okay," Mrs. Queenan tries to soothe her husband.

"May I take your drink order?" the waiter says.

"We can have a 'cold one' now with the new club rules, Dad," Michael says.

"No, we are all drinking water."

The dining room is both casual and elegant. Today's members are regulars—all civic and community leaders, college professors, attorneys, and medical doctors. One family that stands out in casual clothing is the Sampson family.

Britt Sampson is a real estate tycoon, who owns land around the University and also has buildings in Uptown. Dr. Queenan spots Britt at the corner table, where the glass windows show a golf game going on.

"Excuse me, dear, I am going to speak to Mr. Sampson," Dr. Queenan tells his wife.

Christine is busy taking selfies with her phone.

Michael gets up and walks toward the bar. The bar offers an upper-crust ambiance, with leather armchairs, and cherry-wood wrap-around seating. *Since Dad is talking to Mr. Sampson, I want to see what's on the house today.*

"What will you have today?" The bartender asks. Michael's beard and dark hair give him the look of a twenty-something, although he is two years shy of the legal drinking age. The new rules at Emery-wild Country Club don't allow teenagers at the bar. The bartender, a university drop out, forgets to check for Michael's ID, assuming he is of legal age.

"Gin and tonic," Michael says.

"I saw you sitting with Dr. Queenan . . . How's he doing?" The bartender asks.

"He's here taking a break," Michael says.

"You believe all the news about the frats and sororities, the drinking and parties and the police?" inquires the bartender.

Michael's head dips. His drink is passed to him across the oak bar. "I think there may be some frat boys that drink, but not on campus," Michael says. "What happens off campus, we have no control of."

"But Dr. Queenan said in the news he runs a tight ship on campus." Michael doesn't know what to say since his frat, Delta Upsilon Chi, has had several incidents.

Once, a next-door dorm called the police to break up a fight, and campus security negotiated with the police officers to release the frat-house perpetrators. University Security had found John "Jack" Horney, eighteen, of Hackensack, NJ, bludgeoned and bleeding inside the DUC frat house.

Michael grabs his gin and tonic, pulls the stirrer out, licks it, and throws it behind the bar, then walks back toward the dining area, where his family is seated. He opens the double doors to the dining area; the handle hits his drink, and it partially spills onto this white button-down shirt.

"I'm supposed to be over there at the bar when you drink," Mrs. Queenan whispers to Michael, as he sits down next to her. She and Christine admire Dr. Queenan, who is standing on the corner of the dining area next to the Sampson family.

Dr. Queenan greets the businessman: "Hi, Britt. Is this right? I heard you were going to develop some old properties in Uptown?"

"Hello, Dr. Queenan," responds Britt. "Yes, I want to try my hand at building a bar and brewery."

"I want to thank you for working with us to secure more land along Centennial Street," Dr. Queenan says. "We are out-growing our property."

"I am in the pre-construction phase of remodeling an old furniture factory on Church Street," Britt explains, adding, "Do you have any expertise in beer-making, in brewing?"

"I'm afraid I don't. I do know the owner of The Green Truck and The Oak Hills Brewery."

"Tell me more," Britt says. Most of the club members were "empty suits" except for Dr. Queenan. Most of these elite old white men thought Britt was just a cowboy with a redneck background.

"Britt, do you have a moment to meet my family?" Dr. Queenan says—he and Britt now face to face, one in a dark suit and purple tie, and the other in cowboy boots and a flannel shirt.

"Darling, this is the Britt Sampson, who helped us secure the adjacent properties." The forty-something real estate developer meets the fifty-something, very attractive Mrs. Queenan and her two freshmen kids.

"Hello, Mrs. Queenan," says Britt. "Who is this young lady?"

Mrs. Queenan replies, "Hi, Britt—I'll go over and speak to your wife."

Despite the social cachet of the Emerywild Country Club's elite members, their conversations are shallow: the leading ladies of Emerywild gossip rather than discuss women's issues, education, careers, or spiritual matters.

"This is our daughter, Christine," Dr. Queenan tells Sampson. "She is a freshman at the University."

"Hi, Christine. What are you studying?"

"I am majoring in Event Planning," she answers.

"You mean like for weddings and social events?"

"Yes, I think so. I am only a freshman, so I don't have much experience, yet."

"I have an idea," says Britt. Christine's blue eyes get a little bigger. "I'm developing an event space in Uptown. It's going to be a combination bar and brewery."

"A brewery with a full bar?" Christine asks.

"Yes, Uptown needs some new restaurants and bars near the new baseball stadium. I'm going to have a meeting room for social and community events; several community activists would like to have educational events somewhere near Uptown. I am going to need some sharp, fast learners to help me serve my customers. Do you have any experience waiting tables at restaurants?"

"I've never . . ." Christine starts to answer Britt, when her father interrupts.

"I think Christine would make a fabulous waitress at your Church Street Brewery," Dr. Queenan more than hints, with a smile.

"Christine, do you have any knowledge of which wines and beers you'd recommend to potential customers?" Britt queries.

"I'm not sure—they don't teach that at the University."

"How would you handle a customer complaint?" Britt asks.

"Not too many complain about me," Christine says haughtily.

Britt thinks, *These university kids' parents think their kids are God's gift to mankind. I know he is the President of the University, but where I come from, you treat the janitor with more respect than Christine has given me.*

"Well, I'll have you over for an interview as soon as the space is remodeled," Britt says. "We plan to open up right after we get the CO."

"CEO?" Christine says.

"No, CO, Certificate of Occupancy," Britt laughs.

Christine looks at her dad and smiles. "I would love an interview, Mr. Sampson. Do you need a bartender?"

"I'm not sure yet. Just show up, and we will discuss it."

The Church Street Brewery . . . Sounds like a place where I can also have a little off-campus fun, Christine muses. *Can't wait.*

"Dr. Queenan—one more thing," Britt says. "Over here, please." The two men side-step far enough that their whispers cannot be heard by either family.

"Is it true that some parents complained about the frat house party over the Christmas break?" Britt asks. "I heard that the police have made several trips to the University and security has talked them out of arresting any of them on reports of drugs."

"We won't talk about the death a few years . . ." Britt says before Dr. Queenan stops him.

"Let's just say that the news story has blown this incident out of proportion." Then, Dr. Queenan adds, "Christine will make a fine waitress."

"Very well, sir," Britt says. "I look forward to her stopping by for the job interview at The Church Street Brewery."

Chapter 11

NEAL

The meatloaf smell is filling up the house. Mashed potatoes are on the burners and cornbread in the oven. Mama and her two boys are waiting on their father—a construction foreman—to get home so they can eat dinner together. "Mama, have you seen my comic books?" the fifteen-year-old Neal asks.

"I'm cooking supper, Neal," says Mama.

I am only interested in Marvel & DC. I can't find them. I know they're in my room somewhere. Maybe I left them in Daddy's truck, Neal thinks.

Neal gets worried some of his other comic books may be lost.

"You ought to be doing your homework!" Mama shouts from the kitchen.

"Can you help me find them?" Neal shouts one last time.

"Well, eat supper first, Neal," she says.

"Shut up; I'm trying to study!" Neal's brother, Gabe, yells from his room across the hall. The hallway floor is hardwood, and their dog, Fifi, runs back and forth, playing with a tennis ball.

Cardboard boxes, four-feet tall, sit on both sides of Neal's bedroom, with more boxes in his closet—all full of comic books.

I'll go through every single one of them right now; I don't even care about eating, Neal thinks about all the comic books he has collected since second grade. He begins to call out to himself the names and what they mean to him, thinking about quotes from the stories such as Iron Man and Spider-Man:

Iron Man: Demon in a Bottle (#118-128). Are there any real demons in this world?

Sergei Kravinoff: So, now I see through the Spider's eyes. I wear the Spider's skin. I crawl. Now—I am the Spider.

Hobgoblin Saga (#239, 244-245, 249-251), and *The Kid Who Collected Spider-Man (#248): Name is Hobgoblin, and you're just in time for your funeral. That is cool!*

Neal continues to read his comic books, while Mama cooks supper. Neal's older brother Gabe, wearing flannel short jeans and sporting a scruffy beard, enters his bedroom.

"*Avengers: Ultimate Vision (#231-254), Once and Future Kang (#267-269), Under Siege (#273-277),* and *Assault on Olympus (#281-285),*" Neal lists off more books as he fumbles through cardboard boxes while sitting on the carpet floor.

Then, Gabe starts his rant: "I told you to shut your freaking mouth," Gabe says and pops Neal on his head. "I am trying to study."

"Stop! I can't find some of my Spider-Man comics," Neal contends with the older yet smaller Gabe.

"I don't read those things because I am focusing on school," Gabe contends.

Among their school friends, Gabe was known to be small but tough as nails, while Neal was big and friendly.

"I'll get to my homework later," Neal adds. "Did you take any of my comic books?"

"And if I did, what ya going to do about it?" Gabe responds.

"I'm going to tell Daddy when he gets home," Neal says.

Gabe puts his knee into the back of Neal, who is on the carpet floor along with hundreds of comic books spread out around him.

"If you do, I will beat your ass," Gabe threatens Neal.

"You're no help! Get off me!" Neal says.

"Boys, your father is home," Mama yells from the kitchen.

Daddy is tall and well-built. He wears overalls and a baseball cap. When his shoes hit the hallway hardwood, everyone knows it's Daddy.

"What y'all boys doing in here? Your room is a mess, Neal."

"Gabe keeps bothering me, and I can't find my favorite comic books," Neal says. "Did I leave any of them in your truck, Daddy? How do you like my drawings of Spider-Man?"

"Why don't you help me draw some construction plans," Daddy responds. "At least that would make you some money someday."

"Comic books might be worth something someday, Daddy," Neal says.

"About the only thing they'll be worth is kindling for a good warm fireplace," his father responds. "Let's eat, then you can clean up your room."

The two boys follow their much taller father to the kitchen, where Mama has set the table and laid out the meatloaf, mashed potatoes, and cornbread.

"You boys don't get any drink until all this food is ate," says Daddy.

"I'll get you two some tea," Mama responds. "Honey, what will you drink?"

"Water," Daddy says.

Mama slides a tall glass jar under the sink for some tap water. In the 1980s, there was little concern for water quality, especially in a middle-class household with one breadwinner.

"I lost a lot of water sweating and framing those apartments today," Daddy announces. "What did you do today, Gabe, besides study?"

"I just studied, Daddy," Gabe responds. "I want to get into Duke."

"Duke? We like Carolina around here," Daddy responds. "What did you do, Neal?"

"PE was fun, as was history," Neal replies. "But when I got home, I was worried about finding all my comic books."

"How about we go deer hunting this weekend?" says Daddy.

"I'd love that!" Neal replies. "Can I take my 4-10 shotgun?"

"We have church on Sunday," Mama adds. "So ya won't be hunting on Sunday, will ya?"

"What's wrong with Sundays?" Neal responds.

"You know we go to church on Sundays—always have, always will, I guess," Mama explains.

"But First Baptist Church is so boring," Neal says. "All we do is learn about some man who built a big boat for people and animals."

"But sometimes, Daddy don't go to church cuz he says works makes him tired," Neal replies.

"Sometimes, I don't, but Mama will take you boys to church," Daddy says. "We'll go hunting Saturday on the Willard Dairy Farm. Sunday, we can go to church. Mr. Willard told me he's seen a lot of deer running Skeet Club Road. I am right in the middle of one of my best seasons in a long time."

"You mean a ten-pointer, like that one?" Neal asks, pointing to Daddy's deer mounted to the dark pine board wall.

The family of four finishes up eating. Daddy throws an end-piece of pork chop to Fifi.

"I ain't going to church, no matter what," Gabe mutters, as he leaves the dinner table for his room.

———

The next year, Neal enters the tenth grade, and his daddy buys him a 1979 Chevrolet Camaro.

Neal's Camaro is metallic blue. It's a hot car, especially at Southwest High School. The '79 edition of the bow-tie-pony car got a refreshed look with bold new graphics, more streamlined fender vents, and an air-induction hood atop the 185-horsepower 350 V8.

Neal likes to hang out in the school parking lot with his friends before heading toward downtown. This brisk fall day is right in the middle of football and deer season.

"I'm going hunting on the Willard Farm after school," he tells his friend, Dee.

"You can't keep you rifles in the back seat," Dee says. "Principal won't allow guns around school."

"I'm not—I was just cleaning it," Neal responds.

"What's with all the comic books in the floorboard?" Dee chuckles. "Your girlfriend read those?"

About that time, a school bus pulls up beside the two boys. The driver opens his window. The boys in the bus are all staring intently at Neal and Dee.

"Hello, boys," the coach says. "Better keep those rifles in the trunk; the principal will expel you for bringing guns on campus."

"Sure, coach—we're going hunting soon," Neal says, as he shuts the trunk of his Camaro, hiding his 30-30 Remington rifle.

"Hunting won't get you a sports scholarship," Coach says. "What are your plans this year?"

"Why don't y'all try out for the wrestling team," the coach says, through the bus window. "I need a heavyweight." The two boys lie and say they have jobs, but the truth is that Neal likes to hunt more than practice sports, and wrestling is a lot of work.

"I'm working at McDonald's to help pay for my car," Dee responds.

"I'm really out of shape," Neal chimes in.

"Smart wrestlers make good grades," Coach comments. "And I can help you get a scholarship if you work hard."

"I'm also the scorekeeper for the basketball games," Neal adds.

"Sissies . . ." the Coach says and pulls off.

Daddy always wanted me to play football or wrestle. I'm in love with Kimberly. I don't have time for wrestling. She and I like to do things together. I'll do the basketball scoreboard, Neal talks to himself, while standing in the parking lot of Southwest High.

"Catch ya later, man," Dee yells, walking to his car. "I've got to get to work. Shoot an eight-pointer."

"Later," Neal responds, as he sits in his Camaro and turns on the radio.

Neal listens to rock music. He likes AC/DC, Journey, Bon Jovi, and Kansas. Rock music makes him feel like a king in his car. He'll try to impress Kimberly with the music. She is not around today, and he misses her. As he turns on the radio, he hears the Doobie Brothers playing. His Camaro has an 8-track stereo, and he pushes the sandwich-sized tape in to hear the song "Lights" by Journey. Then, he tries to sing.

When the lights go down in the city . . . And the sun shines on the bay . . . Ooh, I wanna be there in my city, oh. Oh, oh, oh. Man, I can't sing that song, but Kimberly will like my car.

He pushes the fast forward button on the stereo, advancing to the Doobie Brothers.

Doo-Doo-Doo-Do-Do-Do . . . Doo-Doo-Doo-Do-Do-Do, Jesus is just alright with me . . . Jesus is just alright, oh yeah . . . He took me by the hand . . . Led me far from this land . . . Jesus is my brother and my friend, sing the Doobie Brothers.

Jesus does not live now. What do they mean? I've never seen Jesus. My brother likes to beat up on me. How can Jesus be a brother and a friend? Neal ponders this, while driving down Skeet Club Road toward the Willard Farm.

As he turns off Skeet Club, he enters a narrow, tree-lined dirt road. The Willard farmhouse is in the middle of what seems like an endless forest. Once inside the forest, milk cows graze on a pasture in front of a tall rusted silo.

Neal's Camaro pulls up beside a tractor and a souped-up '57 Ford. He can see Mr. Willard working behind the silo in a wooded area. Neal's dressed in camo, with boots, and a cowboy hat. He leaves his rifle in the trunk until he is sure Mr. Willard is okay with today's plans for deer hunting on the twenty acres next to Oak Hollow Lake.

"Hey, boy—your daddy said you'd be stopping by," old man Willard yells toward the oncoming Neal.

"Hello, Mr. Willard," Neal says, while extending his hand.

"I don't know you that well yet," the old man responds, not shaking. "Don't need to shake anything—I know your daddy. He helped me build that back porch for my wife before she died."

"What are all these copper pipes for?" Neal asks.

"I make moonshine back here, boy," the old man's eighty-year-old voice crackles.

"But why do you have a radiator next to that brown vessel?" Neal asks.

"You see that '57 Ford?" Mr. Willard responds.

"Yes, I bet you can burn some rubber with that," Neal says.

"Moonshine and fast cars: the two go together like ham and beans, right?" Mr. Willard responds.

"Do you ever race that '57?" Neal asks, as the two sit down on old wooden chairs, while the copper vessel emits steam into the air above them.

"One of the first stock car racetracks built in North Carolina is the one over there on Johnson Street," Mr. Willard explains. "Mean old racetrack to get around, and it wasn't the smoothest track you ever run, either."

"So, you raced that track?" Neal asks.

"The race was promoted by Mary Lee Blair, sister-in-law of driver Bill Blair. It was the seventeenth race of the 1953 season, and I was in it," Mr. Willard brags.

Neal liked history, so he pressed the old man to continue.

"You can't see it anymore from the road," Neal adds, "but some buddies said they tried to deer hunt over there until the Blairs ran them off."

"Blairs don't like anybody on their land, especially hunters," the old man says, as some tobacco snuff slips down the crack of his mouth.

"I read, at the time, it was second in quality only to the Indianapolis Motor Speedway—a National Historic Landmark since 1987," Neal responds.

"Lee Petty came in fifth, and I was eighth behind Lewallen," Mr. Willard recalls. "I drove a '47 Ford with a flathead engine."

Neal nods his head with his mouth wide open.

"Henry Ford was a self-made man, raised as a poor farmer with little education, kind of like me. I call him a genius," Mr. Willard says, and then spits tobacco juice onto the dirt floor.

Neal keeps pressing the question: "Why do you have a radiator next to that brown vessel?"

"That damn radiator is an essential working part," Mr. Willard says, dripping more snuff from his mouth as he reaches under his seat for a bottle.

Mr. Willard never graduated from high school; he grew up during the Depression on Skeet Club Road Farm. He dropped out of school in 1940. Farming and cars were all he knew, and he liked to drink moonshine.

"As the ferment begins to boil, it creates steam, and the steam leaves this boiling chamber," Mr. Willard explains to Neal, bringing the bottle and setting it on his overalls.

Neal can't believe liquor is being made right in his neighborhood.

Mr. Willard continues: "Through the copper tube, it goes into the top of the condenser."

"Condenser?" Neal asks.

"The radiator, yes, submerged in water. The water helps cool the steam as it moves from the top of the condenser to the bottom. When it's complete, it will leave the condenser through these copper tubes and flow into a pot," Mr. Willard explains. "Voila! Mash into moonshine," the old man says with a smile. "Here, try some in this bottle, freshly made."

Neal ponders, *Mama always said you won't be an alcoholic if you don't start drinking.*

Neal knows his longstanding idea of an "alcoholic"—and the old man with the brown paper bag is something he couldn't be farther from right now. But now, sitting next to a moonshiner is both nostalgic and scary at the same time.

It doesn't mean I will have a serious problem. Alcoholics come in all shapes and sizes and levels of severity. It's all about how you use it. I came here to get permission to hunt deer, and now I wonder if I should try some liquor. It might pump me up a bit. I wonder what Kimberly will think. We're supposed to meet up tonight.

"Take a sip," the old man insists. "I call this jalapeño vodka."

Mr. Willard hands Neal a shot glass halfway full, and being a proud, cocky eighteen-year-old, Neal says, "Fill it to the top. What do you think I am, a sissy?"

Mr. Willard fills the shot glass, and Neal takes it. Then begins the most painful five minutes of post-shot coughing and gagging Neal has ever endured in his life.

"God! That burns all the way down," Neal cries.

Between fits of coughing and speaking with a hoarse voice (as the liquor had burned everything on its way down to his stomach), Neal thinks, *What the hell did I just take? And being the crazy man Mr. Willard is, he starts laughing at me and tells me it was jalapeño vodka. No deer hunting today.*

"Tastes good, doesn't it?" the old man smiles again and takes another pull.

"It burns bad," Neal swallows his cough to reply to Mr. Willard.

"The first one burns, but you'll get used to it," Mr. Willard responds. "Hunting and moonshine go hand in hand, boy."

"Okay," Neal says, somewhat subdued.

"There are some ten-pointers back yonder," the old man points into the deep pine forest. "Just don't cross into the Blairs' land or get near Old Mill Road."

Neal continues to sip jalapeño vodka and watch the steam rise above the still, as the two sit for a few more hours under a barn lean-to. By this time, supper has passed, and Mama would be worried. The temperature is already down to thirty degrees, but the spicy vodka is keeping both men warm, as is the hot kettles next to them.

"Damn! It's eight o'clock," Neal yells at the old man.

"What's time, boy, when you're enjoying moonshine?" Mr. Willard responds. "It's Friday night . . . What could be better than reminiscing around some vodka?"

"I better go now, or Mama is going to kill me," Neal explains.

"Alright, well come back, and I'll take you for a ride in my '47 Ford," Mr. Willard offers.

Neal stumbles to find his car. The sun is down, and the forest trees hide the moon. He finds a lighter in his pocket to help him see his way back to his car.

I'm not feeling well, and I miss Kimberly. I think I'll drive to her house. Mama is going to kill me. It did taste good after the first shot. Am I drunk? I don't think so. Neal ponders this as he cranks his car and then makes his way down the narrow, wooded dirt driveway. One hand on the wheel, and one hand on his throat, he tries to handle the burning sensation from three hours' worth of drinking with an eighty-year-old moonshiner.

Neal turns right onto Skeet Club Road, cursing Mr. Willard all the way to Kimberly's house. He pulls into her driveway, seeing only her car.

Neal makes his way to the front door and knocks. The single-story ranch-style house is modest, like his own, for a typical 1980s working-class family.

"What are you doing here?" Kimberly asks when she answers the door.

"Let me in," Neal responds. "I need a place to lay my head—it hurts."

"You reek of alcohol," Kimberly says. "Have you been drinking? We don't allow alcohol in this house."

Kimberly was a devout Christian living out her faith as an eighteen-year-old young lady preparing herself for a career as a nurse.

"I want you to go to church with me and learn about the love of Jesus," Kimberly adds.

"I heard Jesus on the radio today," Neal remarks. "He said he could be my friend."

"I'm calling your mama," Kimberly tells him. "You can't stay here—Mom and Dad will be home in less than an hour, when the movies are over."

"I can't see Jesus, so how can he be my friend?" Neal challenges. "I kind of like jalapeño vodka. It burned at first, then my mind went to a faraway place, where my comic books came alive in me."

"Comic books are fantasy," Kimberly explains. "But God created the universe, and He sent His son, Jesus, to bear the penalty for our sins."

"Sins? I just had a few drinks with Mr. Willard. I didn't even kill any deer cuz I am a good person."

"Even good persons go to hell," Kimberly replies. "Man is inherently depraved because of Adam's original sin."

"How do you know Adam really lived in that garden with Eve?" Neal asks. He rolls over on Kimberly's couch. "Come over here, baby."

"God so loved the world, after Adam's fall, that He gave us Jesus, and we must believe in Jesus to have eternal life, Neal." Kimberly sits on the end of the couch.

"Come here, darling—I want you," Neal says, stretching out his arm toward Kimberly's waist.

"You are not getting me tonight!" Kimberly adds. "And we have had this conversation before."

"What conversation?" Neal asks. "About the birds and the bees?"

"Yes, about sex," she replies. "Sex before marriage is not going to happen."

"We don't have to have sex, just a little hanky-panky," Neal stutters.

"The man that truly loves me will respect my Christian beliefs of waiting. True love waits."

Neal asks her, "How can a good god allow me, a good person, to have trouble speaking? I stutter all the time."

"I don't mind that you stutter or hunt deer or collect comic books," Kimberly states. "But I do not like you drinking alcohol—it is the ruination of many families."

"I can't go home tonight; Mama is going to kill me."

"I care about you, Neal, so I'm going to call her myself. You can't drive drunk."

"Well, I made it this far," Neal says, before throwing up. "Get me a trash can, please."

"Have you drunk like this before?" Kimberly asks.

"Dee and I would have a beer once in a while, but that's it. Don't call Mama!"

Kimberly goes to the den and picks up the rotary phone and rotates the dial: 4-5-4-1-2-3-9.

"Hello?"

"Mrs. Petree, this is Kimberly," she says softly.

"Yes, have you seen Neal? He hasn't come home from school."

"I'm afraid to say that he is at my house, and he is not doing well."

"Well, send him home now!" Mrs. Petree responds. "His daddy and I are terribly worried."

"He's been drinking—you should know that, but now he's with me."

"Drinking!" she says. "I told him he won't be an alcoholic if he doesn't start drinking."

"I'll drive him to your house in a few minutes," Kimberly says softly.

Kimberly drives Neal home; it's only a mile away. She tries to tell him about Jesus again, but he is too drunk to listen—slumped over until she pulls into his driveway, where his mom and dad are waiting.

"You're grounded for a week!" his dad yells, as he pulls Neal out of Kimberly's car.

"Thank you for bringing him home," his mom tells Kimberly.

"I am praying for him," Kimberly responds. "I know you love that boy."

"I do. We all do," Mrs. Petree says. "He just needs a bigger power in his life to guide him, like Jesus guides His sheep."

Neal can barely walk. His dad pushes him inside and drags him to his bedroom, lays him on the floor, and slams the door. "Pitiful!" he yells. "You can't even deer hunt and get home in a timely fashion; instead, you get drunk."

"Loser!" Gabe yells from his bedroom.

Then, a week passes.

Besides deer hunting, cruising Main Street in High Point was Neal's passion. One day, he and Mr. and Mrs. Petree decide to go to Uptown. Uptown was thriving with restaurants, and they liked the Golden Corral. Neal decides to take his parents in the Camaro. Mrs. Petree, who is all of four-feet-nine-inches tall, sits in the front, while Mr. Petree, over six-feet tall, sits on a blue vinyl seat in the back.

"Honey, pull your seat up a bit," Mr. Petree says, while pulling out a cigarette.

"Daddy, put that cigarette out!" Neal yells at his father.

"Boy, I bought this car, and I will smoke this damn cigarette if I want to," Mr. Petree shouts back.

"Now, put that cigarette out. God is watching you two," Mrs. Petree says softly.

Mr. Petree throws the cigarette out the passenger window at the edge of a wooded lot.

"I don't believe all the Jesus stuff," Neal pipes up. "How can a man who lived 2,000 years ago be my friend?"

"You need a haircut, Neal," Mr. Petree scolds, without answering his question.

"Daddy, let me say something," Neals says.

Then, Mrs. Petree jumps in: "Neal, all this drinking you are doing is going to kill your life." Her eyes start to water as she grabs a tissue from her purse. "Jesus loves you even more than I do. You have plans to go to UNC-Greensboro in two months, and there will be drinking all over that campus," she pleads with Neal.

"Kimberly is going there, too," Neal says. "She'll keep me straight."

"You can't always rely on a friend to walk you down the moral path," Mrs. Petree says.

"That's all good, boy, but I told you there's paying jobs right away framing houses," Mr. Petree explains.

"I don't want to frame houses," Neal responds. "I want to live in one."

"You're too lazy, then," his dad remarks.

"Gabe don't believe in Jesus, either," Neal says. "After all that preaching we heard on Church Street, what difference did it make?"

Mrs. Petree says softly, "God is planting seeds in you, Neal, and one day, a seed will turn into a flower."

"A flower?" Neal responds. "I ain't much for flowers, but I do like deer."

The family sits down for dinner, and Neal discusses his summer plans: "Kimberly has invited me to the beach with her church group."

"What's wrong with the youth group at First Baptist?" Mrs. Petree asks.

"They're too cliquish," Neal responds, "and they can't answer some of my questions about the Bible."

"Well, not everyone can," Mrs. Petree responds. "You have to ask God to help you."

"I don't believe in God," Neal mumbles defensibly. "I'm an atheist."

"I don't think you are an atheist. I think you're just confused and don't have all the information you need to make a decision like that." His mother is staying calm.

"What decision?" Neal asks. "I've already decided that Jesus can't be my friend because he is not living here now."

Mrs. Petree thinks, *I've taken the boys to church since they were just three years old. I've led a decent life, faithful to their father. I've tried to be kind to all. I'll just have to wait and see what the Lord has in store for them. God, please touch Neal—he needs it.*

A few weeks go by, and Neal rides with Kimberly's youth group on a bus to North Carolina Beach. He packs his fishing rod. All the kids have Bibles except him.

"Where's your Bible?" Kim asks him.

"I don't need that. I thought we were going surf fishing?"

"This is a Bible retreat," Kimberly explains. "We will have quiet time alone, studying the Bible, and then we'll get together in a group and discuss what we've read."

"College starts in a month, and I don't want to do any studying until then," Neal admonishes Kimberly.

"Come on, let's join the rest at the ocean," Kimberly says.

After having a chat with everyone, Kimberly introduces John, who is throwing football.

"Neal, this is John," Kimberly introduces him to her other friend.

"Hi, John—I've seen you before somewhere," Neal comments. "You go to High Point Central?"

"I graduated from Andrews High School," John replies. "I'm a theology and mathematics major at Yale."

"Let's head back to the house," Kimberly says. The three of them follow the crowd of a dozen or more teens barefoot through the sand.

The group assembles in the living room of the beach house; the surf can be seen through the large windows behind them. The room is quiet.

"Let's all sing a few songs and then have prayer," John explains.

The group sings in unison with melodious accord: *Kumbaya, my Lord, kumbaya . . . Kumbaya, my Lord, kumbaya . . . Kumbaya, my Lord, kumbaya . . . Someone's singing, Lord, kumbaya . . . Someone's crying, Lord, kumbaya . . . Someone's praying, Lord, kumbaya . . .*

"Now, I'd like for each of you to share what's going on in your life at the moment," John says softly, while the others' heads are still bowed, either praying or whispering the song.

"I'll start," says Kimberly. "I have this close friend, and he is so dear to me, but I'm worried about his life."

"Let us pray for him," John says.

"Neal, do you want to say anything?" John asks. "What you say here, stays here."

"Just because atheists don't believe in a supernatural god doesn't mean we don't enjoy each other's company and music and talking about interesting topics, and so on. We're human, you know," Neal says bluntly.

"Neal, I'm worried about you," Kimberly tells him. "God is bigger than you, and He loves you."

"Why are you worried about me? I'm going to UNCG in the fall, too."

"Not worried about school," Kimberly contradicts him. "Your eternal soul!"

"I love soul, soul music," Neal responds smugly.

"Not soul music, but your eternal soul, and where it will be forever," John replies. "Please tell us what is bothering you, Neal."

"I understand that my connection to all life on this planet is biological not because every living thing was created by some agent like God or even Jesus," Neal explains.

John thinks and then mocks: "Well, now, aren't we so privileged to have you, an atheist, tell us how to worship? I guess we should all immediately cease praising God when a nonbeliever shows up?'"

"Let's take it easy, guys," Kimberly interjects. "Let me pray right now because, wherever two or more are gathered, Jesus is with us, and He alone can heal our brokenness."

"Neal, your feelings are the natural outflow of a relational knowledge of, and an encounter with, the son of God, who is alive forevermore," John explains.

Someone in the group comments, "Lets read John 1:1."

"John one, one?" Neal says.

"Religion is always taking credit for human accomplishment. In this case, it's quite easy to demonstrate that those transcendent feelings don't come from a god because atheists can feel it, too," says John.

Kimberly opens her Bible to John 1:1 and reads: "In the beginning was the Word, and the Word was with God, and the Word was God."

"You mean the Bible is what God speaks?" Neal challenges them. "How can he speak this word?"

The room becomes silent. Kimberly realizes this is the first serious question Neal has ever asked about the Bible. Then, John replies, "In the beginning—that is, before anything was formed—God began the great work of creation. This is the meaning of the *Word*, the same as *Genesis* 1:1," John tells Neal.

"I don't believe that Jesus is divine—that is, he is not God," Neal says.

"Let me help you a bit," John says. "The Greek translation means the word 'the word' is the subject of the clause. Therefore, the 'Word was God' is the correct translation and not 'God was the Word.'"

The others could tell Neal was excited to hear this explanation.

"Please, tell me more," Neal asks John.

"The Word is *Logos*, which signifies a word spoken, like a teacher's doctrine or a judge's reasoning, but it is from God's infinite mind—the source of all wisdom to all men and for the testimony of Jesus, and who has fully manifest the deep mysteries, which lay hidden in the depths of the invisible God from all eternity," John explains eloquently.

"My background as a child—I worshipped comic books, and now I worship my Camaro," Neal says. "Just as many of you believe in God because your parents believe in God and because they instilled this belief in you . . ."

"Your parents took you to church?" a youth says.

"The preacher at First Baptist Church never presented it this deep," Neal responds.

"Here's an extra Bible," John offers to Neal. "You want to read over it this weekend on your own, then come back when you have questions?"

"Sure, thanks. I like history," Neal's face looks serious for once in his life.

"The Bible is full of the history of men and women who follow God," John replies. "There are tragedies and love stories."

"Jesus is the true love story," Kimberly whispers, as the room becomes silent again, and the water reaching the beach can be heard in the background.

The group departs for the night, and Neal goes to his room.

In the beginning was the Word, and the Word was with God, and the Word was God, Neal ponders. When was the beginning? Who is Jesus? It's hard for me to understand that God had no beginning.

Neal considers what John and Kimberly said earlier at the group Bible study: *In the beginning was the Word, and the Word was with God, and the Word was God. When was the beginning? Who is Jesus?*

It's hard for me to understand that God did not have to be created. After all, Mama and Daddy made me through sex. But Kimberly says sex is only for marriage. I admire her devotion to her faith and her thinking that 'True love waits'.

Neal thinks back to his comic-book days as a younger teen: *I remem-*

ber reading a comic book called 'God', and I guess I didn't read it carefully enough. I do remember something in one of them. This is crazy
because this comic book is the one I was searching for all these years. I
sat on the carpet looking for 'God' the comic book. Now, is the true God
speaking to me through the Bible in John 1:1?

The comic book 'God' said, "God was lonely. So, God created the angels,
so He would have someone to love Him. And they did. But after a
while, God was curious about just how much they loved Him. So, God
announced that He was going to create humans, a new type of being
that could—unlike the angels—choose to worship or ignore God. They
would live without the tangible, real presence of God around them. And
all hell broke loose.

God, can you hear me? Is that a prayer, or am I speaking to myself?

With his hands on both sides of the pages of *John*, he flips three
pages, one for Kimberly, one for his mom, and one for a friend. His
finger lands on *John 3:16*.

John 3:16 reads: "For God so loved the world that He gave His one
and only son, that whoever believes in Him shall not perish but have
eternal life."

"God, through your word, please speak to me," Neal yells out while
crying.

Neal senses something more than an emotion or casual thought. A
voice, a word: *You can't follow your ways and my ways—you must
choose one. I am your true friend—always have, and always will be.*

And Neal responds, *Lord God, I will trust you.*

Neal stays up all night reading the Bible. In the morning, he tells his girlfriend, Kimberly, about his decisions to follow the teachings of Jesus. Greatly pleased, she believes him.

Two days later, he tells Dee of his encounter with God. The two boys would meet on Fridays to decide between deer hunting and girl hunting.

"Dee, you won't believe this, but God saved me," Neal explains, as the two talk in the parking lot of Southwest High School.

"Does that mean no more girl hunting?" Dee asks.

"Yes, I am a changed man," Neal responds. "In an instant, I became a believer.

"Maybe one day, so will I," Dee replies, "but for now, I am going cruising Main, looking for some babes."

Neal departs for home to see his mom.

After Neal's encounter with God, when he was saved in 1993, he felt the presence of God call him into the ministry in 1994. Six months later, he was preaching in a small country church in Archdale, NC. Later, he becomes the youth pastor at First Baptist on Church Street.

Chapter 12

CONSTRUCTING THE BREWERY

Hammer drills pound Elm Street to break up old concrete, and bulldozers push over the old Little Red Schoolhouse, as dust-filled air rises over Church Street.

"I can save twenty thousand dollars if I hire Johnson Brothers to install the new gas piping," Will says to his construction crew supervisor.

The city of High Point is bustling with excitement as the new baseball stadium is being constructed. When plans were announced to place an independent Atlantic League team in North Carolina, it seemed like a real long shot to many baseball insiders. But the stadium is part of a plan to jump-start growth in the former furniture and textile manufacturing town. The City Council voted to support a baseball stadium and restaurants that could support sporting events—urban revitalization for uptown.

Samp and Dell Architects became the city's chosen design-build team for the first project, the baseball stadium, and nearby bars and restaurants.

As the general contractor, Will knows construction projects' profit margins depend on being tight with his money. He also doesn't tell his clients that it means cutting corners.

"I know you want it cheap, Will, but if a gas pipe is not designed properly, the appliances won't heat up," the supervisor responds. "And, from the owner's sketch, they plan to have a 500,000-BTU gas grill and a 100,000-BTU firepit."

"Gas grill for what? And an outdoor gas firepit?"

"That's right—a gas grill for making grilled meats," the supervisor says. "He wants a firepit with lounge chairs and sectional tables to help create a friendly, romantic ambiance for evenings with the Emerywild crowd, whatever that means," he explains to Will.

The supervisor responds. "And the City Engineer says the connection to the existing underground pipe is not trivial."

"I know he's the owner, but that old building doesn't meet code, and most patrons just sit at a bar with no interest in a firepit or steaks on a gas grill," Will replies. And then says to the supervisor, "I'll call him for clarification and get back to you."

The backhoes, hammer drills, and bulldozers continue along Church Street. The only building that is not planned for demolition or renovation is the First Baptist Church, which sits on the corner of Main and Church.

Will climbs into his truck and backs into the church parking lot before doing a three-point turn around orange barrels. He spots a stocky, dark-haired man picking up construction debris next to the church bus. The man smiles and waves, but Will drives off.

What is it with the church complaining to the city about the stadium and bars in uptown? More and more everyday folks like to have fun, drink a beer, and go to a baseball game, even on a Sunday, Will ponders, as he turns his truck onto Main Street and heads toward his office.

The owner of the old building, who plans to convert it into a brewery, is a forty-something restaurant entrepreneur named Britt—a man with no lengthy expertise in brewing, except his first beer truck—the Green Truck—which he parked on North Main. Wishing he had a brewery near the baseball stadium, and inspired by the way the old building architecture looks, he decides to venture onto Church Street. *I'll just drive up North Main Street to the Green Truck and see if the owner is there,* Will thinks.

Meanwhile, he ponders, *First, let me get the latest architectural and engineering plans. I'll call the architect tomorrow.*

The architect, John, has extensive experience with historic buildings, well surpassing that of the owner and Will.

"There's an abandoned textile mill next to the planned brewery and an underground warehouse full of chemicals," John alerts Will.

"What does the chemical storage room underground have to do with getting the latest plans so the engineer can design the gas piping?" Will is puzzled.

"The city's four-inch underground gas pipe runs next to the chemical storage room, and the brewery is next to that," John replies, assuming that Will understands the inherent danger of that combination.

Will arrives at the Green Truck beer stand. Britt leans back on one of the cozy outdoor chairs next to the truck—a beer in his hand, and a smile on his face. "Hi, Will, what brings you here? No construction work today?"

"Hi, Britt—need to talk to you," Will asserts sharply.

"Will, any news on the construction status of Church Street?"

Will continues: "Listen—when talking to the architect, we were wondering if you really wanted a gas grill stove inside and that ten-foot-diameter gas firepit?"

"Why, yes—sitting outdoors as the sun sets on a pleasant evening naturally draws couples together, creating special moments of . . ."

Will squelches Britt's eloquent soliloquy.

"I found out from the city of High Point that a four-inch steel pipe carrying a hundred pounds per square inch of pressure exists under the street right next to your proposed brewery," Will chides Britt. "The architect found out the abandoned textile mill next to the planned brewery has an underground warehouse full of chemicals. The branch gas line would pass next to the chemical storage bunker and vertically past your gas firepit.

"The city is also concerned about the gas pipe connections to the brewery and other neighboring restaurants being designed and installed properly; if not, then the proposed outdoor firepit is a hazard," Will continues to explain to Britt.

"What hazard?" Britt yells. "Drinking too much beer and driving ain't safe, either, but there ain't been any accidents at the Green Truck beer stand. A lot of my competitors are offering these firepits to attract all kinds of folks. The firepits will be a conversation space, where my customers can spend time warming by the fire and talking over drinks."

"Can't you envision a crackling campfire by the river, creating a soothing nighttime ambiance? The natural white noise will help relax your body and mind; you'll buy more beer and sleep better!" Britt contends, almost poetically.

"Okay, but I hope Samp and Dell and their engineers know how to design the piping, so my subs can install it, and there are no issues with gas leakage," Will warns.

"It's just a pipe; cut it, weld it, and you're done," explains Britt. "Catch you later, Will."

Not wholly convinced, Will worries, *I read about a gas leak that killed two men who were looking for a leak at a hotel using a lantern. An explosion occurred, injuring several guests and killing the two men.*

Will climbs back into his truck and heads south toward Church Street. Indications of an economy that is expanding under the Trump Presidency are exciting High Point—a place where both downtown and uptown have been dead since the 1950s.

As new construction projects and bank loans continue to stimulate the economy, Will hopes for a bright future, but in the meantime, he needs environmental compliance with the city, must deal with the church complaint, and get a gas pipe meter installed for the proposed Church Street Brewery.

The next day, John gives Will a call.

"I have the gas piping design for The Church Street Brewery," he says.

"Great! Any issues?"

John explains what the engineer told him: "The mechanical contractor will need to either replace the main aged pipe with stainless steel and use the new ANSI compression fittings or use a special adapter leading from the old underground pipe.

"The special adaptor will make the transition from the aged gas pipe near the chemical bunker to the new vertical pipe that will feed both the firepit burner and the kitchen appliances," John explains.

"I won't have to dig up the church parking lot?" Will asks.

"No, the main pipe runs along Main Street—north and south—and you will have to trench in the new gas pipe to the brewery," John says. "Underground piping has to be installed with a cover not less than twelve inches."

"A ground cover, you mean?" Will asks.

"Yes," says John.

"Thanks, John; I will stop by and get the plans," says Will.

Still uncertain, Will worries: *The underground bunker at the next-door building is worrisome, but the city says the chemicals are encased in one-inch-thick steel. Right now, I need to get Johnson Brothers started, to meet my construction deadlines, and get some leases signed and make payroll.*

While Johnson Brothers dig the new gas piping trench, the electrician shows up and inquires about the city's electrical service overhead: "Since the appliances will add more power to the brewery building, we need a new set of wires from the transformer," the electrician tells Will.

"That's what the engineer prescribed, so let's use the Johnson Brothers trench so your new wires can go underground," Will agrees.

The National Electrical Code requires that high-voltage wires from a street transformer be encased in conduit encased in concrete to keep the water out and prevent an electrical shortage, which would be a safety hazard.

The existing overhead service drop to the planned brewery building doesn't have enough electrical capacity. An underground conduit of electrical wires would not be an eyesore near the patio and firepit.

"I'll run my conduit next to the gas pipe and coordinate with Johnson Brothers," the electrician tells Will.

"Okay. Let's get going with that work, while I have the plumber ensure the bathrooms are fitted with new water and drainpipes."

Chapter 13

ENGAGEMENT

For Carlton, the overwhelming death of Dorothy was much like the grief he experienced in Vietnam.

Carlton recalls his wife being terminally ill, going through chemotherapy treatments for cancer, and struggling with Lyme disease. Her pain and anguish increased to such a degree that they began to search for ways to end her life. He wanted to die with her. Now, he sits alone in the kitchen of his 1950s single-story ranch home.

American soldiers, like Carlton, suffered through the terror of a jungle ambush during his one-year tour. Dozens of men could die within minutes. For Carlton, an acting squad leader within Alpha Company, the ambush of October 7 came just three months after he arrived in Vietnam, and what mattered on that terrible day was whether you were in the sunlight or the shade. Lying behind a large anthill for cover, Carlton stayed out of the light and watched more exposed comrades get shot running for cover. He later crawled across the battlefield, trying to find anyone who was alive. The bodies had been so shot up that many were unrecognizable.

When he returned home to North Carolina, he thought that he would find peace. He was mistaken. Carlton and his fellow veterans faced scorn, as the war they had fought in became increasingly unpopular.

Carlton joined other Vietnam vets on a float in a Christmas Parade in High Point, and all the servicemen initially felt excited about being back on American soil. But, while civilians along the street sidewalk stopped to watch the veterans, his excitement turned to confusion.

As he sits alone, now, on the sofa, gazing at family photos, he's hesitant to sit on the front porch as he and Dot would. His Vietnam days come flooding back. Carlton thinks, *The Christmas Parade in 1970 . . . I remember wanting to acknowledge the civilians lined up along Main Street. There must have been a thousand folks there. So, I threw up the peace sign, but instead of getting them in return, I got the middle finger.*

Carlton's bitterness from the civilian response to the Vietnam War had bothered him, but he could always count on Dorothy to get him through it. Now, she is gone, and he is lonely. His loneliness resembles being in a desert with nowhere to go, no one to talk to, and no one who seems to care. He is hesitant to join a church or civic group. His neighbors are all working and raising a family.

I found myself going to the mailbox around 5:30 p.m. on a weekday. I normally got the mail as soon as the mailman passed by the house. I liked to see her face. I walked down the driveway, and there she was. She had her head bowed, as though praying. We both reached the mailbox at about the same time. I looked her way and waved; she appeared not to see me. Maybe she did but was afraid. What could she be afraid of? I doubt she was praying—I could only see her hands and that cell phone glued to her face. This generation does not know how to communicate.

They either call or text someone. Whatever happened to a hand-written letter? Whatever happened to face-to-face conversation?

Carlton has been cruising Main Street and the neighboring streets after a few months, since Dot died. When he's not cruising, his new F-150 pick-up truck sits in his immaculate garage, next to Dot's car. He loathes to drive Dot's car for fear of more pain, but he will take his new friend, the F-150, around town.

Carlton wanted to feel young again, and many younger men were purchasing trucks to model themselves after their fathers and grandfathers—men like Carlton, who provided for their families by working "manly" jobs that required brawn and guts, as well as craftsmanship. Men like Carlton, who came along during the days of John Wayne and Steve McQueen—tough guys who were men of action, not words.

But now, Carlton longs to hear words like "honey" and "dear" that Dot would whisper to him, while they sat on the front porch.

Early one morning after eating breakfast, he pushes the AM button and hears Max in the Morning. Max was a throwback in a day and age when radio had become dominated by shock jocks and political talk shows. Max would announce local business advertisements, including Varsity Drive-In, Beeson Hardware, Rose Furniture, and Alma Desk. But it was not the furniture companies that caught Carlton's interest; it was what Max the DJ said next:

His truck was his new friend, and the truck's radio provided brief, but superficial, voices. He liked to listen to WMFR, a traditional AM station with a real live disc jockey, who would announce local news and business advertisements.

The Church Street Brewery will open its doors today. Owner, Britt Sampson, a real estate developer and son of the late David Draughn, says the brewery will provide a unique atmosphere for conversation. The Church Street Brewery will be located within the old Mendenhall Building, which dates to the 1890s and has served numerous functions over its long life, including Plank Street Tailors and, briefly, a night club called Enterprise Lounge, according to the High Point Historical Society.

A unique atmosphere for conversation? Hmmm. Conversation. I wonder what type of folks will visit The Church Street Brewery, Carlton ponders the DJ's remarks.

During his drive home from breakfast, Carlton plans his visit to the brewery. First, he decides to take a slight detour to see the building. He remembers that Church Street is perpendicular to Main and Elm and is along the route he takes from home to downtown.

As he passes the hospital on Elm Street, he remembers all the times he and Dot shared memories there: *I stayed with her from 6:00 a.m. until they made me leave, for months, while she was in the memory care unit. I would have spent the night there with her, but the hospital would not allow it, on account of insurance reasons. I did crawl in the bed with her, and she gave me one last kiss. I'll never forget the tears we shared, even when her mind had failed.*

He turns the corner at Elm and Church and can see a man painting a sign hanging from the corner of the building façade.

The parking spaces on Church Street are full, so he turns right into the parking lot across the street—the one that belongs to the church. From the parking lot, his truck windshield faces the brewery, which is maybe fifty feet away. Adjacent to, and left of, the brewery is an outdoor patio with a second-level porch over a circular knee-high wall. To the right of the patio area is an all-glass façade, and, through it, he can faintly see pendant lights shining on a bar. Carlton thinks, *I hope the interior is cleaner than the outside. They are less than five hours from opening, and the sidewalk still needs cleaning. The windows look pretty clean, though.*

His windshield starts to fog up with condensation, due to the fall temperatures and the sunlight now beaming down Church Street. Carlton turns the engine off, walks across the street, and peeks through the window.

At age seventy-one, with fifty years of real work, his body doesn't move like it used to—one leg drags slightly, and his lower back always hurts. Years of building furniture with heavy hand tools and lifting boxes have taken a toll on the man. Although his hair is thinning and gray, he has most of his teeth, though slightly darkened from all of the years of drinking coffee. What has not lost their color are his radiant blue eyes.

He can see his reflection, as he edges closer to the tall glass front of the brewery façade. Staring inside, looking behind the bar, he can see the brewing equipment and materials: a malt maker, kettle washer, and mash. A man is connecting overhead pipes, while a young lady is arranging menus and other items on a row of stainless-steel tables, each having two high-boy stools next to them. The bright stainless-steel pipes that the worker is installing look impressive. Carlton turns left and walks twenty feet over to the patio and stands between the rock wall and the building's sidewall, which is also all glass.

He thinks, *Nice-looking rock wall around this firepit. That is a big-ass gas heater. I wonder how many BTUs? Why do they need a wood deck over the firepit? I guess they want patrons to be able to see the new sports stadium from here. He continues to ponder: I wonder if any women my age will come to this place. I doubt it—I am getting too old. The opening was announced on the radio, so I think I will find out tonight.*

He decides to visit The Church Street Brewery not to make memories but to find a friend to listen to his pain and heartache and relieve some of his loneliness.

He spends all but five minutes looking around the brewery, then pulls himself back into his truck and heads for home. *I think I'll call Emily and tell her about the place.*

The house is quiet. When he enters, the rhythmic rapping of a wood-pecker can be heard and nothing else. He walks into the kitchen and to the house phone—an old-style rotary phone. It hangs on the dark paneled walls. He puts his burly finger in the wheel and turns it one digit. He moves his finger ten more times to place the call to Fredericksburg, Maryland.

"Hello," Emily says.

"Hi, sweetheart," Carlton says. "Sorry to bother you during work."

"It's fine, Dad," she replies. "Did you go to the pet store?"

"No, I don't want any animals."

"A puppy would be great for you. Especially for your depression and PTSD."

"I don't have any PTSD."

"P-T-S-D," Emily persists. "You've had nightmares since Vietnam."

"I've found a place to hang out."

Emily almost whispers, "I know you miss Mama terribly. A church?"

"No, but next door to a church."

"The Masonic lodge you mentioned?"

"I'm not a Mason, but I know how to make furniture," says Carlton.

"Dad, really? Where are you going?"

"It's called The Church Street Brewery. It's a remodeled place in an old manufacturing building in uptown, next to the new ball stadium."

"You don't need to be drinking beer right now."

"It's not drinks I want, but to meet some folks and just talk," Carlton says. "You should see the big glass windows, and they have a firepit outside."

Emily pauses, thinking of her mama. She whimpers.

"Are you there?" Carlton asks. "Why ya so quiet?"

"I . . . I . . . miss Mama," Emily says, as she cries.

Carlton swallows and looks across the kitchen table to a family photo. Emily's blonde hair radiates from the picture frame.

"You are a beautiful young lady. I love you."

"I love you, too, Daddy."

"I better go now and clean up around the house," Carlton mumbles.

"Daddy? Do you think you will ever get married again?"

"I had a good marriage with your mama," Carlton says, starting to cry.

"She loved you more than life itself, Daddy."

"I better go now; you're getting me all choked up."

"Bye, Daddy."

"Bye, love," Carlton says, and he places the heavy phone receiver back on the wall.

In her sleep, Debra must have felt the change in the weather, for she pulled the blankets up a little closer and brushed her bald scalp. The weather was typical for High Point in October, with a slight breeze and temperatures hovering around sixty—ten degrees cooler than September.

Uncomfortable in the overheated bedroom, Debra awoke before dawn. She thought, *In a month, it will be six months since Don died.* She lay in the dark and silent bedroom, considering her life, thinking about Don. *We met on a starry Carolina night, outside the theatre after the Elvis concert. Your blue eyes pierced through me. We fell in love, and you proposed to me. Then, you were drafted. I thought I needed to be careful and tried to distance my heart from falling in love with you . . . but you didn't let me not fall in love with you; you always wrote to me from Vietnam. There were nights I was so scared you had died in one of those jungle fights. Then, I found out that, like me, you couldn't bear our time away from each other. I had never met such a sensitive and special man. We had our beautiful babies, and you were convinced we were soulmates.* Debra's eyes start to water, as she turns over and sees their picture on the nightstand.

Sometimes, Debra had gone two or three weeks without receiving a letter from Don. After high school classes, she would open the mailbox, and seven or eight letters would tumble out into her hands. On those days, Debra felt reassured that her fiancé was still alive on the other side of the world.

<hr>

But life must move on, Debra thinks.

Lying in bed, she can hear the birds outside her window and a few cars going down the street. The sun rises, and through the hardwood trees, she can see the top of a church steeple in Uptown High Point.

It's a struggle to get out of bed, but she needs to get to her pain medication in the bathroom. Each morning, she likes talking to her daughter, Sandra. Her voice reminds her of Don. Sandra was Don's pride and joy.

Debra's doctors told her that she may not be able to live alone too much longer and that she needed to phone Sandra daily to provide a status on how she feels.

Where's my cell phone? I will call Sandra.

The medicine gives Debra the shakes. Many side effects caused by chemotherapy, such as nausea and vomiting, have to be controlled by more pills, which she takes daily.

Debra crawls to the bathroom and pulls up on the sink to the cabinet. She opens the door and grabs the pill bottle: *I should take all of these and end it right now.* Debra was never suicidal before, but the pain of losing Don has recently tempted her to take her own life.

She crawls back across the carpet to her bed and finds her purse and cell phone on the other nightstand.

"Morning, Sandra," Debra says.

"Mom, glad you called," Sandra says. "Did you take your meds?"

"The doctor said the greatest risk factor for breast cancer was having breasts," Debra says, changing the subject.

"Stop playing with me!" Sandra says. "You have to take them every day, or you will be vomiting all day."

"I woke up and immediately felt nauseous. I crawled to the bathroom."

"I think we need to think about an in-home care nurse," Sandra says.

"If the nurse was a man, I'd let him take care of me," Debra says.

Sandra chuckles: "Now, Mama, who could replace my father?"

"A new man who can pay for the two-hundred-dollar cancer pill," Debra says.

"Okay," says Sandra. "Well, what are you doing for enjoyment?"

"I tried to do some cross-stitch, and the needle poked me," Debra says.

"How about the painting you used to do?" Sandra says.

"Yeah . . . If my hand can stay steady, I do want to try putting my brush to canvas again."

"You remember that brewery you mentioned last week?"

"Yeah, what does the new brewery got to do with my cancer?"

"I saw on Facebook they are having an art class," Sandra says.

"Art class? I've never heard of a brewery teaching anything but how to drink."

Sandra continues, "Anyway, how about we go and check it out tonight, if you feel okay?"

"That would be wonderful," Debra says. "Let me get my bag ready and rest up before we go."

"The Facebook ad said to bring brushes and paint," Sandra says. "The brewery will supply the canvas board. I'll pick you up at 4:00. The art class starts at 5:00."

"I'll be ready, if I don't pass out."

The two ladies chuckle.

"You might see some old friend there, too," Sandra adds, as the two hang up their phones.

"I don't need a cane to walk to the brewery," Debra says. "I think I can manage just fine."

Sandra grabs her mother's bag: "This dang bag is heavy."

"It's got all my brushes and all the colors I need to paint."

"Good. Let's find Britt," Sandra says. "His name was on the Facebook ad for the painting class."

The two women had parked across the street from The Brewery, in the church parking lot. The time is almost five o'clock.

"That is where Don and I were married, over there," Debra says, pointing to the tall white steeple. "I can see it from my window each morning."

After they cross the street, Sandra comments, "This place used to look so run down! They have really fixed it up. Nice big windows, too."

It's a fall day, and the temperatures are hovering around sixty-five degrees outside.

"Looks like some folks have already set up their canvases outside," Sandra says.

The two walk up to the front door, where the hostess is standing. Her name tag says "Christine," and she is a young-looking girl.

"Outside?" Debra asks. "The humidity will not be nice to a canvas painting."

"Hello, we are here for the art class," Sandra tells the girl.

"Yes, the teacher decided to have it outside, rather than in our conference room," Christine says.

"She smells like smoke," Debra whispers to Sandra.

"Mom, not so loud!"

Christine escorts the two to the patio outside the front door. Several other folks are already set up with their whiteboards on trestles.

"There are no more trestles, but we have a picnic table over there you can stay on," Christine offers.

Slightly annoyed, Sandra remarks, "Well, I didn't bring my trestle because the ad said the trestle was provided."

"I'm sorry," says Christine. She then just walks away and opens the big glass door back inside. These women are of no interest to her.

Another voice is heard: "Hello, I'm Debbie—your instructor for tonight."

"Hi," says Sandra. "This is my . . ."

Debra interrupts her daughter: "I'm Debra. I didn't bring my trestle because the ad said . . ."

"I'm really sorry; we had a lot of interest tonight, so we ran out. Welcome," Debbie says. "Take a seat here, please."

Among the six students with the trestles are five women and one man. Despite being outdoors, the patio is enclosed on three sides with the firepit in the center. Overhead, the space is partially covered by second-floor decking. The art class is under the deck, semi-secluded from the glass façade of the brewery and Church Street. A gray-haired man sits in a chair on the street side of the firepit.

Now, the seven students have their canvases set up, except for Debra, who is missing a trestle board. This catches the eye of the gray-haired man staring at the class through the orange glow of the firepit.

Meanwhile, Sandra needs to use the restroom. She gets up from being next to Debra and walks toward the man: "Do you know where the women's restroom is?"

"Yes, go through the big glass doors there and hang a left, all the way down the hallway," the man says, then adds, "I'm Carlton, by the way."

"Nice to meet you, Carlton. I'm Sandra—here with my mother." She points behind her, toward where the sun is setting, above the baseball stadium to the west of the patio.

Carlton sees Debra sitting down and arranging some painting tools. He thinks, *I wonder where Sandra's trestle is?*

Sandra returns to the patio. "Sandra, you need a trestle board," Carlton says.

"You have one?" Sandra asks.

"Yes, something like a trestle board," Carlton says with a smile. "It's a wood tripod, and I think the canvas will fit on it just fine."

"Thank you," Sandra replies.

"Let me go get it from my truck," Carlton says. He heads out the front door with a pep in his step.

Carlton finds the tripod and takes it over to the table where Debra is sitting.

"Hi, I'm Carlton."

Debra smiles shyly: "Hello, and thank you so much." She reaches to shake his hand, noticing his remarkable blue eyes.

"Let me set it up for you," Carlton says. He turns the canvas over to see the name "Debra Culler, January 7, 2017." She notices his blue eyes staring at the back of the canvas.

"That's when I was diagnosed with cancer," Debra says, answering his unspoken question.

"I'm very sorry."

"Don't be—I am over it now," Debra says. "But life will never be the same."

"As for this place, I had a job as a teenager working here when it was a furniture factory," Carlton says. "I made a whopping $1.25 an hour."

"My husband was a fireman."

"Married to you, he was a lucky man." He has appreciated how attractive Debra is: blue jeans, classic boot cuts, tight against her trim figure. Despite her hat covering her hair loss, she looks a decade younger. She is wearing a red blouse with a key-hole neck, and her flat chest is noticeable.

"I beg your pardon?" Debra says.

"He is fortunate to have you," Carlton says.

"He's not here," Debra says.

"Is he home cooking, like a good husband should?" Carlton jests. Carlton has fixed himself up for the evening: new corduroy pants, cowboy boots, and a dark flannel shirt. He wears a cowboy hat unworn since he returned home from the war. He looks manly. He is courteous.

"So, I got your canvas all set up for you to paint," Carlton says.

"Thank you. Are you married?" Debra asks. She is too old to beat around the bush. She notices Carlton has a ring on his finger, blemished and thin, but she spots it like a cat seeing a bird. *Even married men today come to bars,* she thinks.

Carlton sighs: "My wife died six months ago. I needed to get out of the house and meet some new folks."

"Is that why you came here?"

"She died of Alzheimer's," Carlton neither agrees nor disagrees.

"How long were you married?" Debra inquires gently.

"Over forty years."

"Good for you, Carlton."

"And you, Debra?"

"A long time, as well. And, frankly, I barely got out of bed today."

Instructor Debbie tries to get Debra and Sandra's attention. The trio's conversation has distracted the class. "Tonight, we want you to paint birds on a wire. Use your imagination. I will start it for you." The art teacher draws a thick black horizontal line on her bare white canvas. All of the students gaze at the movement. However, Carlton's blue eyes are fixed on Debra.

"Sit down, Carlton," Debra says.

Sandra whispers to her mother, "Mom, you barely know this man."

He pulls the last wooden folding chair next to Debra, who's sitting at the end of the picnic table. The sun has set, and the fire is aglow to their backs. They both feel the heat from this large firepit. Debra pulls out her brush, squeezes some black onto her paper. Her hand trembles, and Carlton notices it.

"The fireplace is too hot for these paints," Debra says. Her hand is shaking, due to her cancer medicine.

"Here, may I help you?"

"A painter must paint it. Well, okay."

Carlton's large, rough hand engulfs her slender fingers, and his index finger helps guide the number seven brush. They make a black line together.

"How'd you do that?" Debra asks.

"Do what?"

"The line is so straight."

"I worked in a furniture factory for thirty-five years," Carlton says. "Our tools were squares and saws, and we had to cut most everything straight."

Meanwhile, Sandra has pulled out her phone and begins to check her emails, while it appears her mom may have found a new friend. What Debra had looked forward to doing, she was now distracted from, by this gentleman, a man who reminded her of her late husband.

"I want to draw two birds," Debra tells Carlton.

"What color?" he says.

"Red," she says, "and sitting next to each other." Debra squeezes orange onto her paper, along with some white, red, and blue.

"ROY-G-BIV?" Carlton says.

"Roy who?" Debra says.

"R for red, O for orange, Y for yellow, G for green, B for blue, I for indigo, and V for violet," Carlton says.

"ROYGBIV, the rainbow colors," Debra says. "But I was never a science person; I always enjoyed English and art."

Debra draws two circles next to each other. Then, she connects each one of them to a larger oval shape, making a torso with wings. She had drawn two red birds sitting on the black wire. In the upper left corner of the canvas, she drew a white circle and filled it in.

"Birds on a wire, with a full moon," Debra announces.

"Can I draw the grass?"

"Carlton, did you ever walk in tall grass?"

"I walked in a jungle back in 1968," he replies.

"You're a Vietnam vet, too?" Debra says.

"It was a landscape so different from High Point," Carlton says. "I never before splashed through paddy fields or stood in an entangled jungle or wandered through the uncertainty of elephant grass."

Debra hands Carlton her brush, as green paint starts to drip off the end onto the picnic table.

"Show me," Debra says.

Carlton's big hands take the brush—he starts from the left, under the moon, and makes vertical strokes, and she is amazed by his prowess.

Carlton smiles at Debra, and their eyes meet. "Green, thick grass for these birds," Carlton says. "The birds are always fed, so what are we complaining about?"

Carlton is captivated by her looks, her conversation, and her attention to detail with the painting.

"Time is up," the art teacher tells everyone.

"This has been so much fun, Carlton," Debra laughs.

"Mom, we better go," interrupts Sandra.

"Can I get your phone number?"

"Sure, eight, eight . . ." Debra starts to whisper.

Carlton flips open his phone and presses his stout finger against the keypad.

"Eight, eight, five, zero, nine, five, three."

"I will call you soon," Carlton says.

Sandra helps her mom back to the car. "You don't even know him, Mom, and you spent the whole time talking to him."

"He was such a gentleman."

"He's old, and you don't need to meet men in bars."

"Well, for starters, a man who had a good, long marriage can be a great catch!" Debra says.

On the way home, Debra thinks, *He probably knows how to love, communicate, commit, and work through problems, like Don did. When a man is in a happy relationship, he pours himself into it. And when it's gone, he's left with the kids (maybe) and his job (maybe). That leaves a giant hole. If he knows what he wants, and is ready for love again, he takes his search for a new partner seriously—and that's the treasure of dating a widower.*

Sandra escorts her mom back home.

"You're like a sixteen-year-old who thinks this is 'love at first sight.'"

"Let's be honest—I am not sixteen anymore," Debra says. "We've experienced a lot this past year: love, heartbreak, successes, failures—and losing Don was hard. And having a loving spouse again is a very real possibility. But, as with all of those other big life experiences, being widowed isn't the end of the story."

Sandra hands her mother her cell phone, her medicine, and the remote. "Here—watch some TV."

"I don't care much for TV right now," Debra says. "I've got someone on my mind."

"Just be careful. Check him out on social media."

"I'll ask my friend, Billie, if she has heard of him," Debra says to reassure Sandra.

"Goodnight, Mom—and I love you."

"I love you, too. Please lock the door when you leave," Debra yells.

"I will."

Sandra is gone, and Debra is tired from the art class, but her mental energy is stored up for Carlton. She phones her friend, Billie.

"Hello, my friend," Billie says. "How are your treatments going?"

A bit abruptly, Debra asks, "Do you know Carlton Jones? I'm feeling a little better, and I met someone."

"You did?" says Billie.

"I met a good-looking man who seems interested in me!" Debra says.

"Where at?"

"The new brewery on Church Street."

"A brewery?" Billie asks. "The one next to my church?"

"Yes," says Debra.

"Why don't you start coming to church with me?" suggests Billie.

"I might just do that one day." Then, Debra adds, "He's a widower—clean-cut, drives a truck, house paid off, gets a social security check, and he's a veteran."

"Carlton who?"

"Jones . . . Carlton Jones, and he worked at the Alma Desk Company."

"Yes, I do remember his family," Billie responds more affirmatively. "They are hard-working, good people."

"Thanks, Billie; I'm glad to hear that. I decided I am going to get in touch with him this week."

"That fast?" Billie says. "What's the hurry?"

"When you find a gem, you don't throw it away."

"Well, the proceeds from the Church Luncheon go to the homeless shelter," Billie says, for some reason. "How are your cancer treatments going?"

"I get sick from all the medicine, but I think the medicine I need right now is Carlton."

Billie laughs.

Debra laughs. "Bye, girl," she says.

"Stay in touch."

"Hello, Debra," Carlton says. "Thought I would call you and see how you were doing."

"I have the painting we did together sitting next to my bed."

"Birds on a wire," Carlton says.

"No, two love birds on a wire."

"That's right, there are two birds there, *in love*," Carlton replies.

"I can't believe we met at a brewery," Debra says. "Is this just a dream?"

"I don't think it's a dream, but our encounter inspired me to write a poem."

"You're a poet?" Debra asks.

"Not hardly," Carlton says. "But painting with you last night gave me a feeling of fulfillment I have not had since Dot died."

"Well, Carlton, I haven't had such a meaningful encounter since Don died, either. What's the poem?"

"Are you sure you want to hear it?"

"Yes, please."

"Okay, here it goes."

He pulls his chair up a little closer to the kitchen table. He pauses for a minute, as his eyes catch a glimpse of Dorothy on the wall. He thinks, *I deeply loved that woman. What would Emily think? God, why did you take Dorothy from me? This is not love at first sight. Can't be. I had so much fun with Debra.*

"Are you listening?"

"Go ahead, Carl," Debra says. She calls him Carl for the first time, and this gets his attention.

I saw two little love birds sitting on a wire,
As happy as can be.

They would kiss each other with their little beaks,
Cuddle up closely touching their tiny cheeks.

It was nice to see your painting, as lovely as could be.
I sat there a while wishing this was you . . . and me.

Then we flew away to the sky above,
Flying side by side, very much in love.

Silence.

The phone is silent because those words have touched her in a way she has not felt for so long.

"Carl, a *real* talent," Debra says.

"I think it's because, for the first time since I retired, I have started to read books, especially poetry," Carlton says.

"That's good . . . good for you."

"I haven't been to the grocery store yet. I was wondering if you wanted to have dinner with me?" Carlton says.

Debra says with a laugh, "As long as I am back before my curfew."

Her laugh is music to his ears. He likes her voice. "I'll pick you up at 5:00, and we can go to Longhorn."

"I look forward to it," Debra says.

"Who's that slender gal you're with?" Carlton's friend asks, as the two run into each other in the men's room at Longhorn.

"Her name is Debra," Carlton says. The two flush their toilets and wash their hands.

"She lost her spouse about the same time as me," Carlton says.

His friend leaves. Carlton strokes his hair one more time and checks his zipper before returning to the dining room.

The dining room was packed when Carlton and Debra arrived. The place is visually appealing, with wooden booths up front, a long and handsome vintage wooden bar with suspended light fixtures, and tables in the back. Rock music—Foreigner's "I Want to Know What Love Is"—was playing at subdued volume. The server is running around from table to table taking orders. Those families waiting for a table at the door appear irritated by the huge crowd.

Debra is wearing a brimmed hat like the ones used for expeditions and hiking. The hat covers her baldness but not her tanned shoulders, which appear attractively above her shoulder-less blouse. She wears jeans again because they fit her slim waist and legs like a much younger woman.

"You look nice tonight," Carlton says.

Debra smiles, her well-manicured hands crossed in front of her in a prayer-like fashion. "Thank you."

Carlton sits straight up. Overdressed, he wears a dark brown suit jacket that complements his radiant blue eyes and salt-and-pepper hair, and he knows he is looking good.

"What did you do today?" asks Debra.

"I mowed the yard and cut back some shrubs," Carlton says. "Things have grown up quite a bit the last six months."

"I have the lawn service do my yard. I'm usually too weak to pull weeds."

"I like pretty flowers, and the only way to have a nice flower bed is to pull out the weeds."

"So, I took up painting to make my own flowers."

"Well, you're quite a painter. Do you plan to paint some more?"

"To be honest, after our bird painting at the brewery, I've been inspired to keep it up," Debra says.

"Tell me, Debra, what makes you tick?"

She chuckles again. "I don't have an alarm clock anymore," she says. "Living with cancer can be horrifying, and I have good and bad days."

"I'm just thankful my ticker still works," Carlton says. He moves his hands forward across the table, as if he wanted to touch hers. Debra notices and moves her hands to her lap.

"I don't know how many nights I stayed with her when she went to the memory care unit," Carlton says unexpectedly.

"You mean you didn't sleep at home when she was about to die?"

"I begged the nurse to let me stay."

"Did they let you?"

"Yes, they broke the rules for me—they would pull the curtain, so when the administrator came by, he couldn't see me," Carlton says.

Touched, Debra asks gently, "You loved her deeply?"

"Yes, I do . . . Yes, I *did,*" Carlton says. He looks down, thinking about love in the past and what he thinks might be love now.

"Carlton, are you okay?" Debra says. She places her hands back on the table . . . this time, with both palms face-down.

"Thank you for your understanding," Carlton says.

The two receive their meals—Debra has a salad, and Carl a filet mignon steak.

"You need to eat more than that," Carlton says.

"The doctor recommended a Mediterranean diet."

"A little steak will build those bones. Here, take a bite," Carl stretches out his solid right arm, while Debra looks at her plate. The piece of steak touches the brim of her cap, and Debra realizes it and raises her head, causing the steak to fall to her lap.

"I'll get it," she says.

Carl cuts off another small piece of the juicy filet.

"No—here, eat this," Carl says.

Debra opens her mouth and takes the small piece of meat. "It just melted into my mouth."

"I'm glad you enjoyed it."

This made Debra inquire, "Do you like to cook?"

"I do enjoy grilling steaks, baked potatoes, and I like a good piece of salmon, but I need someone to cook for." Carl has admitted to Debra and himself that he is lonely.

The two finish their meals. They stare at each other, as if each other's presence makes life just a little more meaningful.

Debra is shaken, puzzled, pleased. *Carl is a life force that has pulled me out of this death trance I have been in for six months. In one evening at The Brewery, he captivated me. Now, he has energized my heart with a meal.*

"I thought we would drop by and have a drink at The Brewery," Carlton offers. "They serve coffee, too."

"That sounds good, but I want to warn you—my medicines make me sluggish, and I usually hit the sheets around 9:00."

"I'll have you home by then—don't worry."

He walks her out toward the car. Carlton's friend is still eating, and Carlton passes him on the way out.

"She's a keeper," his friend whispers.

Carlton, always the gentleman, says nothing, and just nods his head in agreement, as Debra walks slowly in front of him.

"It's a little cooler than the night we met," Debra says.

"When I saw you for the first time at The Brewery, I knew there was something special about you," Carlton says.

Carl helps Debra put her shawl on to cover her bare shoulders. He opens the car door.

"Where's your truck, anyway?" Asks Debra.

"I didn't want you to have to climb up into the truck, so I drove the sedan."

"It's so clean," Debra marvels. "Is your home this clean, too?"

"I try to keep it clean. Grandma always said 'cleanliness is next to godliness.'"

"Are you a God-fearing man? I mean, do you go to church?"

"I used to, but lately I've just been in the dumps and haven't wanted to deal with God," Carlton says.

He pulls his car up beside The Church Street Brewery. "I see a parking spot along the street—we won't have to park across the street and walk."

"It's fine, wherever you want to park. By the way, that church is where I was married—a church service with a minister . . . and God was there, too, I guess," Debra says.

"I'm sure he was. Here, let me help you over the curb. Let's sit inside, this time."

"Can we sit next to the firepit?"

"Well, that will keep us warm," Carlton states.

"But last time we were here, it was too hot. Remember, I said the heat might melt the painting?"

"Yes, I remember, but the two love birds sitting on the wire did not melt away," Carlton says.

"If cancer hasn't killed me yet, I'm not worried about the heat."

Carlton slides two wooden chairs up near the firepit. The flame from the pit extends up above the circular knee-high wall about two feet. Through the glow, Debra can see another couple with their heads turned toward each other. Their conversation cannot be heard, but they both smile at each other with great warmth.

"They look like love birds, too," Debra says. "Is this place a magnet for love, or what?"

Carlton laughs. It's the second time he has felt real happiness in less than a few days.

"It must be a sign," Carlton hints.

"A sign?" Debra says. "What, a sign that two love birds are here?"

"No, that we are laughing together," Carl says.

"I think you are right about that," she says. "I like your laugh, and I like to see and hear you laugh . . . but do you ever get angry?"

"I have no one to be angry with right now," he replies. "I've asked God a lot of questions in the past six months, but I'm not angry, and I don't blame anyone."

"Carl, I think I hurt my daughter when I went out with you."

"What do you mean?"

"She doesn't want me to rush into a relationship because of my cancer, but I haven't felt this good in a long time." Debra turns to her left. She can see a red oval light blinking along the sidewalk—the traffic signal at Elm and Church. More striking is the blinking firelight reflected in Carl's eyes.

Another patron walks up to the couple. He's another older man but dressed in a suit. He holds a short glass filled with chardonnay.

"Hello, I'm Jim. I come here regularly, and I wanted to give you my business card, if you are in need of any legal service."

"Hi, Jim—I'm Carlton, and this is Debra."

"I've been practicing law in this town since 1961 and have represented most of the businesses you see on Main Street."

"We're just enjoying the cool fall air and each other's company," Carl says.

Jim rushes over to the side of the brewery, where the alley leads up to the glass door, and he retrieves another wooden chair and sits down next to Debra.

"Let me tell you about this place," Jim says, placing his glass on the firepit wall.

"That might melt, sitting up there," Debra says.

"It's just a warm fire," Jim says. "I do personal injury cases, as well."

"I'm injured by cancer, not from an auto accident."

"There are plenty of cures for cancer now," Jim says.

"What do you mean, Jim?" Carlton asks.

"Medicine has really advanced in the last few years. For example, twenty years ago, they didn't have prostate removal techniques."

"Nice to meet you," responds Debra, not very warmly, despite the fire. Carlton and Debra remain quiet, staring at the flames.

Jim gets up and leaves. The couple sees him walk around to the other side of the pit and introduce himself to the other couple.

Jim's insensitive comments made them wonder what types of patrons come to The Brewery. They turn and look at each other. Their eyes meet. Two blue and two brown. One man was lonely and now has a companion. One woman was depressed and now is happy.

"Thank you for being here for me," Debra says. "I've enjoyed, so much, getting to know you; you remind me of my late husband, and that is a big compliment."

The hostess comes out and asks about their drinks: "What can I get you?"

"Hi, my name is Christine. Can I get you started with some drinks?"

"We will have two London Fogs," Carlton says.

"Sorry, but we don't sell any drinks from England," Christine says.

"No, it's a coffee made from combining sweetened Earl Grey tea with steamed milk and vanilla syrup," Debra explains. "Can we just have two decaf coffees?

"What is your love language, Carl?" Debra says.

"I try to talk on a date," Carl says, puzzled. "Do I not talk enough?"

Debra chuckles. "No, I mean the five love languages. They are quality time, physical touch, acts of service, giving and receiving gifts, and words of affirmation."

"Oh . . . I see what you're asking. I liked to spend time with Da . . ." Carlton says.

"'Da?' You liked to spend time with Dot?" Debra asks.

"Yes, quality time with her and my two children."

"That's my love language, too," Debra says. "As well as physical touch."

"I do like giving hugs," Carlton says.

"I'm gonna go to the restroom," Debra says, as she yawns.

"I'll walk you inside . . . Or shall we go?" Carlton says.

"Can you take me home? I'm getting a little tired."

Carlton opens the car door for Debra and helps her with her seat belt. As he sits in the driver's seat, he sees Debra nodding off. Passing the hospital, he's surprised—he's not thinking about Dorothy but about Debra. He arrives at her home and wakes her up. The smooth ride kept her asleep for only five minutes.

"Thank you, Carl," she says, her soft voice melodious to him. She tries to extend her arms for him. Instead, his right hand grabs hers, engulfing her whole hand. They are now face to face. A kiss is the only thing left to do to top off this special night.

"You know, I have not been kissed in over a year," Debra says. Carlton has little to say. This moment makes him feel like he has arrived on a different planet. The two kiss, gently at first, and then with passion.

"Let me help you get to the door," Carlton says.

"That would be good."

The cool crisp air is almost as refreshing as the moonlit sky. As his right arm holds her while walking, his left points upward. "A full moon," Carlton notes.

"Like the two love birds in our painting?"

"Yes, ma'am."

He helps her get inside. She opens the side door and turns back around, as Carlton remains still.

"I think I love you," Debra tells him, somberly. "My time is short."

"This does seem magical. It may be that the stars have aligned for us."

"Good night, Carl. Will we talk in the morning?"

"I will call you first thing. Where do you keep the painting?"

"By my bedside," Debra assures him.

In one moment, Carlton's life has changed. He never thought another woman could replace Dorothy. He was wrong.

The next day, Carlton sends her flowers. She places them next to their bird painting. Another day passes before Debra decides she better fill her daughter in on her new friend, since she knows he is more than a friend.

"He sent me flowers," Debra tells her daughter.

"Flowers!" Sandra says. "That is too fast, Mom."

"I think I love him," Debra responds.

Sandra is surprised, but she knows her mother is an intelligent, thoughtful person who knows what love is.

The next day, Carl phones to tell Debra he would be working in the yard most of the day and would call her at night.

Debra calls Sandra again, with good news: "The doctors told me today I am officially in remission."

"Remission?" Sandra says. "That's awesome news!"

Another day passes. Carlton is ready to propose marriage to Debra. He thinks, *Time is running out for me. Is time running out for the two love birds?*

He picks up the rotary phone and dials.

"Sweetheart, would you be up for a ride around town?"

"Sure," Debra says. "You want to ride by The Brewery?"

"No, I have another place picked out this time: Oak Hollow Lake."

Face-to-face time was what they longed for more than being on the phone. "See you soon, darling," Debra says, and the two hang up.

Debra gets a little dressed up, wearing jeans and a fancy sweater.

As Carlton escorts Debra from her home, he helps her get up into his truck.

"It's polished like your sedan," Debra comments, and then asks, "Why did you drive the truck?"

"It's new and fresh—just like you," Carlton says.

Debra smiles and tells him, "You smell good."

"Thanks—I like to be clean, too. I know you like The Brewery, but today, I have a special place we can share my home-cooked meal, at the lake overlook," says Carlton.

"You made me a meal?" Debra says.

"Baked salmon, rice, and veggies," Carlton grins. "The Mediterranean, for sure."

The two arrive at the quiet picnic shelter. From their lakeside view, they can watch the mallards glide on top of the water and the herons fly over it. The sun is up, and sailboats pass them by.

He sits her down and looks deep into her eyes. He has her attention.

They start to eat, but Carlton can't wait to give her some news.

"Like those sailboats, but much faster, life is passing us by," he says.

While she sits on one end of the picnic table, he gets up and starts to walk around to her side. Then, this seventy-plus man gets down on one knee.

Debra turns to see him.

"Debra Jane Willard, will you marry me?" His voice is sharp and distinct. The birds must have heard him, and they scatter from their perch twenty feet away.

Debra's eyes start to water. For a moment, she feels only joy—no pain from the cancer, no pain from depression, no pain at all.

"Carlton Wayne Jones, your unwavering love has been an example of what real love is, and we share the same deep affection for one another," Debra says. "And yes, I will marry you."

Always practical, Debra adds, "And it doesn't have to be some fancy wedding."

Carlton smiles and asks: "Are we going to invite Jim?"

Chapter 14

FIERY DEVELOPMENTS

The fall temperatures in uptown High Point are good for wearing a casual shirt and jeans.

There is baseball and apple pie in the air as their minor-league stadium is being filled with fans for the first game.

The construction of The Church Street Brewery was completed a few weeks past. Sidewalks are clean, electrical power turned on, refrigerators working, as is the brewery equipment.

"Hey, Christine, are you going to sit on your butt all day? Get the guy a beer!" Britt admonishes her.

Daddy got me this job, after I was expelled from Theta Phi Upsilon. Hate him for that, Christine thinks, while grabbing a beer and walking it toward the front of the store, which offers windows with views of the tall church steeple between the bar and downtown High Point.

"I don't see him!" Christine yells at Britt.

My God, she is so clueless. The only reason she works here is because her father is the University president. He primes the brew kettle pumps in the back of the building.

"He went outside on the patio!" Britt yells back, his hands wringing wet.

"Is this all you want?" Christine asks the man standing outside on the patio near the firepit.

Meanwhile, the sound can be heard of a motorcycle traveling through the alley from the north side to the patio. Normally, the adjacent buildings deflect the sound opposite the brewery, making the patio and firepit area seem like a noiseless, wooded campfire site. Only the sounds from the baseball stadium prevail.

Vehicular traffic along Church Street is almost full since some folks are attending the baseball game on the next block. Wednesday afternoons around 6:00 to 6:30 brought several dozen families to the mid-week church services across the street from The Brewery.

The local TV station is on-scene to capture the excitement and interview Britt.

"Given that your other beer place is called 'The Green Truck,' why did you pick a name like 'The Church Street Brewery?'" the reporter asks.

"Well, I was going to call it 'The Plank Street' after the original name of Main Street," Britt recounts. Plank Street was so named because, in the late 1800s, the main road was constructed with planks of wood, not asphalt or concrete.

The town of High Point was chartered on May 26, 1859. It was located at the crossroads of the North Carolina Railroad and Fayetteville and Western Plank Road (now Main Street). This intersection was the highest point on the railroad that stretched between Goldsboro and Charlotte, thus inspiring the name.

"Actually, I had been thinking about the place for a while before they built the stadium; however, none of it ever took hold," said Britt to the news reporter. "We just figured, we've got to keep pushing for it—to keep young people involved in High Point and wanting to come back and stay here."

The reporter notices the firepit and asks, "That is a humongous firepit; tell me the motivation behind it."

"Obviously, the stadium being here is great, but there are so many people we know who are looking for a place to go and have one more drink after most other places close," said Britt. "And we just want The Church Street Brewery to be that place where people can come, sit and relax, have a good time, and make new friends; the firepit offers a place for conversation piece."

As the sound of the motorcycle subsides, the reporter spots a burly man wearing cowboy boots walking through the back alley that leads to the side patio. The patio faces Church Street and the First Baptist Church.

"Is parking going to be a problem for you? It looks as if patrons have to walk from the back side through the alley or park at the church," the reporter asks Britt.

"The church really did not want a drinking establishment next to them, but at least one fella who was picking up trash over there waved at me today, so maybe there is hope for some parking agreement with them," Britt responds. "I better go get the malt machines running because many people expect our signature beer to be served tonight," he tells the reporter, then walks back inside, as several new folks arrive around the patio.

The cowboy walks up on the patio, and the man Christine is serving says to her, "Hello, my name is Jim, and I'm an attorney in town; here is my business card."

She puts one hand on her hip, and with a snobbish tone, says, "I really don't need your card—my daddy handles all my traffic tickets."

"Well, I've been practicing law since 1961 and have won more cases than the number of beers you'll ever serve," Jim says.

"I'm glad I didn't become a lawyer," the cowboy smiles, and he laughs at Jim and Christine. *I ain't gonna serve any more beers after I make enough money to pay back my dad for the wreck,* Christine muses. *And he should not have barred me from Theta Phi Upsilon.*

"I am a personal injury attorney," Jim says, as he leans on the table between the firepit and the sliding glass door.

"I may fix bladders and prostates, but I would never be a personal injury lawyer," Greg says. He and his cowboy boots stroll a little closer to the pit.

Britt sees the group forming on the patio and opens the front door. "Christine, the University reserved the back conference room," he says.

"Well, it's not big enough for much!" Christine sneers.

"We can get about six people in there comfortably," Britt explains. "A professor—David something—is having a Q&A session tonight."

"At a brewery?" Christine replies. "That is weird."

"The door in the hallway leads to the alley, and I need a better lock on it. And put the sign up the professor made!" Britt says. "I told you that needs to be up on the front door, and the yard sign next to the firepit."

She tosses her hair to one side, gives a little grunt, and heads back inside.

Meanwhile, an F-150 can be seen going back and forth in front of The Brewery on Church Street.

Greg and Jim straddle a patio table together. "I'm a urologist; but I guess you figured that out when I said 'bladder,'" Greg says.

"Yeah, I figured. God, I haven't had my prostate checked in five years," Jim responds. "I have a scotch a day, and I'd rather drink than eat food."

"I thought lawyers worked late; it's only five," Greg says.

Jim's deep voice continues pontificating: "Having a drink with a client is good for business," Jim says. "I've secured many million-dollar estates over a bottle of champagne with aging men who need to revise their wills."

"Aging men?" Greg asks.

"Yes, when they get real old, they aren't thinking well," Jim says. "I help them manage their money, too."

"Sounds like elder manipulation to me," Greg says.

Jim just looks down at the ground and slurps his glass of chardonnay.

"That guy looks old, too," Greg says.

Jim smiles: "What guy? I was looking at the two gals over there who just arrived."

"The man in the F-150 who just pulled in across the street in the church parking lot," Greg explains. "I saw the shiny truck going back and forth; now, he is parked and looking straight at us."

"He seems to be gazing at the firepit," Jim chuckles. "I'm gazing at her . . . Well, I'm going to go over and talk to these hot ladies," Jim says. "Do you want to join me?"

"No, I think I will enjoy this nice chair next to the fire," Greg responds. "Take my boots off, too."

Carlton and Debra pull up into the church's parking lot, and both stare before exiting the vehicle. "Looks like there are a few folks already here," Debra says.

"More than the last time we were here," Carlton says. "Word must be getting around.

"Every time we pull into the parking lot, I can't help but think of throwing my garter belt from the steps back toward Church Street," Debra says.

Carlton turns to Debra: "Well, you'll be throwing another one soon."

Carlton and Debra start their short walk across Church Street. They can hear the sound of a baseball bat hitting a ball in one ear and music from The Brewery in the other. The firepit is glowing orange, and the heat can be felt as they pass it walking toward the front door. "Let's check inside with the hostess before we sit down," Debra says.

"Okay."

Meanwhile, Jim—dressed in a suit, with a head of thick, grey, shiny hair—leaves Greg on the patio and makes his rounds inside the bar, where the two ladies are standing. Friendly, laid-back, and affectionate, Jim is like a bulldog, with a cute wrinkly face and a deep voice.

Jim stands next to the bar needing a fresh gin and tonic; the two young ladies are Nadia and Yuan. Each arrived around 5:00 and parked along Church Street. Nadia has on blue jeans and a thick coat, even though the temperature is still around sixty degrees. As Nadia walks in, she recognizes Yuan, who is standing near the front hostess table.

"Hello . . . umm, you are?" Nadia says.

"Yuan—my name is Yuan, but my friends call me Yu."

"Yes, I've seen you in my religious studies class at the University," Nadia says. Nadia spots hostess Christine and makes eye contact with her from across the taproom in front of the bar. The bar runs west to east, about ten feet from the front door for a length of about twenty feet.

"What was the agenda again for the Q&A session?" Yuan asks.

"If I remember correctly, the professor said he wanted to discuss Origin, Meaning, Morality, and Destiny," Nadia says.

"I like the topics because they are not Christo-centric or Islam-centric, yet they allow any religious person to express their world views," Yuan says.

"Precisely," says Nadia.

Christine walks with an attitude, not interested in a Q&A, nor in serving customers. But she does know how to shake her hips. She keeps a pack of cigarettes in her jeans. Tight jeans and a tight T-shirt.

Christine returns a glance at Nadia and walks up to the ladies. "Britt gives me no help here. What are you having to drink?"

"I'm here for the University discussion group. The professor said it would be in the conference room in the back," Nadia explains to Christine.

"Hello, I am Yu—here for the Discussion Group, as well."

"Yeah, I've seen you on campus," Christine responds, as she grabs her drink tray and spots Jim talking to two other ladies in the taproom. "One other person is back there in the conference room—to the left and straight back; watch out for the dust containers; they're hazardous and blocking the hallway slightly.

"The Q&A session is straight back in the conference room," Christine adds.

Both young ladies are staring at each other, not giving off any signals to the men who are starting to enter The Brewery. The women make their way down the west-side hallway. They turn briefly to see the glowing firepit through the tall side windows

"The conference room is to your left and all the way in the back. You want a beer or a glass of wine?" asks Christine.

The renovation of the old building added some pendant lights and fresh new paint in the hallway between the conference room, the kitchen, and the taproom. The conference room is located in the northwest corner, with the kitchen and brewing equipment to the east and the outdoor patio to the west.

The taproom starts to fill with patrons all eager to sit at the new counter and taste The Brewery's signature beer. The space is rustic and casual, with high-top tables fashioned from antique beer barrels and the room enclosed in painted brick walls. Britt designed it so tourists from all over can get a taste of what's available from a variety of beers without leaving the comfort of a barstool.

The taproom is a long, somewhat intimate, space with clear glazing facing the church south and the patio to the west. It provides dramatic and tantalizingly open views of uptown High Point. It lends itself to a rewarding interaction and successfully affords a discerning beer-lover a full appreciation of the beer they are sipping.

"Welcome to The Church Street Brewery," Britt can be heard announcing through the loudspeaker.

He explains to the customers—some sitting at bar stools and some standing—"The beer list usually features a great balance of styles, and there is almost always farmhouse ale and a stout or porter. Please try our signature beer called 'The Rocker.'"

From the large bar, customers can sit and look into the enormous beer production area, where two huge copper kettles are proudly displayed. Nearby, an area with comfortable sofas and chairs provides a more private option for those who want to sit and chat quietly.

The crowd inside hears almost only their own voices. The baseball game can be heard only on the patio. A car's booming speakers can be heard playing rap music. The music gets louder than its source, a beat-up Honda Civic that pulls into the church parking lot.

Meanwhile, the Q&A session is about to receive another participant and the moderator.

Rae, the African American student in Professor David's religious studies class pulls up in the church parking lot that faces the front of The Brewery. He turns down his music and ponders the location. *Mama used to take us to this church when we were little. Sure hope this Q&A session is dope; I need the extra three points. I don't want no damn beer, either; can't afford it anyway.*

As he walks across Church Street, he can see the transparent façade inside. *A bunch of white folk in here*, Rae thinks to himself. *The only reason I'm even coming to this group discussion is to get the extra credit. My exam score was a seventy-three, and I need the three points to make a C and pass the class. Where was God when my daddy left us?*

Rae is dressed in sweats and a long-sleeve T-shirt—dressed down compared to the white and Latino customers. He's struggling to pay his rent despite some federal loans to attend the nearly all-white university. His black hair is neatly parted to match a dark, clean-shaven face. As he passes the patio and firepit to reach the front door, he wonders, *It's warm inside and cool out here, so why so many people on the patio? That is a big-ass firepit.*

Entering by the glass door, his expectations are met—no black patrons at the new brewery, and there is an air of elitism. Christine spots Rae from the far side of the taproom but is serving a crowd of thirty-somethings. Finally, after a few minutes, she makes her way to the front door near the reception desk.

"Are you here to work for Britt?" Christine asks with a chuckle. Then, her face returns to a smirk.

"I'm here for a discussion group—the University Q&A sessions," Rae says politely, as his cell phone beeps.

"Go down the hall to the back; they are in there," Christine says, with a rude tone.

When Rae enters the conference room, Nadia and Yuan are already seated. Rae recognizes both of them from class. "Where's the professor?" Rae inquires.

"We were wondering the same thing," Nadia says. Professor David was running late to his own Q&A session. And there is a reason for it. On Wednesday afternoons, the professor usually leaves campus around 1:00 p.m. and drives to Fayetteville. Precisely at 3:00 p.m., he pulls into a well-manicured condominium community to meet his mistress.

"How did you like the interview with the professor," asks Yuan.

"Mine was pretty interesting, since I still have lots of questions about God," Rae says.

"Although Islam views Jesus as one of the five great prophets in history, I don't believe Jesus is the only begotten son of God," says Nadia.

"So, you are Muslim?" Rae responds.

Meanwhile, Professor David has arrived at the front of The Brewery. The professor is distinguished-looking, and this bar is his kind of place. And his lust signals radiate toward any woman that will talk to him. His briefcase carries his presentations and handouts on religious worldviews.

Katherine says, "You're the professor?"

"Yes, the professor, and I am here to educate the world."

"Let me get Britt," Katherine says.

"Hello, David," Britt says.

"Where is the conference room?" Britt escorts David to the back northwest corner. Like the college students attending his Q&A session, he notices the firepit. "That is quite a patio scene over there," David says.

"We've only been open a week, and every night, that firepit has more than a dozen folks hanging out and chatting till 2:00 a.m.," Britt says.

"Hello, students!" David says. "Glad you made it." David slams his briefcase on top of the lone office table. Six chairs and a long table fit comfortably in the conference room. Joining Rae, Nadia, and Yuan are two older adults, who remain quiet while the students are engaging in a friendly conversation. Rae sits closest to the door to the hallway, while the ladies sit opposite the table.

"Welcome to the Q&A session," David announces. "For an hour, I thought I would offer a summary of my interviews with students in my world religions class."

The students nod their heads. The other two attendees do, too. The adults are thirty-somethings both dressed in white button-down shirts and ties. The professor does not introduce them.

"Tonight's Q&A is not about God but about your world views in terms of origin, meaning, morality, and destiny," says the professor. "You get to interact and debate with each other—I was hoping some people in the local community would join us."

The other two adults now speak up with formidable voices, in plain and simple tones: "We're here to learn about Christianity," the man says. "We believe that Jesus Christ is son of God and the creator of the world. However, we don't believe God the Father and Jesus Christ are one being."

"What are your names?"

"I'm Joe, and this is Kyle," the man says.

"What do you think, Nadia?" says David. "Is Jesus who He claims He is—son of God?"

"We Muslims do believe Jesus is a prophet but not the son of God," replies Nadia.

"What about the origin of life?" David asks next.

Yuan's dark black hair matches her thick glasses, and her head rises: "Origin of life comes from a higher level of power. But I cannot verify my view using scientific methods. So, we have a creator. Life creates everything. Life gives everything emotions."

"But what created this life?" the visiting man said. "I mean who created the life force?"

"Do you believe in life after death?" the professor inquires. "Is there an eternal destiny?"

Yuan says, "I do believe in life after death—I trust eternal destiny."

Yuan's comments must have struck a chord with Nadia's upbringing in Oman and her Islamic faith. "If there is life after death, where does our being go?" asks Nadia.

"Good question," says David. "What is the 'essence' of life after death?"

Then, Joe interrupts and says, "If there is life after death, where does our being go? What is the essence of life after death?"

Yuan says, "We may have soul, and then we can become everything."

"We become everything?" Kyle says.

"We can become sunshine to warm earth," Yuan explains. "After death is a new start for me. Right now, I want to study, then I can find a good job. After these things, I will have a happy life. Before my death, I want to achieve my dream. Then, I can have a new start."

David explains: "What Yuan is referring to is Pantheism—the view that the world is either identical to God, or an expression of God's nature. It comes from 'pan' meaning all, and 'theism,' which means the belief in God. So, according to pantheism, God is everything, and everything is God."

"Yes, that's it," Yuan says.

"This Q&A is becoming very interesting," David comments. "So, none of you are so-called 'born-again Christians?'"

"We are born again," says one of the men.

"You are born-again Mormons?" David guesses.

"Yes, in the *Book of Mormon*, we are told: 'And the Lord said unto me: Marvel not that all mankind, yea, men and women, all nations, kindreds, tongues, and people, must be born again; yea, born of God, changed from their carnal and fallen state, to a state of righteousness, being redeemed of God, becoming his sons and daughters.'"

The professor adds, "The phrase 'born-again Christian' is an expression used by many Protestant Christians to define the moment or process of fully accepting faith in Jesus Christ. It is their experience when the teachings of Christianity and Jesus become real, and those 'born-agains' acquire a personal relationship with God."

"I see—that makes sense," the man says.

"But I'd like to hear from the pastor across the street, at the Baptist church," David says. "I'm sure he has an opinion on it."

"Across the street?" Yuan interjects.

"First Baptist," David replies. "Did you see all their cars in the parking lot? They have Wednesday night sermons over there."

"Mostly old people go to church," says Nadia dismissively. "I go to a mosque."

The professor takes this opportunity to instruct the group: "By the way, the term 'born-again' is originated from an incident in the *New Testament* in which the words of Jesus were not understood by a Jewish Pharisee, Nicodemus. Nicodemus asked Jesus how a man can be born twice. Jesus's response is recorded in Chapter Three of the Book of John, where Jesus told Nicodemus, '. . . no one can see the kingdom of God unless they are born again.' Like with Nicodemus, being born again is not based on your nationality or ethnicity; it is personal. God's gift of rebirth is not through human effort, but comes through God's mercy alone." Anyway, back to the question of destiny and life after death."

Yuan remains insistent on telling about her Chinese beliefs: "After death is a new start for me. Right now, I want to study, then I can find a good job. After I complete these things, I will have a happy life. Before my death, I want to achieve my dream. Then, I can have a new start."

"Jesus claimed to be God," David says.

"I don't believe a man like Jesus can be the life force that created everything," Yuan says.

"Well, folks, do you want to know my belief?" David asks.

They all look wary and curious.

"God is the Master Clockmaker. He made the clock, wound it, and then left it alone."

Having delivered the last words on this subject, David goes on: "Sounds like everyone is having a good time in the taproom. Shall we keep on discussing destiny next, then morality, and meaning?"

"Morality, yes," Nadia offers.

"Is there a moral code you live by, Nadia?" David questions her. "I know you're a Muslim, but American religious views are quite different from those of the Middle East."

"I practice Islam, including no sex before marriage, no stealing, and no murder and being respectful toward people and being honest," says Nadia.

The two men and Rae have a blank look on their faces, as if they can't believe a twenty-something college girl is saying this. *Is she still a virgin?* Rae wonders.

David changes the subject again: "Do you believe in an afterlife? And where will you be when you die?"

Nadia is first to give an opinion: "After we die, there will be a judgment day; God will judge by how each person lived their life—either right or wrong—because He is merciful."

Nadia thinks back to her days as a teenager in Oman and that horrible day of man's evil. She ponders with sadness, *"Give me your burqa and put these on,"* the guard had yelled at me after he threw me on a basement floor.

Nadia starts to cry, as the professor stares at her. For a brief moment, he feels something he rarely shows—empathy. The others at the table are silenced, too.

"What's wrong? Why are you crying? This is just a religion course, and I am not going to fail you."

"I was fifteen, and he was forty. He forced me into the basement of the guard station at the Yemen border, where red stains appear on a damp, sandy floor, and he raped me for two hours!"

The group sits in stunned silence.

"I am so sorry," the professor says. "Folks, we are going to end the Q&A here—thank you for attending and please leave your email and phone number for me."

David, Yuan, and the two Mormon men remain in the conference room chatting. Their intellectual curiosity about religious world views has been temporarily satisfied. But Professor David is not completely satisfied.

"I enjoyed the session," Yuan says. "Thank you, Professor."

"You want to grab a drink, Yuan?" David asks. "Sounds like a good time in the taproom."

Meanwhile, Katherine, the wine connoisseur, has been thinking about what to order on her way into The Brewery. She likes to collect all types of wine, particularly wine from Norway. Short and stocky, wearing a blue dress and a white blouse, she carries a tote bag that catches the corner of the glass door handle as she enters the front door. She mutters, "Damn, it ripped, but I think I can still fit the wine bottles in here."

Christine is on a smoke break outside in the back, at the north side of the brewery, where the alley meets the second parking lot that faces the hospital.

Britt is manning the taproom bar and sees Jim maneuvering. Then, Britt notices Katherine's bag get snagged and thinks, *Where is Christine to help? The customers are starting to roll in. I did this for the University president.*

"Hi, I'm Jim. Here, let me help you with your bag." The fresh white concrete is clean, contrasting Katherine's red heels and Jim's black dress shoes.

"Hi, I'm really fine," says Katherine. "I've seen you at some art council events around town."

"I'm one of their biggest donors. Last year, I donated fifty thousand dollars toward Centennial Station, mostly for operating funds."

"The pace at which most folks live is grueling," says Kathrine. "You race home from a busy day at the office, with food to prepare and laundry piling up . . . The easiest thing to do when I'm standing at the cutting board making dinner is pour myself a glass of wine."

"Are you attending the art events regularly?" Jim inquires. "We need another fine lady like you on the board."

"Wine is the ultimate decompression tool. I'm sorry . . . What about the art board?"

"You look nice tonight," Jim says. The bright red lipstick Katherine is wearing is noticeable throughout the taproom, and she causes a few heads to turn. However, Katherine is planning to purchase take-out tonight.

"Hi, I ordered a few bottles of the Hallingstad, a Norwegian pinot noir off your website earlier today," Katherine tells Britt.

"I'm really sorry, but did you get a confirmation email?"

"No, I did not, but I thought I would stop by anyway."

Jim slides his way into the conversation at the bar with Katherine and Britt: "I've got some extra bottles at my office, if you would like them."

"I beg your pardon?" Katherine is not sure what to make of him.

"Why don't you stay awhile? The first glass of wine is on me," Britt says.

"That would be nice. Fair enough." She notices the firepit through the glass doors and walks over there, carrying her empty tote bag. Although she manages to elude Jim for a moment with the move to the patio, he soon follows her.

Carlton and Debra have settled into a seat in the taproom. Before Jim makes it to the front door, chasing after Katherine, he notices the older engaged couple.

Holding his gin and tonic in one hand and his suit jacket in the other, he winks at Debra. Carlton is staring the other way at the shiny pipes in the ceiling, observing the old timber, and he misses the wink.

"I used to work in this place when it was a furniture factory forty years ago. Same roofing, but now it is all beer equipment, new pendant lights, and glass windows—makes the place look like a spaceship," Carlton says.

Jim pays no attention to Carlton, although he seems to have heard the nostalgic comment.

"It's an old building, Carlton," Debra offers. "Any skeletons in the closet outside?"

"You mean the old storage room along the back of the patio?"

"Yes, seems strange they didn't tear it down so we could see the stadium and hospital to the north," she comments.

"That storage room goes underground twenty feet," Carlton explains. "There used to be some chemicals stored in there."

Jim remains fixated on Debra, despite Carlton's knack for storytelling. Looking at Debra, dressed in her tight jeans, he tells her, "Remember me? I'm Jim."

"I'm Debra; nice to meet you."

"I am an attorney in town—here is my business card." He walks away toward the front door. His bow tie now sideways from bounding around the bar, he can see the firepit ahead of him. The sun has set on uptown and The Brewery.

Carlton looks at his fiancée, and she looks at him. "You want to sit around the firepit before I take you home?" Carlton suggests.

"You mean where you and I painted the birds on a wire? You're so romantic Carl."

Around the firepit, a large outdoor patio space gives customers still another option for sitting, sipping, and dining on treats from the kitchen.

When Jim and Katherine reach the pit, Greg is still sitting in a wooden folding chair. Now, there are at least a dozen patrons either sitting around the firepit wall or standing on the deck that overlooks the patio.

"I wonder what goes on over there in that church?" Greg muses.

"You're more than welcome to visit my church—it's Episcopalian," Jim says.

Greg picks up his bottle of beer off the ground where it sits next to his boots. "They're a bunch of hypocrites," Greg says. "But Neal is not one of them; he's a good man—I just don't believe in what he preaches."

"I did like the Pontius Pilate story," Jim replies. "He did what the people wanted, which is what I try to do."

"Please the people? Sounds like a politician."

Turning his head, Jim booms, "Hey, sexy, warm enough over there?"

Katherine is fully convinced that Jim is a creeper. She notices an acquaintance standing on the deck and makes her way over there. Greg's comments keep Jim fixed in place.

"I went hunting with Neal, the Baptist preacher, a few weeks ago,"

Greg continues. "He invited me to that church, but I declined. Preacher Neal is not a drinker, but he does like to deer hunt."

"Instead of downing deer, you came for downing beer," Jim says. "That rhymes—I'm a poet and didn't even know it."

"Ever heard this song?" Greg starts to sing:

If I could have a beer with Jesus,
Heaven knows I'd sip it nice and slow,
I'd try to pick a place that ain't too crowded,
Or gladly go wherever he wants to go.

Jim takes his coat off, revealing his white button-down shirt and bow tie. "I listen to classical music and jazz," he says abruptly, as though he deserves a medal for it.

"Why is it you lawyers get away with stretching the truth, and we doctors can lose our license for accidentally nicking a man's urethra?" Greg complains.

Jim just mumbles something, and Greg realizes he is dealing with a politician, not a man concerned with the rules of ethical behavior. "I forgot to pay my tab, but that will be fine," Jim mutters.

Greg asks him, "Have you ever cheated on your wife?"

"I may flirt a little, but I have not slept with any of them . . . as far as I can remember, at least."

"If you slept with a woman that's not your wife, you would remember, and if you cheat in your heart, is that not also cheating?" Greg challenges Jim. "I think the Bible actually says lusting is cheating."

"Is watching porn cheating?" Jim counters.

"It's lust, isn't it? Greg says.

As Katherine mingles with her friend on the deck overlooking Jim and Greg, an African American man appears from the alley, which extends from the back of the building under the deck and ends near the glass front door. About the same time, Carlton and Debra are coming out of the front door. Folding chairs line the north side patio wall.

"Who's that black fella?" Debra asks.

"I don't know; I'll get the chairs—you find us a spot around the fire," Carlton says. Debra sits her handbag down in the one open space which is nearest to the Church Street sidewalk.

The African American man is sporting a baggy bean hat, funky jeans, and a shirt around his waist. His white socks contrast a small black container around his ankle. His gold front tooth reflects the light off the firepit. His hands are in both pockets, and he leans back up against the glass sidewall of The Brewery.

"Okay, Mr. Lawyer, is he a terrorist?" Greg challenges.

"I don't know him from Adam," Jim says. "There are no Jihadists or terrorists in High Point, North Carolina, but he might be looking for some fun."

There is a big red sign on the back wall of the patio area that reads "No Smoking." The African American man pulls out a cigarette and lights it. He steadies his body against the glass façade.

Meanwhile, back in the conference room, the Q&A session has neared its end at six o'clock. One of its participants, Rae, decides to skip the final set of questions. He's received his three points of extra credit toward the religious studies class and now wants to explore the bar.

Walking outside, Rae spots the only other black person there. "Yo, homie, what's up?" Rae says.

"What's cracking? I saw the baseball stadium lights on and walked over here," the man replies. "My name is Eric."

"I was here for class," Rae says.

"Class?" Eric says. "Ain't no damn class here where they sell booze."

"Man, you don't fit in here with your dreads, hood, and what's that ankle brace for?" Rae says.

"Man, I was set up," Eric replies. "The judge said I was selling crack to a kid."

"You're not running, are you?" Rae says. "You talking about that cigarette I shared with the kid?"

"Three strikes and you are out?" Rae says. "If you steal candy on your third offense, you're in prison for thirty years."

"Damn right," Eric says. "My trial is set for next week. I'm supposed to stay at my grandma's house under court order."

"Well, what are you doing here? Police will find you real fast, man."

"Grandma lives in Clara Cox, and I decided to walk uptown and find me some snatch," Eric says.

"You can't match these ladies—all from Emerywild . . . or rich white ladies," Rae says.

"How about those two bitches on the deck over there?" The beeping sound from his ankle bracelet goes off.

"You better get back home," Rae urges.

Eric doesn't buy it. "I'm going to hang here and just watch these sexy mamas."

"What's that smell anyway? You farting or something?"

"Might be the food this damn place serves," Eric answers. "You got any snacks I could have?"

"Well, when I left the conference room and came out to the patio, I could hear something strange," Rae states. "A whistling sound from the garbage can back over there," and he points.

Meanwhile, First Baptist Church is about to start Wednesday night services a few hundred feet across the street.

Although the preacher, Neal, knew The Brewery was open, he didn't realize the firepit would glow so brightly that it would shine into his church office window—a stone's throw to the south. He'd been in his study all afternoon preparing for the Wednesday night sermon. His writing desk faces his four-foot-wide window, where he can see the sunset over the baseball stadium. Now, he can't help but people watch those at the new brewery. *I'd like to get some of the beer drinkers to attend our church. What would that take? We have many older members. We need some younger members.*

Members enter the sanctuary. Neal greets everyone and then starts his sermon:

"I've done three funerals already this week. I know our church is mostly an older crowd, and you know this as well as I do. Death comes for us all in one form or another. It might be the death of a beloved parent, whose advanced age has somewhat prepared us for the loss, but whose absence leaves a hole in our heart. It might be the unexpected death of a dear friend, whose departure not only deprives us of a cherished companion but also reminds us of our own mortality. Sometimes, when faced with such tragedies, we become bitter, angry at the world, and perhaps even angry at God. We wonder how a loving God could allow such horrors to take place. I can't explain it all—God is sovereign, but He said He will never leave us or forsake us.

"When faced with this type of tragedy, consider these comforting Bible verses about death. They offer few explanations for life's hardest knocks, but they do remind us that life does not end with physical death. And wherever we or they are in the process, God is always there to support and hold us up. Hold fast to these verses and allow yourself to take comfort in the loving embrace of God. Hear the words from the Psalm 23:4: 'Even though I walk through the valley of the shadow of death, I will fear no evil, for you are with me; your rod and your staff, they comfort me.' The immortal declaration of the 23rd Psalm remains among the most powerful statements of faith in the Bible: 'Wherever we go, from our birth throughout our life and into the passage of death, the Lord is always and ever with us.'"

Across Main Street, cattycorner to The Brewery, the twelve-story Sheraton Towers is occupied by senior citizens, some of whom can see the firepit from their upper-floor vantage point.

Carlton and Debra settle into their chairs, warming their aging bodies. Their faces are aglow with the firelight. "Don't touch that, darling," Carlton says.

"The gas pilot?"

"Yes, I don't know why they have the pilot next to the wall, where we are sitting."

Katherine is toting a bag of wine bottles and sipping her wine on the deck. Earlier in the evening, she snagged her tote bag and is now carrying around plastic bags, as if she just arrived from the farmer's market.

"You enjoying yourself?" Katherine inquires, from the deck above the firepit.

"I am, indeed—nice night," Debra says, as she places her feet up on the firepit wall.

Two other patrons make their way up on to the deck's first level—a squeaking sound can be heard as the deck floor moves with the 4x4 posts.

Katherine and Debra exchange smiles and each continues their conversations while sipping their favorite drinks.

"It's beautiful up here," Katherine says, smiling toward Debra. "If only they would play some Ella Fitzgerald."

"The hissing sound is normal for gas grills," Carlton comments.

"But this is not a grill," objects Debra.

Greg and Jim overhear their conversation. "Do y'all smell anything over there?"

"Not really," Carlton says. "But I hear a hissing sound."

"Do you smell anything?" Greg asks Carlton again.

"No, the Agent Orange in Nam killed the olfactory receptors in my nose," Carlton responds. "I can't smell anything but good home cooking . . . which I ain't had since Dot died."

"It won't be long until we are cooking together," Debra says.

"Are y'all married?" Greg asks.

Carlton starts to smile: "We got engaged just a few days ago."

Greg continues, concerned: "I noticed a rotten-egg smell when I walked from the back through the alley toward the patio, but that was two hours ago."

A young family—a man and a woman and their two children—left the baseball game early. They walked from the direction of the stadium to the west, up the sidewalk in front of The Brewery. They had parked their mini-van right in front of the patio.

"Maybe we are smelling the garbage cans toward the ball field," says Carlton. "Let's ask the family how the game was."

"How was the game?" Debra asks. "Did you notice any garbage trucks on down toward the stadium?"

"No, ma'am," said the father. "But I do smell it here."

"Guys, I see a small flame on the ground over there," Katherine says. Her loud and deep voice carries to the front door, where Eric is standing with Rae.

"I don't see nothing," Eric says.

"That's because you smell like weed," Rae remarks. "The sign says no smoking, and you're leaving blunts on this nice patio."

"That ain't no blunt," says Eric. "That's a damn burning match stuck in a crack."

"I don't see no match," disagrees Rae. "Let me go tell the manager."

"Manager ain't got no time for you," Eric says. "No black man has a friend at this white bar."

Rae pulls open the large glass door and meets Christine, who is texting on her cell phone. "Hold on, you can't come running in here like a wild man," Christine says. "The Q&A is over now."

The bar is packed by this time, around 10:00.

"I need to speak to your manager!" Rae says.

"What's the problem? He can't help you—he's making beer in the back."

"Tell him there is a match burning on the patio that won't go out, and we smell some rotten eggs," says Rae.

"A match burning?" Christine says. "I smoke, and I know a match will eventually burn out—don't worry about it."

Rae is not satisfied: "Come out here and take a look?"

"The city has not come by to collect the trash since we opened," Christine says. "Britt needs to call them."

Rae leaves Christine to see if his classmates and the professor have left the conference room. He hears them talking as he starts his walk from the front door down the hallway that runs next to the indoor wall facing the patio.

"The sign says 'No Smoking', but I do it anyway." Christine yells. "But I don't throw my butts or matches on the patio and leave them burning."

Professor David and his students remain in the conference room. Nadia is adjusting her handbag and hat, while the two Mormon men prepare to leave. Britt leaves the brew room, where he is working on the malt machine, and thanks the group for their business.

Britt discussed the new firepit gas piping requirements with the general contractor only weeks prior, during the remodeling of the brewery. "There is an abandoned textile mill next to the planned brewery and an underground warehouse full of chemicals," the contractor told Britt.

The mechanical contractor who installed the firepit connected its three-quarter-inch gas pipe to the existing two-inch underground pipe. Unfortunately, the fittings on the two pipes were not common. An adaptor was proposed by the engineer who specified particular installation instructions to avoid leakage.

The gas pipe leak in the underground bunker was only five feet from the patio. When the gas-air ratio reaches a certain level, it can be ignited by a single spark—even a static electricity spark will do. The spark ignites the gas, setting off a conflagration. The gas expands as it heats, causing the pressure to reach intolerably high levels. Any walls, doors, or windows in a building space blow out, and the explosion causes great damage to people and property.

So, when Eric chose not to follow the warning sign of not smoking on the patio, he dropped his blunt on top of what looked like spilled beer boiling in a crack. But the bubbling was from leaking gas.

As Debra stood up and walked toward the family ambling along the sidewalk, Carlton remained next to the firepit. When Eric's cigarette butt sparked the gas, it sent a high-pressure wave of hot gas and fire into Carlton's body. The pressure wave landed him in the middle of Church Street, where his fiancée crawled to meet him. Her cell phone was still in her jean's pocket.

"9-1-1, what is your emergency?"

"My fiancée is on fire!"

The force of the blast has propelled Debra and Carlton about fifteen feet, into the street, where the mini-van was overturned.

Eric, the accused drug dealer, had accidentally ignited the leaky gas in the patio crack, and a wave of terror would start. To make the horror worse were the chemicals below the patio, where the main gas pipe ran. These flammables fueled the fire to unbearable levels of heat.

The blast was so intense that the deck above the patio blew some thirty feet in the air, sending Katherine and her friend to make an airborne landing on Church Street. The pressure from the underground bunker opened up the ground like a five-foot-wide volcano. The chemicals fueled the fire, as did the firepit, whose top blew upward and landed in the church parking lot.

The explosion is noted immediately by the umpire at the baseball game; he waves his hands as the pitcher starts his windup: "Stop! Game is stopped!" Most of the three thousand fans see the orange fire ball and also feel groundwaves through the underground, traveling at 12,000 miles per hour, causing bystanders leaving the game early to feel a thump and making buildings shake.

The wave of fire and heat dismantles the side of The Brewery facing the patio. The brewing materials were also flammable. The process includes a malt that is crushed into grist. It is placed in a large drum with heated water and mashed into a substance that is then strained to remove the pulp, leaving wort. Britt's crushing process produced lots of combustible dust in the air and was stored in large closed containers. Some of these containers line the hallway going to the conference room.

The young couple who left the ball game and got back into their minivan are injured. As the woman was placing her baby girl into the car seat, the blast pressure forced the van to roll over on its side, trapping her underneath. The baby is now screaming for her mother.

The blast smashed out the window of The Brewery, knocking holes in the walls. Blood now stains the welcome counter. The explosion blasted a crater into the concrete patio and turned the brewery into twisted metal and broken-down mortar.

The other cars parked on Church Street are damaged, as glass, metal, and debris land on car hoods and trunks. In less than one minute, the street looks like a war zone.

The bodies of the victims, who tried to flee, become strung out along the curb. Eric is no longer leaning on the glass window. The force of the blast has propelled him through the window, and he is now lying on the ground next to the malt machine. Blood is running out of his mouth; chunks of glass pierce his body. The only activity left are electrons flowing through his ankle bracelet.

"It was such intense heat that we couldn't get close enough to it," one firefighter later said. "Once it got to where we could manage it, we had firefighters go in and check what happened."

As Debra's 9-1-1 call was cut off, emergency crews respond to the gas leak slower than needed, according to radio traffic. A four-person crew from the South Centennial Station, about a mile away, arrive within minutes. However, they quickly realize they are dealing with a less-than-routine problem.

"Help us monitor some of these buildings," says an emergency responder on the police scanner. "I think this leak is worse than what I thought."

On its way to the east, the blast wave picked up building materials like 2x4s, rebar, and trusses, as well as glass. Like a push broom, the wave propelled patrons sitting in the taproom to the northern brick wall. Patrons sitting at tables next to the Church Street side were thrown through the weaker glass windows.

"9-1-1, what is your emergency?"

"I'm trapped inside the brewery!" Britt says.

"What is your address?"

"138 Church Street."

"Sir, we have a crew on their way now—they are coming to help you."

"I'm trapped, and no one seems to hear me when I call out," Britt yells. "I can't see anything—I'm trapped under a burning roof."

At eighty-four years of age, Frank is still in pretty good health. He lives on the twelfth floor of Sheraton Towers. Despite the 1950s-style architecture and old plumbing fixtures, he has the advantage that his window faces west. He can see the sun set over the ball stadium.

When the explosion occurred, Frank was sitting by his window watching television. "I could see the explosion before I heard it," Frank declares. "When I looked out the window, an orange cloud was probably 100 feet tall."

"Did you see anything else strange about the orange cloud?" asks the reporter.

"In the middle of the orange cloud was a perfectly round figure that looked like a human face."

Nadia managed to escape out the rear side door to the conference room leading to the alley. The narrow alley had left roof timbers above her, and she crawled under them to safety.

Yuan did the same thing, but one burning timber landed on her back leg.

The professor was not so fortunate. At the time of the explosion, he was mingling by the dust containers, talking to Christine. The flammable dust caught fire, burning his clothes and lower torso. He escaped by crawling out the alley door without any pants.

While Neal is preaching, his safety officer, Dick, runs inside the sanctuary. "Neal, we've got a serious problem on the street—massive fire."

"Everyone, take a minute to pray," Neal commands. "I'm going outside to look." Billowing smoke covers the whole block between Elm and Main Street. Some of the church vehicles are covered in dust and building materials.

Neal steps over some boards and hears the voice of Greg: "God help me . . . God help me!" The urologist lays motionless next to a storm gutter and the church parking lot. His body is burned badly. The patio had exploded, sending flames up Greg's legs and right side, then enveloping his chest. His six-foot-two, 195-pound frame was engulfed in fire. "I tried to crawl toward your church," Greg says.

"Buddy, the ambulance is on its way," Neal assures Greg. He wants to hold his hand, but the skin is missing and only bone can be seen.

Neal pauses for a moment to catch his breath and prays: *God, I know you are a God of mercy, and I ask you right now to be merciful to these people.* He calls his wife, Ashland. Neal can see the sidewalk is bloodied, and timber and metal shrapnel line the street. He hears another voice coming from the building between the patio and the stadium.

"I can't breathe! Please help me!" Katherine shouts from the rooftop. She was standing on the patio deck when the massive volcano-like explosion threw her into the sky and then back down on the next-door roof.

Referring to Greg . . . "Let me help him," the emergency worker tells Neal.

"I hear another voice coming from across the street."

"We'll send the ladder truck to reach that person."

Three ambulances maneuver between the many bodies and over-turned vehicles. The first to be lifted into the ambulance is Greg. "I'll see you at the hospital, buddy," Neal says.

The TV crew has parked along Elm Street and has made its way to the back of The Brewery, where Nadia sits watching the building burn. Although she was not burned, her head hit a burning deck ember as she made her way past the patio to a safer area.

Yuan sits with her head down, her glasses missing. Her right leg has a long cut from a nail she caught it on while trying to exit the rear door.

The professor lies on the pavement with Nadia's jacket covering his naked legs. He moans in pain, "Why did this happen, why?"

"9-1-1, what is your emergency?"

"Can you please tell the fireman there is a man here bleeding and burned badly," Nadia says.

"Help is on the way," replies the operator.

The explosion also produced a somewhat-common mushroom cloud. But something else was not so common. In the pillar of orange and black smoke, an image of a face could be seen. At least that is what Nadia saw after she ran out the back door and looked up. By the time she ran to the end of the back side northern parking lot facing the hospital, the white colored image was of a face with two eyes and a mouth.

"The precision of the image could not be from particles of matter from the patio or The Brewery roofing," Nadia tells Yuan.

"It's like the ink-blot test psychologists use when they ask patients to say what they can see in images," Yuan says in disagreement. "Of course, there is nothing there, no face, but people are seeing whatever their mind focuses on."

"No, this was real," Nadia says. "An image of Jesus."

That evening, many churchgoers also report seeing an image in the sky that looked like Jesus.

Chapter 15

CONVERSION

"Where is the preacher?" Greg writes. "Did he make it past the emergency room?" Greg can't talk now with a trach in his neck. Greg, who was slipping into shock, doesn't remember much about his first hours in the hospital. His wife tells him that he gave the trauma team a hard time about the whereabouts of his cowboy boots and jeans. Both melted in the fiery explosion and had been cut off.

"He's in the emergency room, according to Britt," Greg's wife responds.

"Britt who?" Greg writes.

"The brewery owner, who was inside when the explosion happened. The firepit exploded, and the patio went up like a sudden volcanic eruption; you landed in the street with fourth-degree burns," Greg's wife says.

"The windows of The Brewery all blew out, but Britt was in the back tending to the brew equipment and only received minor injuries," Greg's wife explains.

"Where's Neal, the preacher man?" Greg writes again.

"He's coming to see you and everyone else who was injured," his wife whispers.

"Was it a gas leak?" Greg continues to scribble on the small hospital notepad at a much slower pace.

"The local fire marshal is supposed to investigate," his wife says.

Greg's hand stops moving. His eyes close. His pen drops to the floor.

Neal is making his rounds to all the rooms in the ICU.

Greg falls asleep as Neal enters the ICU room.

Neal can't believe that Greg might not make it.

"The surgeon says skin is an important organ," the wife tells Neal. "And often taken for granted. Until, of course, it's damaged. The burning away of the hypodermis may cause deepening nerve and muscle damage. In severe cases, excessive burns can cause death."

She begins to sob.

Greg was the most severely injured among the patrons of The Brewery.

Neal starts to pray with his hunting buddy.

Greg's eyes remain closed. Only the sound of the breathing machine fills the air. He is unresponsive. A shaken preacher has no answers for this wife.

"Did he say much to you on the hunting trip?" the wife asks.

"We had a great time together, and I almost had him interested in church," Neal says.

"There are other burn victims here you know?" she says.

"I'm on my way now to see them," Neal says.

Neal leaves Greg's room to see the ICU nurse. He runs into a familiar face. A young lady nurse who used to be a church member.

"Hello, Susan," Neal says.

Neal respected Susan greatly. She endured sexual abuse as a teenager by her brother and showed the real power of forgiveness.

"This is Rae," Susan tells Neal.

"What happened to the other black fella?" Rae says.

"I'm sorry, Rae, but Eric did not make it," Susan says. Eric's upper torso and heart was pierced by glass as the explosion pummeled him through the bar window.

"Hello, Rae," Neal says. "I'm the preacher at the church next to the brewery."

"Hey," Rae says quietly.

"How are you?" Neal asks.

"I've been told I have lots of cuts and bruises," Rae says. "They said my arm is broken, and I have twenty-two stiches in my head."

"They're going to take good care of you," Neal says

"Mama took us to your church when we were little, but some folks weren't nice to us," Rae says. "We're from the Washington Drive area."

"I've only been pastor there for a few years," Neal says. "There's no place for racism in my church."

"I don't read the Bible; I like comic books, super heroes, who save the world," Rae whispers.

"Me, too!" Neal says. "I had boxes and boxes of those growing up, as a teen."

"I just don't believe there is proof for God the Father saving the world," Rae explains to the preacher. "My father left me when I was six years old."

"There is a father in heaven that cares for you," Neal says. "What do you like about super heroes?"

"I like Batman—he does a lot of good for people," Rae says.

"I like Aquaman," Neal says. "When folks criticize and ridicule him, his thick skin deflects a persistent onslaught of mean-spirited jokes and insults."

"That sounds cool, preacher," Rae says.

"Some churchgoers said, right after the explosion, they saw a cloud that looked like Jesus," Neal says.

"I didn't see it because the explosion threw me through the glass window back into the bar area," Rae explains. "Will I be okay and get to read my comic books again?"

"Comic books are fun to read, but they aren't real," Neal says. "What is real is God saved you from death today."

"My mama raised me and my ten half brothers and sisters on Hoskins Street," Rae says. "No one else saved me from being poor and black."

"Thank you for listening to what I have to say about Jesus," Neal says politely to Rae.

Susan interrupts their conversation, and Neal turns away from Rae, past the curtain; he can now see the other ICU patients.

"This is Nadia," Susan says to Neal.

Nadia is in better shape than the others. Her only injury is minor bleeding from her head—trauma she received from falling timbers at The Brewery.

"I miss my family so much," Nadia says, looking at Susan.

"Hello, Nadia," Neal says. "How are you?"

Nadia grabs her head bandage, which is now soaked in blood.

"Let me change it for you," Susan tells Nadia. "We need to keep the bleeding stopped."

"That hurts so much when you press the stiches," Nadia says.

"Are you a student and where is your family?" Neal asks.

"In Oman," Nadia replies. "I'm from Oman and I study mathematics at the University."

"I'm no good at math, but the Bible is full of numbers," Neal says.

"I like shapes and patterns," Nadia says.

"God is a mathematician," Neal says. "Actually, he is the supreme mathematician of the universe."

"I saw God today," Nadia says. "Right after the explosion, in the thick black and orange smoke above."

"God in the clouds?" Neal asks.

"Actually, in the plume of smoke that seemed to hover over the brewery," Nadia says.

"The church told me they saw the plume of smoke," Neal says. "It was fiery orange and black, too."

"Yes, the shape of the plume was like a cross, and, on top of it, I could see a distinct image of a face," Nadia says.

"What were you thinking at this moment?" Neal says.

"I instantly felt like I wanted other people to see it because it was so beautiful," she said. "The image resembled the famous Christ statue in . . ."

"Rio de Janeiro, Brazil?" Neal says. "I visit Brazil each year on mission trips to the slums of São Paulo."

"Have you always believed in God?" Neal asks.

"When the explosion happened, before the image of Christ in the smoke cloud, I thought Allah was punishing me," Nadia says. "But now, I believe God is love."

"That's amazing," Neal says. "Jesus saved you from death."

"He was watching over me," Nadia says. "I now believe Jesus did rise from the dead, and makes his face shine on me."

"I'll check back on you again soon, okay?" Neal says.

"Sir, what happened to my professor?" Nadia says, forgetting she was with him right after the explosion.

"I'm not supposed to share confidential medical information, something legal called HIPAA," Neal says. "But I think flammable dust caught fire near the conference room, burning his lower torso."

"I remember now," Nadia says. "He escaped by crawling out the alley door with his pants on fire."

"I'll see you again soon, okay?" Neal says.

"Thank you," Nadia says.

"There is one more female patient that I think will not need critical care," Susan says.

"I'd be happy to speak to her," Neal says.

Neal makes his rounds and then meets Yuan.

They exchange greetings and a few words, but Yuan is mostly silent.

Neal asks if she saw the image of Jesus in the smoke cloud.

The Chinese student gives deep thought to the apparition of Christ but decides to stay with her beliefs of Pantheism.

After visiting all the victims in the hospital, Neal is mentally exhausted and steps outside the ICU to the waiting area room. The room is mostly quiet. Some visitors are reading and some are praying. Neal calls his wife, Ashland, to tell her about the conversion of Nadia.

"Honey, you won't believe this," the preacher's voice cracks. "Wait, Neal, are you hurt?" Ashland replies. "No, I'm fine, praise the Lord, a Muslim accepted Christ, but several others are hurt, badly," Neal says.

Neal is really devastated by the injuries he saw at The Brewery. The terrifying moment when he found his hunting buddy, Greg, in the street, with blood over all his body. "I'm coming up to the hospital, to be with you," she says.

"Some people had broken limbs, some showered with glass," Neal says. "I walked in the emergency room, I saw a few people unconscious and doctors trying to put IVs into them," he adds. "But Nadia, the Muslim, accepted Jesus, truly a miracle of God."

Some of the victims, seriously injured, ended up in the ICU, some with machines keeping them alive. Some are crying. Some are praying. But Nadia remains aware of her vision of the plume of smoke that hovered over The Brewery right after the explosion. The apparition of Christ is now in her heart.

The waiting area room door opens and Susan steps in to say: "Come quick, Neal! Greg's vital signs are dropping, and he wrote, 'I need Neal.'"

In a moment, anything can change.

The Author

Christopher K. Horne, is a native of High Point, North Carolina taught at East Carolina University and now lectures at N.C. A&T State University. He visited or worked in more than 13 countries including Oman, Mexico and Japan.

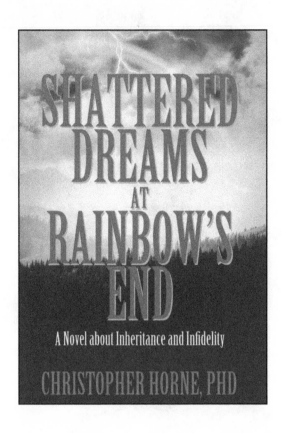

His other novel,
Shattered Dreams at Rainbow's End,
is published by Outskirts Press.

CPSIA information can be obtained
at www.ICGtesting.com
Printed in the USA
LVHW110619291220
675307LV00004B/171